MW00782397

He didn't want to get involved, hadn't wanted to be the one to find the body, but now that he had, he was stuck with the consequences...

"What do you want from me?" Johnny asked.

"Thomas said you knew he didn't kill that man, but he can't prove it," she said. "You know if they find him, he's gonna automatically be guilty and he'll go to the chain gang for the rest of his life or to the electric chair if they can make it happen. That would kill my mama. You can't let them do it to him. You're his only hope, so please help him." There was a long pause and then she added, "Please, Mister Johnny."

Johnny signaled for another bottle of beer as he spoke into the phone. "The Atlanta Police are handling the case. I don't have anything to do with it one way or another." The bartender sat the bottle on top of the juke box. Johnny handed him a quarter then waved him off.

"But you could look into it, couldn't you?" Rachel's voice was cracking. "I—I can pay you some money. Not much, but I have a little."

"I don't know..." His voice trailed off. "I've never done anything like this before. I don't know if I'm the right person."

"What do you mean you've never done anything like this before? You've never worked on a murder case or you've never tried to help a Negro?"

Johnny Morocco hit Atlanta, Georgia in 1953. The former army military policeman changed his name from McDonald and used his military training to become a licensed PI. Johnny's "office" was a pool room called Big Town in the heart of the city. His clients were the players and the occasional lawyer who came in on their lunch hour. Johnny's luck ran out the morning he came into Big Town and found a dead man lying on a pool table. With only Thomas the Negro rack boy in the building, Thomas would be the prime suspect.

Once Johnny decided to help Thomas, he found himself caught between emerging crime syndicates in Atlanta, Miami, and the casinos controlled by Myer Lansky in Havana. Cheating wives, roadhouse murders, imported muscle, marked cards, loaded dice, and a dangerous woman named Rachel were but a few of the roadblocks Johnny faced in his task.

With Atlanta Police Detective Sergeant Jack Brewer looking for both the killer and the money the dead man was supposed to be carrying, Johnny must use all his training and instincts to protect not only himself but Thomas as well. If he fails, they both will suffer the Wrath of The Dixie Mafia.

KUDOS for *Wrath of the Dixie Mafia*

In *Wrath of the Dixie Mafia* by Paul Sinor, Johnny Morocco is a PI in Atlanta, Georgia, in 1953. When he discovers a dead body lying on a pool table, he doesn't realize the trouble it's going to cause him. His colored friend Thomas, who worked at the pool hall where the dead man was found, becomes the prime suspect, simply because he is colored. Johnny is convinced his friend didn't do it, but how to prove it? And since the dead man was supposed to be carrying a large amount of money, the cops and the Dixie Mafia are watching his every move, just in case he's the one who took it. Like his previous book, *Dancing in the Dark*, Sinor has crafted an intriguing mystery with hard-hitting characters and fast-paced action that will keep you turning pages way into the night. *~ Taylor Jones, The Review Team of Taylor Jones & Regan Murphy*

Wrath of the Dixie Mafia by Paul Sinor is a historical mystery/thriller. Set in Atlanta, Georgia, in 1953, it's the story of Johnny Morocco, a former military policeman now a private detective. He's a good man, so when a black man Johnny knows is accused of a murder that he didn't commit, Johnny is honor bound to help him prove it. But what of the money the dead man had with him? The cops and the mafia think Johnny has it since he found the body. Now his life is in danger too. *Wrath of the Dixie Mafia* is a fast-paced, tension-filled mystery with a marvelous central character that you can't help but root for. This is one you'll want to read again and again. *~ Regan Murphy, The Review Team of Taylor Jones and Regan Murphy*

ACKNOWLEDGMENTS

Writing a book, whether it is fiction or non-fiction, is not an isolated act conducted in front of a computer screen, an old-fashioned typewriter, or on a stack of yellow legal pads while sitting in a coffee shop. It is a collaboration of any number of people who help bring the words to life. Many of the people may never know of their contributions by way of a small snippet of dialog, a favorite phrase, or some other act or omission they may not even realize they contributed. In my own case, my fascination with "story" began when my grandmother, whom we called Mama Waller told me stories of what she referred to as the "old days." If she was not the one telling the stories, it was my daddy, a member of America's Greatest Generation, who rode the rails on freight trains, looking for work, survived the great depression and WWII, and loved to talk about it. To them, I owe my ability, if there is one, to tell a story.

To bring this book to life I have had the incredible pleasure to work with two outstanding editors, Judith Geary and Faith C. at Black Opal Books. I thank them for the attention to detail, and Jack Jackson for the cover art work that is spot on.

For their continued advice, encouragement, and suggestions, some of which I actually took, my daughters Colleen and Victoria and especially my wife Jewell for being there when I needed her.

Mistakes, errors, omissions, and other things you don't like or agree with that you may find in this work are mine and mine alone.

WRATH OF THE DIXIE MAFIA

Paul Sinor

A Black Opal Books Publication

GENRE: HISTORICAL/MYSTERY-DETECTIVE/THRILLER

WRATH OF THE DIXIE MAFIA
Copyright © 2017 by Paul Sinor
Cover Design by Jackson Cover Design
All cover art copyright © 2017
All Rights Reserved
Print ISBN: 978-1-626946-97-2

First Publication: JUNE 2017

Published by Black Opal Books **http://www.blackopalbooks.com**

DEDICATION

This one is for my daddy, Ben Sinor, who lived the stories I can only write about and share with those who did not know him. I miss you more with every beat of my heart.

CHAPTER 1

Johnny Morocco stepped off the downtown bus at Five Points in Atlanta a few minutes after seven, walked across the street, and headed for Edgewood Avenue. Even at that early hour in the spring of 1953, the streets were filling with the workers who swarmed into the largest city in the South. Like any big city, Atlanta had its own signature. That morning it smelled of azaleas, fresh brewed coffee, exhaust fumes, and opportunity. Around him, Johnny heard the sound of car and truck horns, an occasional siren as a police or ambulance answered a call, and the chiming of the massive clock at City Hall, mixed with the voices of the city's workers and strangers as they started another day.

Seven was early, even for Johnny, but he had tossed and turned throughout the night as he relived days and nights spent in North Africa and Italy in the army during the war. He usually was able to keep the memories safely hidden away, but sometimes they escaped and attacked him as he slept. The memories and the shakes and sweats they caused were behind him as he headed for Big Town. He expected that, even at this hour, Thomas the rack boy and janitor would already have coffee brewing. A cup of Thomas's coffee and the morning paper would be enough to get him started for the day.

Big Town was a pool room. You could shoot a game for fun, a beer or a couple of bucks. In Big Town the beer was cold, the chili dogs were hot, and no self-respecting woman ever climbed the stairs to the second floor establishment.

It was also where hustlers came for a game. When an out-of-towner came in, the tables cleared and professional hustlers with names like Willie Mosconi and Minnesota Fats took on all comers in a game of rotation, bank or nine-ball. The stakes were as high as the crowd could afford.

There would be no games shot on table number seven this day. That's where a body lay, blood still seeping from the hole in his chest.

When Johnny tried the street level door leading to the second floor where Big Town was located, it was unlocked. Good. Thomas was on time. He usually came in about seven in the morning to restock the beer cooler, put the chili on to cook and clean up after the previous night's crowd left. Atlanta had a two a.m. closing time for pool rooms, bars, and the other places considered unsavory, but its lax enforcement was tolerated by the city fathers.

With a light breeze blowing, many of the men on the street wore jackets. The jacket Johnny wore was not so much to protect him from the possible chill, but to cover the .45 automatic pistol in his shoulder holster. This was the same style weapon he carried for the five plus years he served in the US Army, in North Africa, Italy and in the Occupation of Japan. During that time, he carried it in a holster on his hip. Now it rested in a brown leather shoulder holster with a large US embossed on it he purchased at an Army/Navy surplus store for fifty cents. This was the kind of holster used by men who were assigned to tanks. The holster he picked out of the pile on the table at the store had a small dark brown spot on the corner which could have been either blood or a scorch mark from a fire. Either way, Johnny felt the holster had already suffered as much as it could, and he would be safe wearing it.

As he pushed open the door, Johnny saw Eddie, the local bug runner making his morning stop at the shoe repair shop that occupied the ground floor of the building he was about to enter. Eddie was making the payoff delivery. The *bug* was the name given to the lottery, although illegal, played by many of the people of the city. The owner or one of his two family members who worked there had picked the right numbers and won. Eddie would return in the afternoon to pick up the slips for the numbers played that day.

Eddie held up a hand, acknowledging Johnny. The smell of leather and shoe polish rushed from the open door as he stood there. The old man who owned the shop had been a refugee from Eastern Europe a few years before the war started. The locals said that during the war no American military person could pay for having his or her shoes repaired or shined in the shop.

"Morning, Eddie. What was the bug last night?" Johnny asked, referring to the three digit number taken from the closing stock market report in the *Atlanta Journal* each evening.

"Nine three seven, Mister John. Always a good number for Tuesday." Eddie was in his late teens, still close enough to the farm to retain the belief that colored folks addressed white men as mister.

"Check with me on Friday. I've got a good number I want to play." As Johnny stepped into the stairway, he noticed the bulb at the top of the stairs was out and the only illumination in the entryway was the natural light from the early morning sun. As soon as he stepped inside he was hit with the odor of stale beer and day old bar rags. Missing was the smell of fresh brewed coffee. Johnny took the steps two at a time until he reached the top.

The well-worn wooden stairs ended just in front of the main bar. By the time he reached the top of the stairs, Johnny expected to see Thomas either behind the bar or mopping the floor. Thomas lived with his mother and sister in a section of Atlanta known as Cabbage Town. It was not far from the center of the city, yet Atlanta, and all it had to offer, might as well have been a million miles away for most of the people who lived in Cabbage Town.

Thomas walked with a limp from an injury he received during WWII. It was just after D-Day and medical treatment, especially for the few Negro units on the front was catch-as-catch-can. Once when one of the men in Big Town made a joke about Thomas's limp, he said he had earned it the hard way in France. That gave Thomas an instant boost in stature with all the men who had also served.

The large room that was Big Town was divided in half by the bar. Each half had two rows of seven pool tables. The walls were lined with tall wooden chairs where men sat while they waited for their next shot on the table. The bookies and players sat in those chairs when they listened to the bank of radios broadcasting the day's selection of baseball games.

"Hey, Thomas? You got the coffee ready?" Johnny stood on the landing at the top of the stairs and looked around. Like the stairway, the room was unusually dark.

"Thomas?" he called cautiously and the feeling that something was not right formed a shiver running from the back of his neck to the tips of his fingers. He usually liked to go on more than instinct, but it was something he trusted and, when it happened, he responded.

To the right, a light was shining over one of the tables. Overhead, suspended horizontally from two five foot lengths of black electrical wire was a three foot long florescent light. It was kept from swinging by cables which ran from the corners of the light to the high ceiling where they were secured. A second wire ran the length of the room over each table. This wire had a row of wooden numbers which could be slid across with the tip of the pool cue. The players kept score with the numbers. In the middle of each row of numbers was the larger number identifying the table.

The only light over table number seven was shining down. It was the only light in the room which was on as Johnny walked toward it. Johnny knew what the light was shining on. The only question was when the "what" would turn into a "who?"

Johnny cautiously approached. It was an instinct born of war and, within the next few steps, he knew what he was going to find. Lying on table number seven was a body. The blood draining from the body stained a dark circle beneath his left shoulder on the green felt of the pool table. A blood-red stain had stopped spreading on his chest. His white shirt looked like someone had poked a small hole just under the pocket on the left side, leaving him the ultimate in a broken heart.

Johnny reached into his own shirt pocket and pulled out a pack of Lucky Strike cigarettes. Carefully placed behind the pack of cigarettes was the small, black, Zippo lighter he had carried throughout the war. With its square edges, it stood upright between his own flesh and whatever might invade it.

"Maybe if you had one of *these,*" he said as he flipped open the top, spun the wheel. and touched the flame to his cigarette, "you'd still be here."

Johnny looked at the lighter he had carried and remembered the man who had been saved when a lighter in his pocket took the hit and stopped a bullet. From that day on, Johnny and almost everyone he knew who was there at the time, carried a Zippo in the shirt pocket over their heart. He hardly ever used it to light cigarettes, and a lighter probably wouldn't stop another bullet for the next hundred years, but it was always there. Just in case.

Johnny sensed the movement before he heard the sound. He quickly turned toward the noise, squatted slightly, and listened. As he heard it again, he pulled his jacket open so he had quick and easy access to his weapon. The sound was like a door being opened or closed. Johnny was not foolish enough to simply walk toward it. With one dead man on the table beside him, there was no way of knowing if the noisemaker also wanted Johnny to go for a Daily Double. That was a bet he had no interest in.

Johnny had a license to carry, so without waiting to see or hear anything else, he eased the .45 caliber automatic from its resting place in the holster. He maintained the crouch as he walked toward the sound.

Johnny took several steps and saw the source of the sound. It was Thomas.

"Don't shoot me, Mister Johnny. I ain't had nothing to do with that argument back there." Thomas held his hands in the air. Behind him was his mop bucket with the long wooden handle of his mop protruding like a flag pole awaiting the raising of the colors. The smell of stale mop-water filled the air.

"Do you know what happened here, Thomas?" Johnny holstered his weapon.

"Oh, Lawdy, Mister Johnny. That man's dead, ain't he?" Thomas had already begun to back up as he spoke. "I got's to get out of here. They find a dead white man in here wit' me bein' the only colored man around, I'll be hanging before the sun sets." He backed away and almost tripped over the mop handle as he headed for the door.

"Not yet, Thomas. You need to talk to me before you leave." Johnny took Thomas by the arm and led him to the table where the man lay. He walked around the table and, for the first time, saw the weapon lying next to the body. "What time did you get here this morning?" He turned to face Thomas.

Thomas was shaking. "'Bout the same I do every day. Little before seven. I catch the bus at six thirty and it takes me to Five Points. I walks from there. Take about five minutes." He looked at Johnny, his eyes wide with fear. "I swear on my mama's grave, Mister Johnny, I didn't do that man no harm." He took a step closer to the body. "Oh, Lawdy, that man done died right there on that table. I got's to go. I got's to go right now, and I ain't never coming back. You know that's the truth, Mister Johnny. No matter what you say, the po-lice gonna say it was me. Ain't no getting 'round that."

By this time, his shaking was making it hard to understand his words. He was still talking as he turned and headed for the steps.

CHAPTER 2

Johnny had arrived, in more ways than one, in Atlanta in the spring of 1952. Two years earlier, he was still in the army and was known as Sergeant John McDonald.

When the war in Europe ended, Johnny was sent from Italy to Japan as a part of the invasion forces. When the two atomic bombs ended the war, invasion forces quickly became occupation forces. Unlike his time in North Africa and Italy, in Japan, as a military policeman, he had it made. He had his own jeep and a nice place to live. His off-duty companion, Miko, was a young, attractive, Japanese college student who lost her family during the war. For about the cost of a hamburger and a Coke back home, he could have her for a week. She stayed with him for almost six months before moving in with a lieutenant who graduated too late from West Point to make the war. The butter-bar volunteered to come to Japan to make his mark during the occupation.

The first thing he did after taking Johnny's companion was to get drunk and throw up in front of General McArthur one night at the officer's club. The next week, Miko came back asking if she could be Johnny's special lady again. By that time, he had orders ending his tour in Japan.

Five weeks later, he was assigned to a military police detachment at Fort Benning, Georgia.

The war had ended, most of the military forces had returned home, and life in uniform became routine. When Johnny was a teenager in West Palm Beach, Florida, he boxed at the local YMCA and then moved on to be city champion in the middle-weight division of Golden Gloves. He boxed a few matches in North Africa and in Japan, but at Fort Benning, he joined the boxing team and gained a reputation as a scrappy fighter who took some of the hardest shots his opponents had and always came back for more.

Across the Chattahoochee River from the city of Columbus, Georgia, the gate town for Fort Benning, was a small Alabama town that resembled any city the old west of the late 1800s had to offer. Phenix City was known around the world as a wide-open Mecca for prostitution, gambling, and drinking and where the cost of having a rival killed was well within the budget of even the lowest ranking private at Fort Benning. Prior to WWII, General Patton had threatened, or rather promised, the mayor that if one more of his men was found floating in the river, he would bring an entire armored division's tanks across the state line and level the city. With Patton gone and the threat removed, it was business as usual for the city of multiple sins.

Johnny's training and his ability with his fists meant he spent many nights as a military policeman roaming the streets of both Columbus and Phenix City, looking for drunk or missing soldiers. Most were quickly found in the numerous whore houses, while a few were never seen again.

It was not unusual for Johnny and his partner to visit several of the better-known bars and whore houses in Phenix City and Columbus. They got to know a few of the women and some of their regular customers on a first-name basis.

One night on a joint patrol with a Columbus police officer, they pulled a car over that was being driven by a drunk driver. The driver turned out to be the wife of the mayor of Phenix City. Johnny volunteered to drive her home when they recognized who she was. They knew if they gave her a ticket it would be torn up as soon as her husband made one call the next morning.

The drive home turned into another hour sitting with her as she drank coffee and told Johnny how miserable she was. Before he left, she pulled him to her, and with whiskey breath that could peel wallpaper, she gave him a long lingering kiss. The kiss and the potential it held were not lost on Johnny. That night led to several other late night rendezvous and ultimately getting caught by her husband.

Within twelve hours of the mayor coming home unexpectedly and Johnny leaving through a bedroom window, he was out of the army and standing at the Muskogee County line. He had a duffle bag at his feet and his thumb out, facing south and home to Florida.

e∕ɔe∕ɔ

In West Palm Beach, he tried to make it in several jobs. He drove a milk truck, sold tires at an auto store and worked as an insurance salesman. Each lasted a few days or at the most a couple of weeks. Johnny didn't want to live with his parents, so he took a room in a boarding house that was home to other recently discharged veterans who, like Johnny, were still looking for their place in post-war society.

One evening the telephone in the downstairs sitting room rang. A former first sergeant from an infantry unit who was now working as a house painter answered it.

"Hey, Johnny, it's for you. He didn't say who it was. You want me to find out?"

The man was dressed in white coveralls splattered with paint and smelled of alcohol. One night Johnny learned the smell could come from real whiskey or paint thinner. He was sitting on the end of the porch in the early evening shadows when the painter came home. Johnny watched, first in curiosity and then in fear, as the painter took the top off a can of a paint thinner made from denatured alcohol. He placed several slices of bread over an empty, and hopefully clean, paint can. Johnny watched him pour the alcohol over the bread to filter it. When the second can was full, the man noticed Johnny and offered him a drink. The drink was quickly turned down and the offer was not repeated. Johnny had watched as the can was emptied, one drink at a time.

"No, I'll get it." Johnny sat at the top of the steps leading up to the old house while he read the evening paper. He folded it, placed it on the step, and walked into the house.

The main room was a large area which had once been part of the living room of a very expensive home. Now it was divided into two rooms. One still served as the living room, but the other half had been converted to another bedroom when the war started and the military came to town. With more men in town than rooms, everyone with a house rented their spare rooms to the military. This house was owned by an older couple whose children had all moved out long ago. The house always smelled of furniture polish and kitchen grease. Johnny stood by the now thread-bare couch as he picked up the handset.

"Hey, Johnny!"

He recognized the voice on the other end immediately. It was David Gladstone, a man he had known since they were in grammar school. David joined the navy the day after Pearl Harbor, and they had not seen each other in over six years when Johnny came home. Once they both returned to West Palm Beach, they had met by chance in a bar one evening, and the war and its separation soon ceased to be a topic of conversation.

"Yeah, I still got my camera. Film? Yeah, I got some of that too." Johnny spoke while the painter, whose name he did not know, sat at the end of the couch and listened.

"Hang on a second." Johnny put his hand over the mouthpiece and turned to the eavesdropper. "Don't you have something to do someplace else?"

The painter started to protest, then slowly rose from the seat and walked away.

"Okay, I'm back. I can meet you at that place on Okeechobee Road in an hour."

He replaced the handset and climbed the stairs to his second floor room. In earlier times, his room had probably belonged to a young boy, as there were three sets of initials carved inconspicuously low into the baseboard. Each had a heart around them with a plus sign in the middle. In each set, one pair of initials were the same; the others were different. When Johnny saw them he thought of his youth and lost loves. He often wondered if the boy went to war, and if so, had he made it back, but he didn't have the nerve to ask the owners of the house.

Johnny pulled his camera from the back of the small closet in his room. He had traded for it on the black market in Japan. It was one of the best available and he got it for two cartons of cigarettes. Smokes were worth more than money in occupied Japan. You could get a woman for a week for a couple of packs. For a carton, Johnny found out, the women did things he had never even heard of until he got to Tokyo.

He pulled the camera bag from beneath a pile of cloth-

ing, slung it over his shoulder, and went downstairs. Tonight he had a *job*.

ⒺⓈⒺⓈ

Johnny pulled his car into the white crushed shell
parking lot of the drive-in restaurant on Okeechobee
Road. Two long sheds with tin roofs where cars pulled in
with their noses pointed to the sidewalk led from the
sheds to the inside of the restaurant. The car hops, old
Negro men in white shirts and black pants, quickly ran
from the building to the cars as they pulled in. As soon as
Johnny cut the engine, an old man was standing by the
open driver's window.

"Evenin' Suh. What'll it be tonight? The beer's cold,
and the barbecue ain't. Only thang that'd be better is if
you had a lady friend with you." He leaned closer as he
dropped his voice. "Course, if you was a mind to, I 'spect
we could find you one of them too." When Johnny didn't
respond, he changed his patter. "It sho' is hot tonight, but
I think we're gonna get some rain. You know, when you
gets to be my age, you can almost feel the rain in your
bones afore it even crosses the county line. You just wait.
Someday, you'll be old, and you'll know what I mean."

"Just bring me a sandwich, sliced pork, and a Pabst.
Tell 'em to put some extra hot sauce on it, too. I'll pass
on your other offer." Johnny didn't want one of the wom-
en they were pushing from the bar. He'd seen too many
guys get more than they bargained for when they got a
girl sight unseen.

One of the things his mother sent him when he was in
the army was an occasional bottle of hot sauce from the
barbecue stand. He doled it out almost a drop at the time
to liven up the endless boxes of K-Rations. When they
got to a location where they had real cooked food, the

sauce even made the powdered eggs somewhat palatable.

Johnny turned the dial on the radio as he waited for his food. All he was able to pick up was a station in West Palm Beach that came in with very little static. He alternated rolling the windows up and down. With them down, the mosquitoes were all over him, but with them up the heat was stifling. He was in the process of rolling them down again, when the passenger's door opened and David Gladstone slid into the front seat.

"Easy on the cloth. They're still not making covers that'll fit this one." Like most returning vets, Johnny didn't have a car. He drove the old 1937 Plymouth sedan he borrowed from his dad. He already had his eye on a 1941 sedan. It was rusty red in color, and he had driven it a couple of times when he went to the used car lot where it sat. He had almost enough to buy it, but, like everything else in his life, it would have to wait

There weren't any automobiles made from 1941 until the war ended. After the Japanese bombed Pearl Harbor, all automobile assembly line production was dedicated to turning out Jeeps and other pieces needed for the war. It took a year to get things back to normal on the lines after V-J Day.

"You got your camera?"

"You told me to bring it, didn't you?"

"Don't get your ass on your shoulders. If we do this right tonight, we'll split twenty dollars. How's that sound?" David leaned across the seat when the car hop brought a tray with Johnny's sandwich and beer.

"Hey, tell that ol' Jake to bring me a sandwich and a bottle of whatever it is you're drinking." He handed Johnny a fifty-cent piece. "And I want my change, too."

The old man opened the two legs of the tray and hooked the back lip over the window. He adjusted them so that the legs rested against the driver's door and held the tray steady and level at window height.

"Here." Johnny handed him a quarter for the beer and fifteen cents for the sandwich. "He's gonna give you the tip when you bring another sandwich and another beer." He placed the fifty cent piece on the corner of the tray.

"Another Pabst, suh?"

David leaned across the front seat and spoke to the car hop. "Damn right, and it better be cold if you expect to keep that change."

"Don't you gentlemens worry. I'm gonna earn that tip."

☙☙

It was barely dark when they pulled from the drive-in and headed south on Okeechobee Road. The winter had passed and with hardly a notice, spring had turned into early summer. The almost tropical climate of West Palm Beach meant many flowers were in full bloom. Oleander bushes, heavy with white blooms and enough poison on each bush to kill a dozen people lined the sides of the road.

"Up here, turn right." David pointed to an upcoming intersection. "It's about a mile on up from here."

Johnny slowed for the light. "Don't you think you might want to wait a little longer?"

"Wait. Why?"

"If you're trying to get a picture of the woman with her boyfriend, you might want to give them time to get undressed and in bed."

A large truck loaded with vegetables from one of the many farms closer to Lake Okeechobee crossed the road in front of them. The smell of fresh-cut celery filled the night air as it passed.

David shook his head. "They ain't got all night. The guy's married to some Jap broad he brought home in 'forty-six, so he's got to hurry so he can get home to her. The husband that hired us said the little wife's always sitting at home, like nothing's been going on, by nine when he gets back from bowling on Thursdays. It's almost seven now, so that don't give them much time to do the nasty."

Johnny drove slowly down the street. They passed several houses still showing damage from the hurricane of 1949. One house had its roof completely lifted off in one piece and then dropped into the back yard. The walls of the house still stood. Windows—cracked, broken and missing—told the story of the neighborhood's compassion for the former residents. In all likelihood, once the storm passed, the people who lived there came back, salvaged what they could from the rain-soaked interior and left town. That is, if they themselves survived the storm's fury.

"Does he know she lets this guy in every week?"

"He must. He's giving us twenty smackers to prove it." David leaned out the window to get a good read on the house numbers. "Slow down, we're getting close. He said the address was One Hundred Fourteen Chickamauga. That house we just passed was Two Hundred."

Johnny depressed the clutch and slipped the long, floor mounted gear shift into second. The extra torque on the engine slowed it without the use of brakes and the accompaniment of lights, in case anyone was curious about the strange car in the neighborhood.

"Look. Over there." David pointed across the street. "The guy's supposed to have a 'thirty-four Buick. That must be it."

Parked on the side of the road was a massive black sedan. The four-door car was a favorite of gangsters of the

Depression era. It was heavy, fast, and had doors that, when opened, formed a wall from which to shoot.

"You ever shoot a Thompson, Johnny?"

"Yeah, I had one for a couple of months in North Africa. Why?"

"Just wondered."

"You didn't say anything about a Thompson. Is this guy supposed to have a gun?"

"Naw, everything's gonna be okay. Trust me." David opened the door as they rolled slowly and silently down the street. "Let me out here for a second."

Before Johnny could say anything, David jumped from the car and headed for the Buick. Even in the waning light, Johnny saw the massive switchblade knife as David flicked it open. With a deft motion, David made two stabbing moves as he walked quickly across the ground in front of the car and both front tires hissed as they lost air pressure. He was back in the car before Johnny was fifty feet from where he had jumped.

"Okay, pull over and park. It's time to go to work."

They walked slowly toward the front yard of the house at One Hundred Fourteen. Two doors down, an old man sat on his front porch. He gave them a half-hearted nod in polite recognition of their presence.

"Just go up to the front door like we know the folks here. He gave me a key, so pretend to knock and while you do that, I'll unlock the door. The bedroom's across to the left. There ain't but three rooms, so we won't have any trouble finding it." David held up a black skeleton key that probably fit half the front door locks in the city. "You just get that camera ready. We need to get them together in the bedroom. It don't matter what they're doing, just so long as they're doing it in the bedroom."

They approached the house down a walkway in the front yard. The sweet smell of night blooming angel trumpets filled the air. Both sides of the cement walkway were lined with roses and other flowers in full bloom. A large bush with red flowers that Johnny did not recognize partially covered the small front stoop. They stood in front of the door while David slipped the key into the square black metal lock and turned the white door knob. With hardly a sound, the door swung open. Both men quickly stepped inside.

"Over there," David whispered as he pointed to the left. "That's the bedroom." The sounds coming from the room left no doubt that the people in it were making love in the most primitive manner.

"Damn. Listen to that." David had to suppress a giggle.

Johnny hesitated as he unsnapped the cover from the camera. He reached into his pocket and pulled out two flashbulbs. He placed one in the flash attachment and put the other one in his mouth ready to use as soon as he popped the first one out.

Johnny saw the low stool before David did. With a flash bulb in his mouth, he could only mumble before David tripped over it and fell into a table holding a lamp. Within seconds of the lamp crashing to the floor, the man was out of the bedroom and headed toward them. Johnny held his ground and got one picture.

The photo showed a naked man with a baseball bat in his hand swinging it in Johnny's direction. The next photo, if he had been able to get it, would have shown that same man connecting with the bat breaking Johnny's arm as he and David ran for their lives.

ℰℰℰ

Johnny's broken arm kept him from working his job as a laborer on a construction crew. He normally carried bricks and mixed and pushed wheelbarrows filled with cement for the experienced brick layer. With no job, he had to move back home and, for the next six weeks, Johnny lived on his mustering out pay from the army. He did not collect all of his pay while on active duty so when he finally got to a pay master he was amazed at how much the army owed him.

He still slept in the room he had occupied in his parent's home as long as he could remember. As an only child, Johnny had been one of the lucky ones in the crowd he ran with. He didn't have to share a bedroom, wear hand-me-downs, or fight over who sat where in the back seat of his dad's car. He also had no one to blame when he got caught at something his parents did not approve of, and he got caught a lot.

By the end of the first month, Johnny knew it was time for a change and, once he decided to change, he went for the gold ring.

ℰↄℰↄ

"More coffee, Johnny," his mother asked as she took the aluminum percolator off the stove.

"No—yes, pour me another cup and have a seat, Ma, I want to talk to you and Dad."

"What's up, son?" His father was shoveling a fluffy, buttered biscuit in his mouth as he spoke.

"I'm getting my cast off tomorrow, and I think it's time I left home—"

"You know you don't have to do that, son. It was just bad luck that you broke your arm. Nothing else," his mother said as she sipped her coffee.

"Sometimes I think if it wasn't for bad luck, I wouldn't have any luck at all."

His mother sat heavily in a chair. "Johnny, you can

stay here as long as you like. You know we don't mind. We've missed you so much during the war."

"I know, but I can't live in my old room forever. I'm going to Atlanta. To—to—start over. I need to get away from here. Not you two, but here. This city. The people I know and who know me. I've got to make a fresh start, and I want to do it in Atlanta. I'm sorry, but I've made up my mind." He noticed when he rose from the table his mother was wiping tears from her eyes.

All of that was behind him. He had made the change he wanted.

Once he got to Atlanta, Johnny McDonald changed his name to Johnny Morocco. Six months later, he had a license and worked as a private investigator in Atlanta, Georgia.

CHAPTER 3

The Atlanta Police Department was housed in a gray stone building on Decatur Street. From the outside, the stones looked like they were rescued from the rubble of a medieval castle destroyed long ago. Inside, whether you were a police officer, a petty criminal, or a family member of either, you might as well have been in the castle's dungeon. Dark and dank, it smelled of stale cigarette smoke, urine, and sweat. It was the frightened sweat of the men and women, pulled from the streets for crimes they may or may not have committed, mixed with the sweat of honest work from the few cops who tried to make a difference.

Detective Sergeant Jack Brewer was not part of the latter group. He got the gold shield of a detective ten years earlier when he was forty one. In those ten years, he bullied his way into and out of every scam known to the department. He was credited with two justified shootings, and at least five suspensions for offenses ranging from excessive force to kickbacks.

He was the first person Johnny called.

"Brewer, here. Who's this?" His voice had the edge of a lifelong smoker, punctuated by periodic coughing spasms.

"Sergeant Brewer, it's Johnny Morocco. You working

the day shift today?" Johnny stood by the pay phone and watched the steps leading up to the second floor as he spoke.

"Why? You wanna take me to dinner? I go at noon and—" Before he could finish, he began to cough.

"No, but I got something here you may want to see."

"If you're at Big Town, it's too early for any of the usual low-life's to be there. What'd you do, hit the bug?"

In the background, Johnny heard the sound of another detective as he interrogated a suspect. The man was obviously in pain as the detective told him in no uncertain terms what he was about to do to him. As he listened, Johnny then heard him do it.

"No. This is serious," Johnny said. "I don't want to say anything over the phone, but you may want to come down here and bring a black and white with you. A meat wagon's probably a good idea, too." Johnny hung up the phone before Brewer could ask any more questions.

For the entire time he'd worked as a private investigator, Johnny had used Big Town as his office and primary source of employment. Most of his work came from the men who frequented the pool room. Even they occasionally needed a PI to gather information for a divorce or a lawsuit. Two of the regulars who stopped by and shot a game of pool on their lunch break were local attorneys. Another was an insurance agent. He got work from them on a regular basis.

Johnny walked back to table number seven. The man was still there and he was still dead. There was no doubt about it. Johnny took another cigarette from the pack, lit it, and pulled the smoke deeply into his lungs. He let the smoke roll from his lips and out his nose as he leaned over the body.

For a fleeting second, Johnny was back in uniform. Back in North Africa. Back in the war. Before he stepped off the transport ship that carried him to combat, Johnny had seen only one dead body in his life. He attended his grandfather's funeral when he was in first grade. He remembered how much he wanted to talk to the man he called Papa just one more time. His father said he could talk to Papa but the old man could only listen. For the rest of his life, every time Johnny smelled roses, his first thought was of that day. One dead body in his nineteen-year-old life. He broke that record the second day he was on the sands of North Africa.

In his mind, he was standing up in the passenger's seat of an army Jeep. He had on goggles to protect his eyes from the sand and a cloth was draped over his mouth and around his neck to keep the sand out of his clothes. Nothing worked. Every pore, every opening in his body filled with sand the day he stepped off the transport and landed into the middle of a war fought between the three greatest tacticians and megalomaniacs on either side—Patton and Montgomery for the Allies and Rommel for the Germans. Johnny stood in the Jeep, his mouth grinding sand with every word, his lungs filling with it with each breath, and looked at the dead men lining the road. Uniforms and philosophies were of no matter. They were all dead.

British, American, and German forces tried to recover their dead and bury them, but in many cases, by the time they were able to go look for them, they had been claimed by the desert sands. They were the first casualties of war Johnny had seen. Unfortunately, they would not be the last.

Johnny felt the bead of sweat form on his upper lip as he regained his composure. He walked around the table to get a better look at the man. He was wearing nice pants and a white, long-sleeved dress shirt. His feet were covered with two toned brown and white shoes, and he was wearing white socks. Johnny looked at the shoes for a long minute. There was something about them that seemed familiar. He couldn't place what it was at the moment. Surely it would come to him eventually.

The shirt was starched and nice looking except for the large red stain and the hole where the bullet entered his chest. There was probably an even larger hole in the back where it exited, and it was a sure bet the stain was much larger there than in the front.

The man's eyes were open, and it looked like he was staring at the corner of the light hanging overhead. Johnny looked up and smiled as he wondered if the dead man's last thought was to worry about the spider web covering the end of the light and why someone hadn't cleaned it off.

Johnny was still looking at the man's body when he noticed the corner of a piece of paper sticking out of the man's watch pocket. Using the tips of his fingers, he slid the paper out. It was a receipt for a round of golf at Flat Rock Golf Course, a popular course just south of Atlanta.

Somehow the golf ticket didn't go with the Model 1911 army .45 caliber pistol lying beside the body. Whoever shot him wanted the search for the murder weapon to be an easy one.

Johnny sat on the end of the table next to number seven and stared at the body. "Is there something you want to tell me? Am I overlooking anything that could tell me who you are or what happened?" He spoke aloud to the dead man knowing if those questions got answered, they would not be verbalized by the man in front of him. He was still sitting when he heard someone call his name.

"Morocco? You up there?" Sergeant Brewer was chugging up the steps. By the time he got to the top, his breathing was already labored. "This better not be some kinda bullshit hustle."

The detective had passed his fifty-second birthday. He

had spent most of those years with the Atlanta Police Department, first as a beat cop in the West End section of the city. When he made detective, he perfected his style of clothing from the many second-hand stores he shook down on the beat. He was wearing a brown suit, a wide tie, and he held a brown felt Stetson fedora. He stopped at the top of the stairs, pulled a soiled handkerchief from his pocket, and wiped the sweat from his face as he looked for Johnny.

"Over here. You can make up your own mind if it's a hustle or not." Johnny sat on the edge of the table across from number seven and waited for Brewer to come to him. It was almost nine and time for some of the regulars to start making their way to the pool room. Like Johnny, some of the men, especially, the bookies, spent all day there during baseball season.

"I got a black and white downstairs. You owe both of them a beer next time they come up." He made his way toward Johnny. "And if this ain't—" He stopped in mid-sentence when he saw the body on the table. "You kill him?" Brewer's hand was cautiously, and without his even noticing it, reaching behind his back for his weapon.

"No. He was dead when I got here. He almost bled out. It's all over the table." Johnny hopped down and walked toward Brewer. He held his hands in front of him, palms out.

Brewer dropped his reach and pulled a small notebook from his shirt pocket. He walked to the table, bent over, and looked at the man. "Whadda you think? He's been dead...what...two hours?" He picked up the dead man's hand and dropped it on the table. "He ain't even started getting stiff, yet." For the first time, he noticed the gun lying on the opposite side. "You carry a forty-five don't you, Johnny?" He took out his handkerchief, wrapped it around the pistol, and dropped it into his jacket pocket.

"And I'll bet we got your prints on file from when you got your PI ticket."

He turned to face Johnny. "And let me guess. You left your piece at home today. Am I right?" The detective reached into his other pocket and pulled out a single long wooden kitchen match. "You got a cigarette?" He held out his hand.

Johnny slowly pulled his jacket back to reveal his weapon still strapped in the holster. With his other hand, he reached into his shirt pocket and pulled out his cigarettes. "I'll bet you're smoking Luckies, today. Right?" Johnny tapped the pack against his outstretched index finger and a single cigarette popped loose.

"One of my favorites." Brewer flicked the end of the match with his thumbnail, waited till the flame stabilized, and touched it to the tip of the cigarette hanging from the center of his mouth. He took a deep pull and walked around the table where the body lay. "Looks familiar. Have I seen him in here before?"

"Could be. There's a lot of men who come in here, shoot a game or two, and leave. Maybe he was one of them." Johnny pulled a cigarette for himself from the pack. "Maybe you shot a game with him. That's where you know him from."

"I don't think so. He's dressed a lot nicer than the average low-life that calls this place home. He don't look like a hustler, either." Brewer stopped at the side of the table, looked closely at the blood stain on the man's shirt. "You ever see somebody shot when you were in the army?"

"Yeah, a couple of times."

Brewer continued without looking up. "How many did you shoot?"

"I've got an appointment with a client this morning. So if you don't need me any more—"

Before he could finish, Brewer struck like a mongoose on a cobra. He grabbed Johnny by the front of his shirt and pushed him against the wall. "The only appointment you got today, or any other day 'till I tell you different is with me. I got a stiff on a pool table and a two-bit loser who thinks he's Sherlock Holmes that calls me and tells me I better get my ass down to a hang-out for every petty thief, bookie, and hustler in Atlanta. That's what I got. What you better have is a reason for me not to drag you down to the castle and drop your ass in the dungeon."

Brewer slipped his hand inside Johnny's jacket and pulled it back, revealing the weapon still in its holster. "Maybe you're like one of them cowboys in the movies. You know, the ones that carry two guns."

Johnny knew from experience that Brewer was not as friendly as he seemed on the surface. He had a reputation throughout the city as a cop who was not above breaking a law or an arm when it came to getting what he wanted. And all he wanted was a closed case. Guilt or innocence was determined by the courts. Brewer supplied the fodder for the justice system to grind.

"Okay. Okay, I was just doing my civic duty. I come in here, find a dead man on one of the pool tables, and you're the first name that pops into my mind to call." Johnny gently placed his hands atop Brewer's and tapped them in an effort to get the man to loosen his grip. Nose-to-nose, Johnny could smell the sweet, rose-tinted scent of Brewer's hair tonic.

Brewer removed his hands and stepped back. "You just caught me at a bad time, that's all." He raked his big hands over Johnny's shirt, as if to smooth out the wrinkles. "The wife's been after me to consider some other line of work. One that pays better, you know what I mean?" He began to walk toward a row of pin-ball machines sitting against the wall. "I was thinking maybe a car salesman. Everybody's getting new cars now. Whadda you think? Would you buy a car from me?"

"Would you want your customers to sign the papers before or after you shook them down and slammed them against the hood of the car?"

Even Brewer laughed at that. "You know I ain't that bad…am I?"

It was not unusual for Detective Sergeant Jack Brewer to visit Big Town with his hand out. Everyone knew that gambling was against the law in Atlanta, but it was over-looked unless there was a politician who needed a cause. To keep politicians from servicing that cause in Big Town, Brewer was the man the owner called when he heard of any actions directed toward him or his business. During football season, Brewer usually played a parlay card each weekend. He never did it in person, but every-one knew the runner who brought it in was working for Brewer.

"You got a nickel?" Brewer turned to face Johnny. He was standing in front of a Shooting Gallery game. For a nickel, the player got to fire twenty electronic shots at a variety of targets.

"Here." Johnny handed him a five-cent coin.

"Tell you what, gimmie two and we'll see who's the best shot. You win and I let you go home. I win, and—" He hesitated, smiled. "—and you come with me."

"Don't you think you should be working on solving the murder of the dead guy back there instead of bum-ming nickels from me?" Johnny reached into his pocket and pulled two nickels from his change. He handed them to Brewer.

"Bumming? Did I say I wouldn't pay you back?" He dropped the coin in the slot. The targets behind the glass ran from side to side in an erratic dance. He swung the short rifle from one to the other and hit eighteen out of twenty targets. "As for our friend, the stranger currently residing on table number seven, that one's wrapped up. It's in the bag already." He leaned against the machine and pulled another match from his jacket pocket and held it up in a motion for another cigarette.

"Wrapped up? You know who killed him?"

"Course I do. All's I gotta do is go pick him up."

"Who do you think killed him?"

"No thinking to it. I already know who done it." He looked around and saw the mop and bucket sitting in the aisle. "You open the place today?"

"No. You know Thomas always opens and makes the coffee while he cleans up."

"Then why ain't he here? He have an appointment to get his conk done?"

Johnny met Thomas when he first came to Big Town. Thomas was already working as the rack boy and janitor. No matter where he was or what he was doing as soon as he heard someone yell "RACK!" he made his way to the table and racked the balls for the particular game they were playing. He had been doing it so long, it took mere seconds for him to place the balls in perfect order for rotation, eight-ball or nine-ball. Each rack cost ten cents which was either tossed to Thomas or dropped into one of the corner pockets. He usually got a nickel tip after racking a game or two for the steady players. Johnny had been there the day Thomas explained about his leg.

"I'll tell you why he's not here. First, I don't think he did it and, second, you do and he knew what would happen to him if he was here when you arrived."

"I knew you soldier-boys stood up for each other, but I never thought a white man would do it for the likes of a rack boy."

"You have no idea who he is or what he did during the war. Where were you in June of 'forty-four? Rousting drunks and pimps to keep the streets of Atlanta safe for the folks back home?" Johnny pulled out another cigarette and without being asked, handed one to Brewer. "Thomas was part of a Negro unit called the Red Ball Express. They drove trucks full of supplies from the beach at Normandy to the men who were cleaning up the mess the Germans left behind as they ran for Berlin." He took a long drag and let the smoke slowly slip from his mouth. "One day his truck took a direct hit from a German anti-tank weapon. The truck rolled over and caught on fire. Thomas was thrown out and it broke his leg. His relief driver was trapped in the fire."

"I suppose Thomas was a hero?" Brewer lit another one of Johnny's cigarettes.

"You figure it out. Thomas went back to the truck and pulled the other guy out. The bone was sticking out of his leg the whole time. That got him a Purple Heart and a Bronze Star." Johnny stopped talking.

"He tell you this and you believed him?'

"I believe he deserved more than to know he was coming back to Atlanta and the best he could hope for was to ride on the back of a garbage truck or mop floors in a pool room."

"Your heart-warming story is tugging at my heart strings."

"I wish I could believe that, but you'd have to have a heart. You and me and everybody else in Atlanta knows you don't."

Brewster smiled and turned toward the mop and bucket. "I'd like to stay here and trade stories with you but unless you've taken up mopping floors, I'm gonna go get me a gimp-legged nigger named Thomas."

CHAPTER 4

It was not unusual for Big Town to be half filled and buzzing with regulars by mid-morning. Many of them came from the boarding house and hotels, many no more than flop houses, scattered all over town. Some of the men rode the bus, some walked and a few drove from where they lived to the pool room. They spent the day hustling pool, betting on baseball, football or basketball games depending on the season or generally trying to figure the next angle that would make them a few bucks.

Some were married with working wives. A few actually had jobs themselves. That small group came in after work or on their lunch break. The two things most of them had in common was a general dislike of the police, anything or anyone who had to do with them, and anything that resembled a regular job. Some took part time or day labor jobs; those lasted only long enough to get back to their seats along the walls in Big Town.

When they began to arrive that morning they were not happy to see their favorite hang-out filled to the brim with blue suits when they topped the stairs.

Johnny heard the owner, Henry Belcher, before he reached the top of the stairs. Like most of the men who frequented Big Town, the owner had a nickname. He opened the pool room in 1949 with money he inherited when his mother died. A player himself, he spent most of his time and all of his money betting on baseball. By owning the place, he had the opportunity to make a few bucks from the other players. That was enough to keep the place open and operating. The owner, like many of the men who frequented the pool room, would bet on any sporting event. Also like the others, he was always looking for an edge. Once he managed to buy a hockey player. The player, whose name and team had long been forgotten by most of the men, had dogged a couple of shots thus insuring the other team won. The only problem was that Henry could not get anyone in Atlanta to bet on a sport they did not understand and most of them had never even heard of. It cost him the price of the bribe and he couldn't place a single bet on the already determined outcome of the game. Once the word got out that he fixed the hockey game, he was given the nickname Hockey Doc.

"What the hell's going on?" Hockey Doc made his way up the remainder of the steps. He pushed aside a young uniformed Atlanta police officer.

"I'm sorry, sir, you can't—"

"The hell I can't. Get out of my way before you get hurt." Doc stopped at the top of the flight. "Thomas? Thomas? Did you let all these people in here?"

Johnny came to him. "Take it easy, Doc, Thomas is not here." Hockey Doc brushed by Johnny when he saw another group of uniformed police officers in the middle of the room. Beside them were three men in white hospital uniforms. Another man was pulling a tall step ladder over to the end of table number seven.

"Will somebody tell me what the hell's going on and why I've got so many cops in here people will think I'm giving away donuts?" He turned toward Johnny. "You know what this is all about?"

Johnny took him by the arm and led him to a chair along the opposite wall. "I'd say having a dead man on one of the tables was a good guess." He paused to allow his comment to sink in. He pulled out his pack of Luckies and offered one to Doc, who quickly accepted.

"A dead man? Is it one of the regulars? What was it, heart attack?" Doc took the cigarette and offered light, and when he fired it up, he pulled deeply from the cigarette. "Wait a minute. If he had a heart attack, how'd he fall on the table? You said he was *on* table seven. Not beside it or under it. Something ain't right here, Johnny. What's going on?'

"I think he's been in a couple of times, but I can't remember his name." Johnny hesitated. "But that's not important. Somebody shot him."

"They shot him on the table? Shit. The bullet must have gone into the slate. You know how much it's gonna cost to get a new piece of slate?" Doc dropped the half-smoked cigarette on the wood floor, crushed it beneath his shoe with a twisting motion of his foot and walked toward the activity.

A man with a camera was now standing atop the next-to-the last step of a six foot ladder at the end of the table. He was leaning toward the middle of the table as he took photos of the dead man. As each flashbulb popped, he pushed a button on the back of the gooseneck attachment and the bulb was ejected and dropped to the floor. Doc crushed one beneath his feet as he walked up.

"You gonna clean up your own mess. This ain't what I pay Thomas for." Doc looked around. "Where the *hell* is he, anyways? You seen him, Johnny? He's never late."

"Why don't we let the cops do whatever it is they need to do, and I'll tell you everything I know? Let's go to your office."

Without waiting, he led Doc to the small room that

served as an office and occasional bedroom for the owner. The office had a large old wooden desk, two chairs and a small couch. The walls were covered with large, out-of-date calendars kept only for the photos of scantily clad women. They posed while holding cans of motor oil or a variety of automotive parts. Others were posed in skimpy lingerie. Doc sat and Johnny stood.

"I got here early this morning. I'm supposed to go over to a lawyer's office and pick up some papers he wants me to serve. He wanted me to meet me here at nine, 'cause he didn't want anyone in his office to know he was using me. I came in and there was nobody else here, except Thomas, and I didn't see him right away." Johnny took a seat on the couch. Doc swiveled in the chair to face him. "Not all of the lights were on like normal, so it didn't feel right when I was coming up the steps, you know what I mean?"

Doc nodded. "Yeah, like something ain't right, but you don't know just what."

Johnny continued to talk to Doc as he pulled off the shoulder rig and opened the bottom right drawer of the desk. He had an agreement with Doc to let him keep his pistol and holster in the drawer when he was in the building. "I looked around and saw something on the table. By the time I got back there and saw it was a stiff, I saw Thomas in the back where he keeps his mop bucket. He panicked when he saw me. Said he had to get out of here."

"You think Thomas done it? I know he carries a knife, but they all either have a knife or a straight razor in their pocket. But you said this guy was shot."

"No, I don't think he did it, but Brewer does."

"Brewer? How'd he get involved in this already? Did you call him?"

"As soon as I found the body."

"I guess he'd probably get the squeal anyways. He's been working homicide for the last year or two." Doc motioned for Johnny to give him another cigarette. "From what you said, this would probably be a homicide. Not too many guys'll shoot themselves on a pool table. Why does he think Thomas killed the guy?"

"Because Thomas was working, and he left before Brewer got here. In his world that's an admission of guilt. Plus if you noticed, the dead man is white and Thomas ain't. Thomas was smart enough to know Brewer would make that connection right away. He left as soon as he saw what had happened. He told me he had nothing to do with it, and I believe it. He was as surprised to see the body as I wa—" Johnny was interrupted when a young police officer came to the door.

"Mister Belcher, we need to talk to you. You want to do it here or you want to come downtown with us?"

"Look outside the window, Junior. We're already downtown. I ain't going nowhere with you or anyone else wearing a uniform. You want to talk? Do it here and do it fast. I got a business to run."

Over the officer's shoulder, two men in hospital whites were rolling a stretcher with a body covered in a white sheet. They had it tucked tightly around the body, so in death the former occupant of table number seven now looked like a week's worth of bundled up dirty clothes being rolled to the cleaners.

The officer took out a small notebook, folded the cover back and pulled a pencil from his shirt pocket. "I'll need your full name and address."

"How about we trade? You tell me the name and address of the man you just scraped off one of my tables and I'll give you mine." Doc looked at Johnny for support and approval. A slight nod was sufficient.

"No need to be that way, Hockey Doc, I'm just—"

"Hockey Doc? How'd we get on first name basis? My name is Mister Belcher to you, Junior. Only my friends call me that. And we ain't even been formally introduced."

"You want to be a hard-ass, Mister Belcher, I'll show you hard. We'll keep cops up here investigating everything and everyone so long that the only business you'll have is the officers buying cokes and crackers if you're lucky. You want to play that way, it's your call."

Doc looked at Johnny.

"I was the first one here today," Johnny said. "I've already talked to Detective Brewer. Mister Belcher, here, arrived only about twenty minutes ago."

The officer turned to Johnny. "So, what? Are you his lawyer or something? Detective Brewer said all of you guys stuck together. Something about honor among thieves is what he said." The officer closed his book and walked away. "I ain't got time to play grab-ass with you people. Let the suits figure out who done what to who."

They watched as he walked out of the office and left the pool room. Several of the regulars had gathered outside the door during the exchange and were now waiting to see what happened next. Johnny and Doc ignored them and went to the counter to get a cup of coffee. By that time, the seats along the wall were also filling up as the news spread about the dead man.

Like Hockey Doc, most of the other men who frequented Big Town were known only by their nicknames. The first time Johnny walked upstairs and became a part of the Big Town culture, he was immediately taken by the colorful names the men used. Even though they had distinctive names, he felt like he was looking at cars in a used car lot. If you walked through the lot you'd find Fords, Chevrolets, a Studebaker or two, and maybe even a Cadillac or a Packard. Stand next to each model and you knew it was distinct, but if you stood back and looked at the lot as a whole, all you saw were used, worn-out cars. They all looked the same, most had the same problems and many, like the men at Big Town, were probably not fixable.

Men with names like Oots, Slim, Haboo, Preacher, Red, and Crip gathered in small groups to discuss what had happened. Preacher, the oldest of the group, alternated between hanging out at Big Town and standing on a street corner, Bible in hand, graphically describing the road to ruin.

He once left for several months when he started a church that held services in an old gas station that was closed on Sunday. He soon came back and now could be counted on as a poker player if he could find enough money to sit in on a game. He was the first to approach Johnny and Doc.

"You ain't gonna lose your license or nothing, are you?" he asked Doc as he placed a five cent piece in a quart jar on the counter and poured a cup of coffee. The men would cheat a stranger and sometimes each other out of his life savings if given the opportunity, but they all paid their tab at Big Town.

"I didn't have nothing to do with it. I don't even know who the guy was." Doc turned to Johnny. "You said you knew him?"

Johnny topped off his coffee from the large coffee urn which had once sat in an Army mess hall. He still took it without cream or sugar after years of black coffee in the army. "I said he was in here a couple of times. I recognized him but I don't know his name."

Doc looked around as the last blue suiter left the room. The chalk mark was still on the green felt covering of the table where the body had been when the cops arrived. Blood stains had ruined the remainder of the felt.

"I should have shook his ass down for the cost of fixing the table before they took him out of here."

CHAPTER 5

B y three in the afternoon, everyone in Atlanta who was out of doors, and most of those inside buildings, were soaking wet. From mid-May to mid-September, the daily humidity was usually as high as the actual temperature. By mid-afternoon storm clouds gathered in sufficient quantity to darken the sky, drop the temperature a few degrees and create enough wind to blow debris all over the streets, soon followed by booming thunder and the crack of lightning as the storm hovered over the modern, new high-rise landscape that was becoming Atlanta and drenched everything and everyone. The storm lasted only long enough for the ground to be teased with a scant resupply of the moisture which the Georgia summer quickly fried from it again.

The afternoon Johnny walked out of Big Town was no exception. He had spent most of the day there after talking to the cops working the death. When he left Big Town, Johnny was wearing a white, short-sleeved shirt and brown pants. He carried a light sports jacket over his shoulder until he got to the street. Since he had retrieved the shoulder rig from Doc's office, he had to slip on the jacket. When he pushed open the door leading to the street, the heat hit him like a warm, wet blanket.

He heard the first roll of thunder as he walked down

Whitehall Street to the hamburger joint on the corner. He wasn't particularly hungry, but the two large fans spinning at either end of the diner offered a short respite from the heat. At the counter he ordered a burger and fries. As he waited he glanced around the diner looking to see if he recognized any of the other patrons.

This was a favorite place for the men from Big Town who were coming or going and wanted something different from the spicy but limited menu served where they spent most of the day. For forty cents, they could get a decent hamburger, a plate of fries so greasy you left an oil slick on your evening bathwater, a cup of coffee with unlimited refills and a piece of pie. Placing a half dollar on the counter when you sat down guaranteed the waitress a ten cent tip and that your coffee cup never ran dry.

Johnny took a seat and placed two quarters in front of him when he ordered.

He found a copy of the *Atlanta Constitution*, the morning newspaper, on the stool next to his. Johnny opened it to the sports section and read the box scores for the teams in the Southern Association. The Atlanta Crackers were first and the Chattanooga Lookouts were only one game behind.

He was checking the line-up for the evening game between the Crackers and the New Orleans Pelicans when he was jostled as the stool next to him filled with another body. Without looking, he knew who it was.

"Lemme have the comics, will you? I want to see what's happening to the Phantom. They got him in a cave, and some guy's about to pull off his mask." Detective Brewer motioned for a cup of coffee as he took the seat. "You think you'd pull the mask off the Phantom if you got the chance? It'd be like taking it off the Lone Ranger. Some people just don't need to have others know who they are."

Johnny put his part of the newspaper down. "You're taking this someplace, right?"

"Smart. You should be a detective. You ever thought about that? Maybe you could get hired in some little shithole town down in South Georgia. A place with three cops, one car, maybe an old motorcycle to catch speeders if they got a speed trap set up. I'll bet a town like that has a need for a detective to figure out who's stole old widow Jones drawers off the clothes line."

The waitress slid a mug of coffee in front of Brewer. "This gonna be it or you want something to eat?" She stood in front of them, order pad in her hand.

"I'd like something to take home with me. What time do you get off?" Brewer smiled at his feeble attempt at a pick-up line.

"Why would I want to go home with you? You already got one asshole living there. There's no room for another one." She closed her pad and walked to the other end of the counter.

Johnny had to laugh as he looked at Brewer. "I'll bet you've been saving that line for just the perfect opportunity, haven't you?"

"I'll tell you what I did save. I saved your ass."

"From what?" Johnny picked up his coffee mug.

"You know I could have run you in this morning if I wasn't such a nice guy." Brewer took a drink from his coffee and waited for Johnny to respond.

"Yeah, I suppose you could have, but you and I both know I didn't do it. I'm not even sure I know the man. I think even you'll have to agree you probably need to know the victim in a crime like this to have a motive."

Brewer nodded in agreement.

Outside the café, a fire truck sped by, its lights and siren breaking the stillness of the post-thunder-storm afternoon.

Brewer pulled three photos from his jacket pocket. "Take a good look at these and tell me everything you know about the subject." He placed the photos on the counter. Just as Johnny picked up the first one, the waitress came with his order. As she placed the plate with the burger and fries on the counter, she noticed the photos.

"He dead?" She sat the second plate with the pie beside the photos.

"Now what makes you think that? Maybe he just likes to pose lying down on a morgue table with his eyes closed." Brewer slid one of the photos around so she could get a good look at it. "You ever see him in here? Maybe early this morning?"

She studied the photos for a minute. "He does kinda look familiar, but I can't be sure. Unless he was a big tipper, I'd never remember him." She placed the photos back on the counter. "You may want to talk to Peggy. She comes in at five and gets off at three. You just missed her."

"See, that's called detective work." Brewer reached across and picked up one of the greasy fries off Johnny's plate and took a bite.

Johnny swiveled sideways on the low stool. He held up his hamburger. "You want a bite of this to go with your fries?"

"Keep that up and I may reconsider my decision that you're not a suspect." Brewster scooped up the photos and put them in his pocket. "'We'll talk some more later." He stood up. "You got enough change there to pay for my coffee. I'll catch the bill next time."

"That's why no waitress will ever remember you, Mister Big Tipper." Johnny finished his meal, read the sports section, folded the paper, and placed it on the stool when he left.

He stepped out on the sidewalk and let two people

with large umbrellas pass by him. They must have been tourists, he thought, as no one in Atlanta used umbrellas. The rain lasted ten or fifteen minutes, and if you got caught out in it the best way to stay dry was to slip into an open shop's doorway or take refuge under an overhead canopy. Carrying an umbrella was just not worth the return. As soon as the two passed him, he melted into the crowd on the sidewalk. He had taken but a few steps when he heard his name called from a doorway.

"Mister Johnny?" The person who called his name stepped beside him and walked at his pace. "Is there some way I can call you tonight? I can get to a phone anytime you can."

The woman walking beside Johnny was a very attractive young woman in her mid-twenties. She was about five feet six inches tall and even as she hunkered beneath the umbrella, he could tell she had a very nice figure. Her skin was the color of cream, lightly dusted with coffee. "I'm Thomas's sister. He said you could be trusted. He needs help."

Johnny did a double take because she had to be at least half, if not more, white.

The streets were filled with shoppers, office workers, and those with nothing to do. The people were both white and colored, but they were not walking together. Without speaking, Johnny nodded his acknowledgement to the woman. With her a few feet behind him, he walked to a bus stop where he stood near the light post. His companion recognized what he was doing and stood slightly to the right with the post almost between them. Here they could talk without raising eyebrows.

"Did Thomas tell you where to find me?"

"He said you usually went to Jack's for something to eat about this time every day." Her voice gave away her nervousness. "I took a day off from work to find you. We really need your help, but I can't talk to you here. Can I call you someplace tonight? Anywhere. Just for a few minutes. Please?"

Johnny looked at her. Her eyes were filled with fear and pleading. They were also unusually light for someone who claimed to be Thomas's sister.

"I'll be at the Emerald Lounge at eight. The number is Euclid two, two, six, one. Can you remember that?"

"I'll call you at eight." She turned to walk away, stopped and came back. "My name is Rachel." She stepped back and disappeared into the crowd on the sidewalk.

In spite of himself, Johnny watched her walk away. The sway of her hips and legs revealed she knew she was being watched. If she was doing it just for him, he thought as he shook his head, he was not sure if it was working or not.

Johnny walked the three blocks down Whitehall to Five Points, where he waited for the bus to take him to his rooming house. By the time the bus came, the clouds had cleared away and the sun was beating down with a vengeance, lest anyone forget the rain and its relief was only temporary.

There were only three other people waiting to get on the bus when it stopped. As soon as it pulled to the curb, the rear door opened and several people got off. After Johnny boarded in the front, an old man with a cane slowly stepped on the first step, grabbed the metal hand rail, and pulled himself into the bus. As soon as he dropped a token in the fare box, he made his way to the back of the bus marked *Colored Seating Area*.

Johnny pulled the cord above the window, and the bell rang for his stop. The driver slipped to the curb and Johnny got off across the street from the old brick boarding house where he lived.

When Johnny first arrived in Atlanta, he stayed in a cheap hotel not far from the bus station. With no job and no contacts in the city, he had to take what he could find. His first job was as a cook in a diner across from his hotel. It was there that he met Henry Lewis. Henry was a bookie who lived in the same hotel and ate at least one meal a day in the diner. After watching Henry for several weeks, Johnny's police training kicked in, and he realized he was doing his daily tally at the table each morning. When it came time for the Kentucky Derby, Johnny had a horse he wanted to play.

Henry was sitting at the counter when Johnny placed his breakfast in front of him. At the time, Henry had the sports page open.

"You know anything about horses?" Johnny asked as he poured a second cup of coffee for Henry.

"Enough to know they're hard to pick." Henry looked up from the paper. "How 'bout you? You a railbird? You follow the horses?"

"I bet on them some when I lived in Florida. Dogs, too. I have one in the Derby I really like. I'd like to put a fin on him." Johnny slid a five dollar bill across the counter toward Henry. "You know any place that'll cover the bet?"

Before Henry could answer, another customer rapped his knuckles on the counter to get Johnny's attention. Johnny left the five on the counter when he walked down to the other man.

"What's a man got to do to get some food around here?" he demanded and slid the nearby napkin holder to his place.

"No problem. Take a look at the menu and I'll be—"

"I don't need a menu. I already know what I want." He cut Johnny off in mid-sentence. "I want eggs over, country ham, two biscuits, grits, and some of that stuff you put in cups and call coffee." He almost threw the menu at Johnny as he slid it across the counter.

From his seat at the end of the restaurant, Henry was watching the action as it unfolded.

Johnny drew a cup of coffee, and reached beneath the counter to pick up a set-up for the man. As he placed it in front of him, he hesitated. "If you don't mind, I got a question for you."

"What is it?" The man looked up from the morning paper he was folding as he propped it up between his plate and the napkin holder.

"How many people do you see working behind the counter here?"

"I see you, but I'm still not sure you're actually working."

"Good. Real good. But look around. Who do you think is gonna cook the food you just ordered?" He leaned down to eye level with the man. "You see a cook anywhere? I'll give you a hint. It's gonna be me, and while I'm cooking, I'll probably remember how nice and friendly you've been to me since you got here." He stood to his full five-feet-ten-inch height. "You sure you don't want to take your business and your attitude someplace else this morning and start over?"

Without comment, the man stood and left.

Johnny watched him leave and then returned to stand in front of Henry.

Henry nodded. "I'll keep this five in case I happen to run across someone who can get down on the horses. Who do you like?"

"His name is Hill Gail. He's going to be Eddie Arcaro's mount. I think that's an almost unbeatable combination."

A week later, Arcaro rode the horse to a Derby win, and Henry paid Johnny fourteen dollars. Johnny and Henry had been friends ever since. It was Henry who suggested Johnny put his military police talents to use and get his private investigator's license in Atlanta. It was also Henry who introduced him to Big Town.

Henry took Johnny there one Saturday to listen to a baseball game he was booking. The chairs along the wall were filled with men paying rapt attention to the games being broadcast. Henry used Big Town to listen to the ball games and conduct his business. That day, he was booking fly balls in a game between the Washington Senators and the Cleveland Indians. The Senator's pitcher had just come up from the minors and the Cleveland players were hitting balls all over the park, most of them in the air. Henry lost his shirt that day, but Johnny was hooked on Big Town and the men who called it home.

Just after getting his license, Johnny moved to the place where he now lived on Ponce de Leon Avenue. It was an old neighborhood, quiet, few children, enough bars and restaurants to add variety to his evening's drinking and meals. And it was on the bus line. Just what he wanted.

At ten minutes to eight, Johnny walked down the street to the Emerald Bar. It was a small place that served a decent steak and a drink worth paying for. They had a juke box that was not too loud if you were on the phone, and loud enough to dance to if you were one of the men who brought a wife or girlfriend.

"Evening, Johnny." Without asking, Ray, the bartender slid a bottle of Johnny's brand of beer down the bar where it landed almost dead center in front of him.

Johnny picked up the bottle and nodded his greeting to Ray. He wondered if Rachel really was going to call and what she wanted.

As he sat, sipping on the beer, he realized he had thought entirely too much about her since meeting her in the afternoon rain. He unconsciously shook his head to clear the thoughts.

At exactly eight, the phone on the wall at the opposite end of the bar from the juke box rang. Ray walked toward it to answer, when Johnny stood.

"I think it's for me, Ray. I'll get it."

He pulled the receiver off the hook on the fourth ring.

"Hello?" There was silence on the other end. "Hello?"

"Is—is this the Emerald Bar?" a female voice asked. Wives and girlfriends often called looking for the man in their life, so it was not unusual.

"This is the Emerald. Are you Rachel?"

CHAPTER 6

The Rio Vista Supper Club was a not-so-well-kept secret. The two-story building overlooking the Chattahoochee River was a popular destination for dining and dancing. Tony Ventura and the All Stars had headlined the entertainment on the upper floor restaurant for as long as anyone could remember. The best item on the menu was a Kansas City steak dinner with baked potato, salad and hot rolls made daily in the kitchen's bakery. The music was mostly Tony's rendition of songs popular on the radio of the day or those from the big bands of the past decade. The club had one of the few liquor licenses in the city so the patrons could get a highball, or a glass of wine. There was Champagne for the ladies and special celebrations. As good as those features were, that was not the reason most of the guests came to the Rio, as it was known.

Patrons arrived at the Rio Vista Supper Club in Lincolns, Cadillacs, and a few older Packards. As soon as they pulled into the parking lot, an attendant opened the car doors for them to exit, and the cars were parked in a lot between the building and the river. When they stepped from the cars, the men were dressed for a night on the town. The majority of them wore suits and ties, many of them still wore hats, and it was not unusual to see a tuxedo or two. Their ladies, many of whom were actually their wives, wore cocktail dresses, heels and enough jewelry to make a cat burglar chase his tail. Most came to enjoy dinner and perhaps to dance. Downstairs held different attractions.

Downstairs, accessible only to special clients, was a full service casino. Slot machines lined the walls and blackjack dealers, craps and roulette tables stood ready for any guest who wanted to try their luck. Guards stood at the only two doors leading into or out of the casino.

Unlike those found at the other underground gambling rooms in the Atlanta area, these guards were not off-duty cops on the payroll. These guards were imported muscle. Rowdy customers or bad losers were given the opportunity to apologize to those they offended. If they chose not to do so, they were escorted out of the room. Rumors abounded about them being escorted all the way across the parking lot and into the river below. A serious offense at the Rio Vista met with serious consequences.

The Rio was the main casino for a new group in town. Atlanta had dealt with invading Yankees, carpet baggers, the Ku Klux Klan and the impact of World War Two on the local economy. This new group, known as the Dixie Mafia, had the potential to be more devastating than all of the others combined.

Atlanta was a cultural oasis in the middle of a turn-of-the-century desert of lifestyle and thought. Thirty miles in any direction from Five Points you were on dirt roads with clapboard houses. The occupants wore overalls, grew what they ate and thought education was a waste of a good field hand's time. Atlanta was as foreign to most of them as the Pyramids.

The Dixie Mafia also saw Atlanta as a Pyramid of sorts. It was filled with treasure waiting to be plundered.

They started organizing bootlegging operations and

distribution during the Prohibition era. Their talents were refined with black market operations during the war. With several military bases in the area, a bomber plant in Marietta and the expansion of the airport at Chandler Field, there was a lot of money to be made if the persons had no loyalties to anyone or anything.

After the war, the returning GIs had a lot of money to spend and not much to spend it on. Ever the one to discover a need and fulfill it—slot machines, juke boxes, prostitution, and whiskey in the multitude of dry counties throughout the South felt the not-so-gentle touch of the Dixie Mafia. They continued to make a lot of money, mainly because they did not care who got hurt in the process.

Throughout the South, in the larger cities like Atlanta, New Orleans, Miami, Memphis and Nashville, you could find casinos to rival the newly created gambling Mecca of Las Vegas. The Rio was the premier spot for Atlanta.

The black 1952 Cadillac Fleetwood pulled to the entrance of the Rio. The parking attendants knew immediately who was in it. They rushed to open the doors on both sides for Abraham Salem and his girlfriend. Abraham was married and had two children in a private school on the north side of Atlanta, the only school in town that was both prestigious and admitted Jews. Early in his rise to the top of the local heap, Abraham had been trapped in a warehouse he and another man had set on fire. Before he could get out, his face was severely burned, earning him the nickname of "Jew Ugly."

The last person who was not an intimate of Abe's who called him that to his face had disappeared, never to be seen again.

"Good evening, Mister Salem. I'll take good care of the Caddy. You just go on in and have a good time." The valet was a young man who knew enough to immediately forget the names of anyone who arrived or left the Rio in case he was ever asked. For that he made more in tips on the weekend than most family men made in a week.

Salem did not respond to the young man other than to casually hand him a dollar bill. Salem walked ahead of the striking brunette who was his companion for the evening. She was left to follow him.

Inside, he was immediately greeted by several of the regulars. Like a king surveying his domain, he hesitated long enough for everyone to notice his arrival. He took the opportunity to quickly see who was there that he needed to acknowledge or who needed to acknowledge him. As he made his way to his reserved table, glasses were raised in a toast, hands were offered for a handshake and occasionally a close associate introduced him to his lady for the evening.

At his table, the maître d' pulled out a chair for the lady and one for Salem. Before either of them had settled into the seats, another man was pouring them a glass of champagne. "Our special tonight is filet mignon, just like you like it. I took the liberty of having the chef start one for you and the lady when I saw you arrive."

"You must think I'm a big tipper, Ernie." Salem shook out the napkin and placed it in his lap. "Or do you treat all the thugs in here like this?"

"Just you, Mister Salem." Ernie hesitated. "And of course, the lady." He reached over and pulled the linen napkin from the table in front of her, popped it open, and placed it on her lap.

"You're good, Ernie. I'll remember that later." Salem took a sip from his glass and motioned for Ernie to lean close to him. "Go downstairs and see if Joe Skinner is in the house. If he is, tell him to come see me. Don't let anyone hear you tell him." He folded a bill and tucked it into Ernie's pocket.

The band started a new number, and several couples left their tables for the dance floor.

"I wish you'd dance with me. It's not so hard. I taught lots of guys—"

Salem cut his companion off in mid-sentence. "Then why don't you have one of them bring you here, buy you dinner, a bottle of champagne, some nice clothes, and maybe they'll dance with you?" Abe stood, tossed his napkin in the middle of the table. "I gotta go to the can. You stay here."

With that, he disappeared down the hallway.

૯౧౬౮

Joe Skinner was at the craps table when Ernie approached him.

The table rail was filled with players. Each person had his, or occasionally her, stack of chips rolled out in the tray in front of them. Several players had impressive racks with the high value black and gold chips in them.

Joe had the dice and had, just two rolls previously, rolled his come out number. The marker was placed on the nine indicating Joe's point. He had covered most of the numbers on the layout and was taking the payoff for his last roll which was a six when Ernie came to stand discretely behind him.

Ernie was in a jam. His duty was on the floor upstairs taking care of the guests. However when Abraham Salem gave him a mission he had to carry it out.

If Joe's luck held and he didn't roll a seven soon, Ernie could find himself standing there for a long time; he dared not interrupt the man in the middle of a good run.

The stick man captured the dice, flipped them several times to the land with a five and a four showing and slid them back to Skinner. "The point is nine. All bets are down."

Skinner took the dice and handed them to the tall blonde standing next to him. She was almost as tall as Skinner in her heels. She wore a tight fitting green dress that accentuated every curve, and she had plenty of them to display.

"Here you go, Virginia, you like to blow on things, see what you can do with these." His comment was met with laughter from those on the rail and no embarrassment from Virginia as she did as she was told.

Virginia, with the crowd's encouragement, blew on the dice and then held them in her right hand. She shook them close to her right ear and, with the crowd around the table yelling, tossed them to the far end where they bounced off the upswing of the table and rolled to a stop in the middle of the FIELD play area. One dice quickly showed a two, the other spun on its edge and finally land- ed with a five showing. With Virginia rolling a seven, Joe's run was over.

"Good run, Joe. I made a bundle off you," one of the men standing next to him joked as he watched Joe's chips raked from the cloth.

"I'm sorry, Joe, I'll do better next time." Virginia held his arm in an obvious promise to make up for her loss of the dice.

Joe turned to order a drink when Ernie slid beside him. "Mister Skinner, Mister Salem is upstairs. He'd like to see you." He hesitated, "without anyone knowing."

Without acknowledging his presence, Joe spoke to Er- nie. "Tell him I'll meet him in the office in ten minutes."

He took Virginia's hand from his arm and placed it in Ernie's. "Take Virginia upstairs and get us a good table. I'll be up after I talk to Abe." Joe Skinner was the only person Ernie knew who called Mister Abraham Salem

"Abe." Maybe others had, but they probably were some-place between the Rio and the Gulf of Mexico where the Chattahoochee River ended its journey.

Ernie escorted Virginia to a table only two over from where Abraham Salem was sitting. Once she was seated and he had taken her drink order, he went back to Salem.

"Mister Skinner will meet you in the office in ten minutes."

"Was that ten minutes from when he told you or from now, Ernie?"

"I suppose it was from when he said it, Mister Salem. And that was about three minutes ago. I had to bring his lady up and—"

"No, what you had to do was go give him the message I told you to deliver. And then, if there was one from him, you had to bring it to me. We got guys outside who park cars and guys in here who park people. Do this again and you'll be working for one of those two groups." Salem stood and walked away.

A very large man standing by the door moved at the same time and followed Salem through the kitchen to the Rio's office.

The office was small but well furnished. It was used by a number of people. The manager of the Rio almost had to make a reservation on the weekend to get into it. It was a place where strategy was planned, profits were dis-tributed, disagreements were settled and contracts were awarded. These contracts were not for road paving, house building, automobile purchases or delivery of meat to the Rio. The contracts awarded in the manager's office were serious. Deadly serious.

When Abraham entered, his bodyguard stood outside the door. Joe was already inside pouring a drink.

"Scotch, okay?" Joe poured a second drink for Abra-ham when he entered.

"That's good." He picked up the glass, touched his to Joe's and took a drink. "Not bad. Where'd we get it?"

"It came in from that shipment that went to the country club. Three cases of scotch and another five of bourbon. There'll be more next time."

Abraham walked around the small office, touched a few things on the desk, took another sip of his scotch, and then sat behind the desk. If it was a power play to let Joe know who was the senior person in the room it worked. When he sat, he motioned for Joe to take a seat.

Joe poured both of them another drink then took a seat in a large cloth covered chair in a corner to the left of the desk.

"I been thinking, Joe."

"That can be a dangerous thing, Abe, depending on what you been thinking about." Joe had been born in New York and even with over twenty years in the Deep South, he still had a Brooklyn accent on some words. His "you" always came out as "youse."

"Havana."

"You thinking about going?"

"Not me, you, Joe. I'm thinking about you going to Havana."

"Why do you want me to go to Havana? We went last year, remember? There's a lot of action down there, but it's too far away. Ain't it?"

"You gotta start thinking bigger, Joe. We got airplanes now that go all the way across the states without stopping. You can grab a plane from here to Miami, spend the night and be in Havana the next day. That makes it as close as driving to New Orleans."

"Okay, so what's there now that wasn't last year?" Joe reached for the bottle and poured another drink. He slid the bottle back without pouring one for Abe.

"Casinos with lots of money. That's what's there. All

we got to do is get into the middle of them and we can lay off as much cash as we can bring back."

"I suppose you have a way to get in on the action?"

Abe smiled and took the bottle from the middle of the desk. He took his time as he poured another drink, swirled the stolen amber liquid in the cut glass tumbler and held it up for a toast.

"I don't, but you do."

"How do I have a way to get in?"

Abe smiled at his old friend. "How long you been banging that broad, uh, what's her name, that you brought here tonight, Joe?'

"Uh, you mean Virginia, that the one? I don't know, maybe six months. What's she got to do with my plan?"

"What do you know about her, Joe?"

"I know she's got great tits—"

"I'm not talking about what you two do in the bedroom or wherever you take her. I mean, what do you know about her personal life?"

Joe starred at him for a silent moment.

"What do you know about her husband, Joe? You do know she's married, don't you?"

"Yeah, I know. But he's never around. Some kinda traveling salesman or something." Joe was leaning forward in the chair. Abe had his undivided attention.

"A salesman? Any idea what he sells or where he goes when he leaves town?"

"Her husband's activities are not high on my list of conversation topics. All's I need to know is that he's out of town, and he ain't coming back when I'm with her." Joe hesitated. "Don't I?"

"I think you better find out where he is when he travels, and what it is he sells."

"You want me to go up and ask Virginia, or are you going to tell me?"

"He works for Saint Louis Games. That mean anything to you?"

"SLG? The card company? He sells dice and cards?"

"The very one. And guess who his biggest customer is
about to become?"

When Joe and Abe touched glasses for their final toast
that night, Abe had initiated a plan which would take the
Dixie Mafia from a disorganized group of backwoods
petty thieves and a few sophisticated men like Abe and
Joe to a force to be reckoned with in the world of crime.

CHAPTER 7

Saturday morning, Johnny rose at six like he always did. He had no real place to go or anything to do, but his internal alarm clock said it was time to get up. After talking to Rachel the night before, he stayed at the Emerald bar a little longer than usual. He drank a little more than usual and, this morning, he felt it a little more than usual. His mouth tasted like the entire Russian Army had marched through it with muddy boots.

Outside his window at the boarding house, he could hear the sounds of birds as they communicated with each other from their perches in the oak trees that dotted not only his back yard but the entire neighborhood. Some of the bird sounds, he thought as he lay in bed listening to them, were warnings about cats or other animals in their territory. Some must have been male birds looking for girl birds, or vice versa as he wasn't sure how it worked in the bird community. One particularly loud and annoying one must have been the neighborhood gossip, for every time he or she sounded off, several others quickly joined in and drowned out the sounds.

"Why can't you just look for worms or pick up an acorn and be about your business?" he asked aloud as he continued to listen.

Having had enough with his conversation with the

birds, Johnny slipped from the bed, and dressed in only white boxer shorts and a cotton tee shirt, he started the day. His room at the boarding house was sparse, but it had everything he needed. His bed was a twin with a mattress so soft he had to bolster it with a piece of quarter inch thick plywood so it didn't sag. He had a small closet where he hung his two suits, a raincoat that he kept when he left the army, and an overcoat that he hardly ever wore.

He bought the coat the year before when Atlanta had one of its annual weeks of below freezing weather. He saw the coat in the window at a men's store on Peachtree. The timing of the sale was perfect. Johnny had just gotten paid for chasing down a guy who owed a furniture store over five hundred dollars. His fee was twenty percent of what he collected, so he had a fresh C note burning a hole in his pocket.

On one wall was a dresser where he had the top drawer filled with the neatly folded shirts he picked up twice a week from the laundry at the corner on Ponce de Leon Avenue where he caught the bus to town. Shirts, washed, ironed and folded were twenty cents each. He could splurge a buck a week on nice shirts if nothing else.

The second drawer was filled with his socks, boxer shorts and undershirts. That left two drawers for a couple of pair of work pants he wore on occasion and a sweater which would have been much better off hanging on a rack in the closet, but it was something he never got around to doing.

In the center of the top drawer, between the neatly stacked shirts, lay Johnny's .45 automatic. He kept it there out of habit. There was no need to hide it as he had a license, and leaving it in plain sight was no problem since he never had any visitors to this room. For him, placing the gun in the drawer was something he had done every night since he got it, and he felt comfortable doing so.

Each room had a small table and a chair. The bathroom with the tub and shower were down the hall and used by Johnny and the four other occupants on the top floor. Five people, including the kid who lived with his parents in the two big rooms downstairs shared the bottom floor bathroom. The walls of his room were painted a dull shade of green over plaster and lathing. If you tried to hang a picture, you wound up with a hole the size of a golf ball as the plaster cracked and crumbled around the nail. That was reason enough for Johnny not to hang anything on the walls.

Still in his boxers, coffee pot in hand, Johnny walked down the hallway to the bathroom, found it unlocked and entered. He quickly stood over the toilet, placed one hand against the wall and aimed for the open bowl beneath him.

After he finished, he brushed his teeth and filled his coffee pot from the white porcelain sink.

Cooking in the rooms was prohibited, but each occupant had a hot plate and a coffee pot. Back in his room he placed the coffee pot on the hotplate and took down his shaving kit, clean boxers and slipped a towel from the rack where he hung it every day when he finished showering. He walked back down the hallway and found the bathroom still empty. He locked the door, stripped and took a quick shower. By the time he finished and returned to the room, the coffee was ready.

On Saturdays, Ruth Gittens, or Miss Ruth as she was known by her boarders had breakfast on the table at seven. There was a twenty minute window of opportunity at each meal. Miss it and miss the meal. The amount you paid at Miss Ruth's was based on one of two systems. You could rent a room with or without meals. If you paid to eat there, you got breakfast and supper. Even those, like Johnny, who didn't pay for their meals got breakfast on Saturday morning.

"Morning, Miss Ruth." Johnny pulled out a chair from the old dark mahogany table as he took a place beside one of the other men who lived on the second floor.

"Good morning, Mister Morocco. I heard you come in after eleven last night." She spoke without looking up from bringing in a plate of biscuits from the kitchen. "Is everything all right?"

Miss Ruth treated the single men in her boarding house like her sons. She looked after them, made sure they got enough to eat, occasionally did some sewing of buttons and small rips in shirts and pants and generally made your business her business.

She placed the pan of biscuits on the table, stopped and looked at Johnny. He knew the look. She was not going to return to the kitchen until she had an explanation of why he had returned home at a time that was, in her opinion, far too late for any person to be out at night.

Now everyone at the table was looking at Johnny.

"Go ahead, Johnny, tell her why you was out last night. We all wanna know." Harold Dotson was a bus driver for the city of Atlanta and had lived at Miss Ruth's place longer than any of the others.

All the people who lived there knew Johnny was a private investigator, but they knew very little about what he or any other person who was a PI did for a living.

"Strictly business. I had to watch a warehouse to see if I could determine who was stealing from the place." He reached for a platter of fried eggs.

"Did you have to shoot anybody?" A small voice rolled in from a table set in the corner for the only child who lived in the building.

"No, Scooter, I didn't shoot anybody." Johnny turned

to face the six-year-old boy. "I didn't even see anybody the whole time I was there."

"Well, if I'd been with you, I'd sure shot somebody with that big ol' gun you carry." He made a pistol with his thumb and forefinger and pointed it toward the table. "Pow, pow! You're all shot." Before he could reload, his mother came to the table and stood in front of him.

"Young man, you stop that right now. I'll have none of that at the table. You want to play like you have a gun, you go outside to shoot at people."

Johnny finished his meal and returned to his room. As he walked from the table, he wondered what the people there would have thought if he told them where he really was last night and especially who he was with.

CHAPTER 8

Rachel was hesitant to talk to Johnny when he answered the phone at the Emerald. "I—I don't know if I should be talking to you or not. Thomas said you're friends with that detective who came out here to the house and talked to Mama and me."

"Believe me when I say if you're talking about an Atlanta Detective named Brewer, that guy doesn't have any friends." Johnny held the phone in his right hand and covered his left ear with his left hand. "What did he say when he came over there?"

"He said he knew Thomas killed that man, and if we'd tell him where he was, he wouldn't hurt him." She hesitated. "I think that was a lie, don't you?"

"Do you know where Thomas is?"

There was a long silence on the other end of the phone.

"Rachel, you still there?"

"I am, but I'm not sure I want to answer that question."

"Okay, let me ask it another way. Is Thomas all right?"

He could almost feel the tension leave her voice as she answered. "I think he's okay. He didn't really tell me where he was or what he was doing but I think I know."

"What do you want from me?"

"Thomas said you knew he didn't kill that man, but he can't prove it. You know if they find him, he's gonna automatically be guilty and he'll go to the chain gang for the rest of his life or to the electric chair if they can make it happen. That would kill my mama. You can't let them do it to him. You're his only hope, so please help him." There was a long pause and then she added, "Please, Mister Johnny."

Johnny signaled for another bottle of beer as he spoke into the phone. "The Atlanta Police are handling the case. I don't have anything to do with it one way or another." The bartender sat the bottle on top of the juke box. Johnny handed him a quarter then waved him off.

"But you could look into it, couldn't you?" Rachel's voice was cracking. "I—I can pay you some money. Not much, but I have a little."

"I don't know…" His voice trailed off. "I've never done anything like this before. I don't know if I'm the right person."

"What do you mean you've never done anything like this before? You've never worked on a murder case or you've never tried to help a Negro?"

"Now wait just a minute, you can't—"

Rachel cut him off in mid-sentence. "If it makes you feel any better, Thomas and me are not really brother and sister. We're cousins and the lady we both call Mama is really our grandmother. Our mothers were sisters. Our grandfather was a white man. You saw me and you know I've got white blood. My daddy was white, too, but Thomas's mother was a very angry woman. She wanted to find the blackest man she could so her children didn't have any white features at all. So Thomas is really part white, too. My mother felt just the opposite. I have a sister in Detroit who is passing and nobody knows."

"Passing? I'm not sure I know what you mean."

"She's so light skinned she's passing for white. She looks like she came from Italy or Mexico or someplace like that." She hesitated. "I know you noticed when we were talking that I'm not much darker than you. I've even thought about passing myself."

Johnny recalled, when she stepped out into the rain beside him, he did notice that she was not only light skinned, but a very nice looking woman as well.

The juke box began to rumble as two nickels were dropped into the slot and a record was selected. A couple walked hand-in-hand to the small dance floor and stood as they waited for the music to start. Soon Patti Page started lamenting about her loss of a partner during a waltz number as the couple slowly circled the floor.

"I can meet you someplace. Tonight if you want. And give you some money if you'll help Thomas."

"Meet? Where?" He almost laughed at the thought of a place where he could meet Thomas's sister or cousin or whatever she was without one of them getting hurt. He had heard Thomas mention once that he lived near Cabbage Town. If she lived near or with Thomas in Cabbage Town, it was a place where Johnny would not be welcome after dark. She certainly could not just come walking into the Emerald, wave at the bartender and take a seat across the table from Johnny.

"There's a little bar on Peachtree not far from you. I've been there before. With men. White men. And nobody said anything."

She gave him the name and told him she was two blocks away from the bar in a phone booth.

Johnny sat in the booth alone for a few minutes. He had to think this one through if he could. The first question that came to mind was simple. Why was he trying to help Thomas? He didn't know him that well. Johnny knew he or his cousin couldn't pay even his normal fee, and he had never worked on an investigation that included a murder. He placed the beer bottle on the table and ran his finger around the edge of the neck. The glass was smooth and cool to the touch, but it was still glass. One tiny crack and it could nick you. The crack could grow and cut. A drop of blood from a nick, then more from a cut and then—who knew? He picked up the bottle, tilted it to his mouth and, hoping the smooth lip had no way of cutting him, downed the remainder of the liquid.

He was going, but was it to help an innocent man who was also a fellow veteran or a woman he just met and would be as deadly as a rattlesnake to him if he handled her the wrong way?

Thirty minutes later when he pulled up on the street outside the club on Ivy Street, Rachel was standing beside the phone booth where she had made the call. In the dim light from the booth, a streetlight overhead and the glow from the club's sign she looked anything except Thomas's sister.

Rachel wore a light blue dress that could have gotten her arrested on any number of street corners in Atlanta. The dress was tight at the hips, came to mid-calf and had long sleeves. She was smoking a cigarette and Johnny knew from the way she held it and took drags from it, she was just doing it for show. She did not inhale the smoke and, as soon as she got a mouthful, it was quickly expelled in a cloud.

He parked the car and walked back to where she stood.

"Rachel?" He knew it was her, but still called her name.

She dropped her cigarette, quickly crushed it beneath her foot, and turned in his direction. "Yes. I'm glad you came." She held out her hand, then quickly dropped it before Johnny could decide if he wanted to take it or not.

"Look, I don't know if this is a good idea. I mean—"

Rachel cut him off again. "I know what you mean. If you don't want to be seen with me, I understand, but at least let me try to convince you to help Thomas." She hesitated for a moment, and then nodded toward his car. "Is that your car?"

"It is." Johnny was driving a 1937 Chevrolet two-door sedan he had taken as payment for a job from one of the players at Big Town. It was actually worth more than the job, and the guy was supposed to pay Johnny and reclaim his car, but so far the bill of sale written on paper intended to hold a chili dog said the car belonged to Johnny.

"We can ride in the car. Nobody will see us and if they do, just tell them I'm a whore you picked up." Without waiting for his response, she walked toward his car.

Johnny drove for over an hour. They went down Peachtree to Five Points, took Whitehall until they picked up Lee Street, and headed toward the West End section of Atlanta. Johnny knew that some of the houses in West End had been taken over by Negros so it was not unusual to see both races in the same neighborhood.

"Did you grow up in Atlanta?" Rachel asked as they drove.

"No. I was born in West Palm Beach, Florida, and spent my life there till I was drafted in ' forty-two." He pulled up to a stop light and watched an old man barely make it across the street before the light changed.

"You were in the war?"

"Yeah. North Africa, Italy, and then they sent me to Japan. I got there two weeks after they dropped the bomb."

"That must have been horrible. The bomb, I mean." She took a moment and looked at the man beside her. "I know the war was bad and all, but the bombing must have been especially bad if the pictures I saw in *Life Magazine* were true."

"They didn't even come close."

"Thomas doesn't talk about it much, but I heard him tell a friend who was in the navy about getting wounded and some kind of medal. They were drinking, and I think that's the only reason he talked about it. His friend called him a hero."

For the remainder of the drive they talked about Thomas and Rachel and how they grew up. She told him how their grandmother took them both in when first Thomas's mother left home, and then when Rachel's mother was killed in a yet-unsolved murder.

"After she was killed, they wanted to arrest my father, but then the police saw me and realized he was white. Nobody, not even my grandmother, thinks he did it, but it didn't matter. No white man was going to be arrested for killing a Negro woman." She reached into her purse and pulled out a pack of cigarettes. "You want one?" She offered the pack to Johnny.

He waved her off as he down-shifted the car and spotted an entrance to a small city park. Johnny pulled the car into a parking space just inside the entrance. "We can talk here for a few minutes." He shifted sideways in the seat and turned toward her. "Okay, we're only gonna have this conversation once. You tell me everything I want to know and don't hold back, you understand?"

"I never hold back." She spoke through a cloud of smoke.

"And if you're not really going to smoke that thing, get rid of it." Johnny took the cigarette from her hand and crushed it in the ash tray beneath the dash board.

"I thought men liked women who smoke." She shifted toward him and pulled one leg beneath her on the seat.

"We can talk about what men like and don't like some other time. Right now, we're talking about Thomas and how to save his ass." He looked deeply into her dark eyes. "That is why you wanted to meet me, isn't it?"

Rachel reached into her purse and pulled out an envelope. "I told you I had some money to pay you. If I wanted to meet you for any other reason, you'd be the one paying." She pulled the top back on the envelope and dropped it on the seat between them. "I may not be able to pay as much as your regular clients, but maybe it won't take as long to find out who really killed that man in the pool room."

"I need to know where Thomas is. You do know, don't you?"

"I said I think I do, but I'm not sure. He may be living with a cousin of ours in Hapeville."

"Just how many cousins do you have in this city?"

"You don't know a lot about us, do you?"

"Us? You mean you and Thomas?"

"No, I mean people like Thomas and me. All we have is family. We have to keep up with them because we never know when we'll need help. We can't go to a bank or a finance company when we need money. We just have each other." She softened a bit. "That's why it's so important that you help Thomas. He and I have lived like brother and sister for so long that that's how I feel about him. He's blood. It doesn't get any closer than that."

She was still looking at him when another car pulled into the parking lot. Although it was on the other side of the paved strip, she quickly turned toward Johnny. "You want me to duck down or lay my head in your lap?"

Before he could answer the car pulled to a stop and cut the lights. Once again, it was quiet and all that concerned them was their discussion in the car where they sat.

Rachel gave a little laugh as Johnny pulled a cigarette

from his pack. "You've never done this before, have you?"

"Done what?"

"Been out with a colored girl. I though all you white boys had to change your luck at least once in your life."

"I'm not out with you. I'm trying to figure out how to help a little guy who is probably in more trouble than he ever thought possible. Right now, I don't give a shit what color he is. If he's not guilty he shouldn't have to hide." Johnny pulled a match from the small box in the ash tray and clicked the end of it with his thumbnail. The flame flickered for a second and then caught.

As he touched it to the end of his cigarette, Rachel pulled a cigarette from her pack and placed it in her mouth as well. He was about to blow out the match when Rachel caught his hand in both of hers and pulled it toward her. Leaning forward, she lit her cigarette from the match and then carefully, with pursed lips, blew the match out.

Johnny grabbed her hand. "Game's over. If you want me to help you and Thomas, cut the shit and play straight with me. I want to know where I can find him Monday morning. If you don't know, then you find out. If you can't find out by Monday morning, you call me and that's the last conversation you and I will ever have." He did not notice the small smile that slightly turned up the corner of her mouth as he started the car, put it in gear and pulled out of the parking lot.

The ride back into Atlanta was made in silence until they got to the intersection of Moreland Avenue. "Where do you want me to drop you?"

"Anyplace on a bus line is fine. I can catch one on almost any corner around here." Rachel looked out the window and did not face him when she spoke.

"You take that money." He pushed the envelope toward her on the rough brown fabric of the seat. "Put it in your purse and keep it."

"How am I supposed to pay you if you won't take my money?"

"You asked if Thomas was a hero? He saved a guy in 'forty-four so now maybe it's time somebody did something to save him." Johnny glanced in her direction as he drove. "I'm doing this as a favor for Thomas, not you."

He pulled the car up to a light and waited for it to change to green. Outside the car, the summer night was heavy with heat and humidity that did not disappear when the sun went down. Almost every house they passed coming and going to the park had someone sitting on the front porch. The lucky ones had a rocking chair that's motion gave them the false sense of cooling off. Others fanned themselves with cardboard fans on flat sticks advertising funeral homes or churches.

Many of the neighborhood kids still played in the streets. Some were on roller skates strapped to their shoes, some had games of "flies and grounders" going beneath streetlights between the traffic. He passed one old pickup truck with the tail gate down and a group of five or six gathered around sharing a watermelon.

The light changed and he crossed the intersection, pulled to the curb and slipped the car into neutral. "You call me at Big Town Monday morning. If you don't call by ten, don't call at all." He hesitated, waiting for her to open the door and leave.

Rachel looked at the envelope. "Are you sure you don't want this money?" She hesitated a second. "I'm not a whore. I have a job. I worked for this money and earned it honestly. You can call the Grady Hospital and they'll tell you I work in the laundry. It's hard, honest work. Like you do. Hard and honest."

She held out the envelope in one last gesture.

"I told you it was a favor, didn't I?"

Rachel folded the envelope and put it back in her purse. "Okay, I understand favors." She opened the door and slid out. When she closed the door, she walked around in front of the car, taking her time till she got to the driver's side window.

Johnny had his left arm resting on the edge of the car's window frame. Rachel leaned down and placed her hand on his bare arm. "Like I said, I understand favors. And now I owe you one."

Her fingers trailed across his skin as she turned and walked to the bus stop.

CHAPTER 9

Ask anyone on the streets of Havana Cuba who was in charge and they would tell you, "Batista runs Cuba. Meyer Lansky runs Havana." Lansky ran it through his gambling empire in all the major hotels, race tracks and free standing casino operations in Havana.

Gambling first came to Cuba in 1919, but it was nothing like what Lansky brought when he hit town. Originally designed to cater to the Cuban populace, it was a combination of low money bets placed on roulette, craps and other table games or on the national lottery. By the time the Americans of the Roaring Twenties discovered this little bit of Sodom off the southern coast of Florida, the casino owners had discovered another way to make money. Marked cards, shaved dice, mechanics imported from illegal casinos in the US and dealers banned from European casinos were on the payroll. By the mid-twenties, the suckers were never given an even break and the casinos started a long, steady downhill slide. All of that changed when Fulgencio Batista came to power.

He saw the casinos as a way to help finance the lifestyle to which an up and coming Caribbean dictator ascribed. Shortly after taking over the country, he offered the casino operation to Lansky.

In less than two years with the casinos under Lansky's

rule, the corruption was gone and the tourists were back.

The first full service casino in Havana was small compared to the legal ones in Vegas and even the illegal, but overlooked, ones in Miami Beach. Set in the Nacional Hotel, it had a total of ten table games and twenty-one slot machines. It was opened by a seasoned casino operator from Las Vegas. He knew what he was doing in Las Vegas and tried to do the same thing in Havana. Unfortunately, Havana was not quite ready for a legitimately run casino.

Batista knew he could make a fortune on the casinos, but he also knew he did not have the experts within his trusted circle of friends and supporters to make them work. He had to look outside the Cuban people for that. He contacted Lansky and made him an offer he could not refuse. As soon as the head of one of the largest Mafia families in the United States stepped off the plane in Havana, he smelled money.

Lansky placed his trusted Lieutenants in the San Souci Hotel, the Capri and eventually in the Nacional. Even the supposedly state-run lottery answered to Lansky. The change in the operations meant that for the average tourist who came down from the east coast and the local player from Cuba, there was no need for marked cards or shaved dice. There was enough money flowing through the cashier cages to satisfy even the insatiable appetites of the Mafia.

But even the Mafia can't resist temptation. This time it wasn't the established, old line Costa Nostra, but the upstart syndicate known as the Dixie Mafia that wanted a piece of the action.

During the years after the Depression and into World War Two the two homespun industries that began to take hold in the South were illegal whiskey and gambling. Whiskey was so widespread that almost every family had someone who made whiskey or home brewed beer. It was all tax-free and illegal. The whiskey was made and bottled in stills set deep in the pine forests of Georgia, the swamps of Louisiana or the hills of Tennessee. The market was every country store and gas station in the state. Pay enough to the county sheriff and a judge or two, and your business flourished until a politician needed a platform for an upcoming election.

Gambling was different. It was not a one-person operation like a still. Gambling was done in roadhouses or supper clubs in some of the bigger cities in the states. Because of the size of the operation, organization was inevitable. Local men associated with the Dixie Mafia worked the tables, dealt the cards, tended the bars and made certain that the money stayed in the house.

When the first illegal casino was planned for Miami, two factions wanted the action. The old-line organized syndicate and the local Dixie Mafia. Heads were broken, bodies were found floating in Biscayne Bay and no one could determine how to share. Finally a compromise was reached, Miami went to the Mafia and, as a part of the deal, a small take from the casinos in Cuba was promised to their Dixie counterparts.

That money was for Abe Salem, the head of the Dixie Mafia, and Joe Skinner was responsible for delivering it to him.

ᕙᕗᕙ

Otis Hightower loved being on the road. No factory job for him. No, sir. He wanted to jump in his car, load his sample case into the trunk and head out. One week, he'd head north from Atlanta toward Chattanooga. There were only two gambling houses there, but a lot of the bars on the highway bought his punch boards. In a good week, he could sell fifty boards, and with a profit of fifty cents a board, he'd clear twenty five dollars just on them. That didn't count the decks of playing card and counter stands containing twenty pair of dice he sold at most of the gas stations and truck stops. All things considered, he'd bring home at least fifty dollars cash after he paid for gas and expenses on a trip to Chattanooga. And that was his worst territory.

Otis got up and headed for the bathroom as soon as the alarm began to ring. He had been lying in bed, listening to the clock tick for over an hour. He always did that when he was heading for his biggest accounts in Florida. His wife Virginia lay next to him. She didn't move until the clock jarred her awake.

"Oh, God. Is it time to get up already?" She pulled the pillow over her head to drown out the sound.

"It's Monday all over the world. A new week and a new adventure," Otis responded in a much-too cheery manner for Virginia. They were at opposite ends of the spectrum when it came to sleep habits. Virginia was a night person. She could sleep till noon or later every day if left alone. Otis went to bed by ten every night and was awake by six-thirty every morning even if he didn't have an alarm clock. He even awoke at the same time on the weekends.

Virginia rolled over and pulled the pillow from her head now that the alarm had been silenced. "You seem to have all the adventures. My week is going to be the same as last week, the week before and next week as well." Virginia stretched, pushing her arms over her head while yawning. Her blonde hair was mussed from sleep and from her and Otis having made love the night before. She wore a long, satin nightgown to bed. As she slid across the bed, the smooth material felt cool against her warm skin. Without thinking, she rubbed her hands across her flat stomach and felt the liquid softness of the satin against her body. She smiled as she remembered who gave her the nightgown.

She heard the shower as Otis stood in the bathtub and let the water run.

"Make sure you put the curtains inside the tub. I don't want to mop water again after you get through," she yelled from the bedside where she sat. She reached over to the nightstand and pulled out a cigarette from the pack Otis left lying there. He had a new lighter he picked up some-place on his last trip to New Orleans, and she used that to fire up her first smoke of the day. By the time she pulled the first drag of smoke deep into her lungs, she heard the water pipe clank in the walls as Otis cut off the flow. She knew he'd shave in the bathroom and in five minutes he'd be standing naked in the bedroom.

Otis was not a big man, but he carried himself and his weight well. He stood about five eight, and weighed just shy of one ninety. He had a head full of brown hair, ears slightly too big for his head and a noticeable scar on his right forearm where a piece of shrapnel sliced it open one spring day in France. Seeing him like that was a sight she had grown tired of so long ago she couldn't remember.

"Where you going this week?" She called out.

"Oh, I got a good trip scheduled. This one's gonna make me a lot of money." Otis almost sang the words as he replied. "I may have to stay all week and not come back till Saturday or Sunday." He opened the door and walked out of the bathroom. He had two small pieces of tissue paper stuck to his face to stop the blood from shaving nicks. "You don't have a problem with that, do you?"

Virginia stood and touched his arm. "Oh, baby, you know I don't like it when you stay out of town so long at one time." She smiled. "But if that's what it takes to get you to move up in the company, I guess you gotta do it."

She dropped the satin gown, walked away, and entered the bathroom naked. She knew he was watching, and even better she knew he wanted her.

Twenty minutes later, she stood in front of the stove and, with a deft motion, flipped two fried eggs in a pan then slid them onto a plate which she set in front of Otis. She quickly cooked two more and put them on a plate for herself. Toast popped out of a stainless steel toaster, and as usual, it was burned to a light crisp on one side. Otis took his knife and scrapped off the burned part as Virginia sat down.

Otis had fixed the coffee pot the night before. It was ready for a flame to be lit beneath it which he always did every morning when he got to the kitchen a few minutes before Virginia did.

"You never did say where you were going this week," she said as she drank coffee from a large white cup.

"Florida. I'm going to try to get all the way to Miami. That's why it may take me all week to go there and come back. It's two days down and two back, so if I try to do it in one week, I'll not have much time for work."

Virginia was thinking of a week without him being home. She was especially interested in his being gone on the weekend. "Don't worry about me. I'll find something to do. Maybe I'll go to a movie if you're not home this weekend. There's a new Bette Davis one coming on. Remember, we saw the previews when we were at the Roxy."

"Yeah, you and Mae can go."

Virginia worked as a bank teller and sometimes went to lunch and movies with another teller named Mae. At least that's what she told Otis. If he ever came to the bank and actually wanted to meet Mae, Virginia was prepared to say she had quit unexpectedly that very morning. Mae was an excuse, not a person.

"I gotta pack some orders to take to the post office this morning." Otis had turned their small second bedroom into his warehouse and did all his packing and shipping from there. The walls were lined with shelves he had built and they held boxes of assorted styles of playing cards, dice, both loose and affixed in pairs to cardboard counter stands, and punchboards in an endless variety of sizes, styles and prices. On one wall was the prize that went with the punch boards if they had one. The most popular ones were purchased for the money prizes. Virginia knew that some of the salesmen had the key to the punch boards and knew exactly which little hole to punch in order to win. If you knew which one held the winner, you simply went to a friend's territory, punched the boards and split the money. Otis said he never did it, but Virginia wasn't sure he was that honest.

He would be in there for an hour or more and Virginia had to catch the bus in fifteen minutes. When she finished dressing, she called out to him. "I'm leaving. I'll see you in a week or so, right?"

Otis walked out of the room to respond. "Yeah, I'm getting a late start today. And I gotta go out to a place here in Atlanta I been trying to get into for a long time. I got a call and they want to meet me."

"Really, which one's that?"

"You ever heard of the Rio Vista Supper Club?"

CHAPTER 10

April in Atlanta meant the azaleas were in full bloom. Peach, apple and cherry trees that had weathered the winter were dropping their blossoms all over the city. The city, known as the Dogwood Capital of the World was reveling in its reputation. It was a gardener's dream come true.

The seasons at Big Town were measured by the professional or college sports that were available for betting on. Fall began when college teams took to the field followed by the pro teams. The winter was taken with basketball and everyone's battle cry was "just wait till April!" that's when baseball season began, and every man there was convinced this was his year to clean up.

Just as Atlanta's Dogwood Society waited for the first bloom, the men at Big Town waited for the first pitch. Baseball was the lifeblood of the gambling crowd at the upstairs pool room just off Edgewood Avenue. Games were broadcast on the radios along the wall from Spring Training all the way to the last game of the World Series.

Johnny drove to Big Town that morning. He wanted to have his car close by in case Rachel called with information on Thomas's whereabouts. Rachel—Thomas's sister or cousin or whatever she was. He had tried to push the conversation he had with her that night out of his mind, but every time he did it crept back with a vengeance. He wanted to help Thomas because…and that's where it ended. He kept telling himself that Thomas was a nice kid and could not have killed the man he found on the pool table. He had no obligation to help him and didn't know anything about him other than what he knew from seeing him and talking to him at Big Town. They were both veterans but their paths never had and never would cross in any setting other than the pool room. But then Rachel stepped into the picture.

Hers was a simple request. *Help my brother.* Johnny had heard that before. He'd taken a case once when a lawyer hired him to find his own brother. The lawyer's brother had returned to Atlanta after the war, spent a couple of years working at a printing plant and then just disappeared. He'd spent some time at the veteran's administration being treated for what they called "shell shock" from his time in the army. The lawyer gave Johnny all the information on the man, handed him a photo, gave him his last known address, and sealed the deal by saying, "Find him. He's my brother."

It took three weeks but Johnny had found him in a flop house lying on an old blanket he'd been given by the Salvation Army. He was too malnourished and too drunk to care if he was ever found. Johnny cleaned him up, got him a room in a dollar-a-day hotel, and fed him for three days before he told his brother he had found him. By then, he was almost presentable.

Johnny collected his fee, got the expenses for the clothes, hotel, and food for the man and forgot about it. One day about six months later, one of the other regulars at Big Town mentioned that the lawyer's brother had gone on another bender. This time he had been found, not by a PI, but by a garbage man. He was lying dead in an alley when they came to pick up the garbage behind the apartment where he lived. Johnny later heard that the lawyer paid for his brother's body to be shipped home for burial. Unlike most of the men who died in alleys in Atlanta, he had a family who cared for him and wanted him home.

Johnny hoped Thomas's fate would not mirror that man's.

There was a parking lot across the street from Big Town where Johnny parked when he drove into town. When he pulled in, he recognized a couple of cars that belonged to some of the men who would be sitting around the walls of the pool room when he arrived. To say the cars belonged to the men was a stretch. They were driven by the men, but they were owned and financed up to the tip of the radio antenna by as many loan companies as would let them have money. Most of them would be repossessed at least once before the last pitch of the World Series in October.

He left the car and walked toward the booth where an attendant stood with a ticket stub in his hand.

"Here you go, sir. You gonna be all day?" The attendant handed Johnny his half of the stub. The other half would be stuck beneath the windshield wiper blade on the car.

"All day." He placed the stub in his pocket and continued to walk.

As he was about to cross the street, he saw one of the many newspaper vendors that called the streets of Atlanta their sales territory. Like most of the men at Big Town, they were an unusual lot. Most had been selling papers, both the early morning and afternoon editions for years. They usually worked a five or six block area and one did not cross into another's territory.

Across from Johnny was the one everyone called Boots. Boots was of an indeterminate age. It could have been mid-thirties; it could have been mid-fifties. He was short, wore his hair long and always wore jodhpurs and riding boots. No matter the weather, he could be seen, newspapers beneath his arms and always in his jodhpurs and boots.

Johnny crossed the street and opened the street-level door to enter the building. As soon as his shoe touched the first step, he heard the unmistakable sound of a rack of pool balls being broken. He looked at his watch. It was only five after nine and a game was already in progress. Most of the players would not start arriving until about ten. The first baseball game came on the radio at noon. Games would continue late into the night. Chicago, Kansas City, St. Louis and Detroit games always started an hour behind Atlanta time, so they were the last ones booked at night if they were playing at home.

When he reached the top of the steps, a player everyone knew as Red was shooting a game of nine-ball with a man Johnny did not recognize. He was probably a new man in town who just wanted to kill some time and shoot a game. If he was a hustler who came specifically to pick up some money games, he was much too early.

When Johnny passed Red, the man who stood well over six feet tall and weighed in at about two hundred fifty pounds was leaning on the pool cue, waiting for the other man to take his shot.

"Morning, Johnny." Red rubbed the blue square of pool chalk on the tip of his cue as he spoke.

"Red. How's it going?" Johnny kept walking.

"You ain't found no other dead men, have you? We don't need to lose no more tables." Red looked around to see if anyone else was laughing at his joke.

The only one to respond was Hockey Doc who was working behind the counter. "Red, you keep talking that shit, and you can just get your big ass out of here." He did not like anyone talking about what had happened the previous week. "I don't need you to jinx this place no more than it already is."

Johnny passed by Hockey Doc and leaned across the counter to speak to him. "Have I had any calls this morning?"

"Ain't nobody had any calls today. No wives looking for their husbands, no loan sharks verifying employment, no bill collectors thinking they're calling somebody's house. If I had as many people on the payroll as claim to work here, I'd be stumbling over employees." Hockey Doc pulled a bar rag from beneath the counter and wiped it down.

Johnny, like everyone else had heard that diatribe many times. Most of it was true. Many of the men listed Big Town as their place of employment and gave the number of the pay phone in the booth at the end of the counter as a way to reach their boss. When a loan company or almost anyone else called to verify employment, Hockey Doc always told the caller that the person was his best employee and had worked for him for years.

The coffee urn was steaming when Johnny grabbed a mug and placed it beneath the spout. He was pulling the handle when the phone rang. Normally Thomas would have answered, but with him gone and no one hired to replace him, it became the responsibility of anybody who was standing nearby to answer it.

"Big Town. Whoever you want ain't here." A man Johnny knew only as Pete spoke into the handset. "Who? Mister Johnny? Hang on."

He covered the mouthpiece and yelled. "Is there anybody here called 'Mister Johnny'?"

"I'll take it." Johnny walked to the end of the bar and reached for the phone.

"Who the hell you know that calls you Mister John-

ny?" He held the phone in front of him, but did not release it.

"You hold that phone for another second and you'll be
calling me more than mister." Johnny snatched the phone
and stepped sideways to shield his voice, but did not turn
his back on the man.

"This is Johnny Morocco." He knew from the silence
on the other end of the line that it was Rachel. "Hello?"

"It's Rachel" Her voice was barely audible above the
noise in the background from wherever she was calling.
That, combined with the pool game going on two tables
from where Johnny stood, made the conversation difficult.

"Do you have an address for me?'

"Yes, I mean no. Not an address with a number and
everything."

"Then I don't think I can help you." He knew he should
have placed the receiver back in the phone's cradle. He
knew he should have broken the connection. He knew all
of these things, but he ignored them.

"Please, don't hang up. I—I know where he is, it's just
that the place doesn't exactly have an address. You ever
heard of Plunkett Town?"

Every city in the South and probably in the entire
United States, for all Johnny knew, had at least one section of town where Negroes lived. It usually had its own
unique name. Plunkett Town was one of those places. It
was just far enough south of Atlanta not to be an actual
part of the city, but close enough so that the residents
who had a job could catch a bus to work. Bounded by the
main road out of town to the south on one side and railroad tracks on the other, it was a community within itself.

The houses were mostly clapboard and tarpaper shacks
without plumbing, electricity or running water. The roads
were hard-packed red clay until it rained. Then the streets

turned into a quagmire of thick red paste that stuck to everything and everyone. In the summer that clay was ground into a fine powder by the hundreds of feet, cars, push carts and animals that called Plunkett Town home. The powder in turn became a fine dust that settled on the area like a dark red fog. It would have been impossible to get an accurate count of the number of people who called Plunkett Town home. If an outsider ventured into the conclave and knocked on a door, no matter the reason, the person he was looking for was not at home. Furthermore, that person was completely unknown to the resident of the house. There were few exceptions, one of whom was the insurance man.

The "policy man" as he was known in the community, was always a white man who traveled the streets of Plunkett Town with complete impunity. He collected the dimes and quarters that it took to keep policies in order. More important, he paid out the money when someone died, or in many cases was killed. He was the only outsider who knew the secrets of Plunkett Town, but as a part of that confidence, he never betrayed their trust.

"He's in Plunkett Town?"

"I think he may be living with a relative out there. If he is, you'll never find him by yourself. If you want to go out there, I can go with you. I'll have to ask for a day off. I don't know if I can get it or not, but if you want to go, I'll just stay out of work that day and we can go together."

"I don't want you to lose your job over this." Johnny took the receiver from his ear and leaned back on the stool in the phone booth. He closed his eyes and tried to think of what he was getting himself into. After a moment, he spoke back into the handset. "Look, see if you can find out for sure if he's there. If he is, tell him I want to meet him at the caddy shack at Flat Rock Golf Course.

It's only a few miles from there. He can hitch a ride or walk if he has to. I'll meet him there Sunday morning about ten. You got it?"

"Flat Rock Golf Course Sunday at ten." There was a hesitation on the phone. "I don't work on Sundays. You want me to go with you? I can miss church if you want me to."

"No." As soon as he said it, he felt like he answered too quickly. "No, let me meet him alone the first time."

"How will I know what he told you if I'm not there?"

"I didn't realize you and I were working together on this. I'm the only one who needs to know what he says." Behind him Red was picking up two dollars off the table. He smiled as the other man put his cue back in the rack and headed for the door. "If you want to know if I find out anything, you can call me at the Emerald. I'm usually there at night."

"Thank you for doing this. For Thomas. For both of us." Johnny heard a male voice yelling Rachel's name in the background. "I gotta go. My boss is looking for me." The line went dead.

CHAPTER 11

The Rio Vista Supper Club was built on the eastern bank of the Chattahoochee River for several reasons. The castle-like structure was a perfect fit for the high bank overlooking the green forests of Atlanta's suburbs to the east and south. With the land sloping down from the peak at the river's edge, putting in a second story to level the structure was a piece of cake. The lower level was accessible through the kitchen from the parking lot or from the staircase leading down from the main floor on the inside.

The river itself provided one of the best security measures for the Rio. The steep bank dropped straight into the murky, reddish-brown water. No outcroppings, no rocks, nothing stood between the water and anything, or in some cases anyone, who was dropped from the bank.

It was no secret that when a body turned up floating in the river sometimes as far south as the Georgia/Alabama border in Columbus, a courtesy visit was made to the Rio. For years, any dead body found floating in the river north of Phenix City, Alabama was credited to the Rio. Those found near or below the famous place in Alabama, near Fort Benning were credited to Phenix City.

Since the Dixie Mafia was deeply involved in both the

Rio and also many of the activities in Phenix City, there was a good chance that all of the bodies in the river were a direct result of a Dixie Mafia issue.

Otis Hightower knew as much about the Dixie Mafia as most people in the South did at the time, which was not much. What he didn't realize when he pulled his two-door Chevrolet Bel-Air into the parking lot was that he would soon have more information about them than he ever wanted.

The lot was almost deserted when he pulled in. There were only four other vehicles that he could see. An old Plymouth pick-up truck was sitting in the far corner of the lot, a green Studebaker and a newer Cadillac were parked near the entrance. Otis pulled his car beside the Cadillac, opened the door and got out.

He went to the trunk and opened it to retrieve his sample case. He picked up a couple of extra punch boards and a prize box that contained a small wooden box that resembled a pirate's treasure chest. Inside the chest was an assortment of soaps, powders and perfumes. This was one of the prizes on one of his most popular boards since every man on the road liked to take a chance on winning something for the ladies back home. If the weather was cooler, he'd have a treasure chest like this one filled with candy. With the exception of money, chocolate was the number one prize he had.

Otis held the treasure chest in one hand, reached into the trunk, grabbed the sample case by the handle, and swung it out. He tucked the chest into the crook of his elbow, closed the trunk and then headed for the entrance. As was his habit he did a practice introduction aloud to himself as he walked.

"Mister Skinner, good to meet you. I'm Otis High-tower. High, but not high when it comes to prices." He smiled at his old worn-out joke and repeated the introduction several times. Otis always did the little speech to himself to make certain he did not forget the customer's name.

The entrance to the Rio was a large wooden door. The hinges and all the lock hardware was made from black strap iron. From the looks of it, the pieces could actually have been made in one of the remaining blacksmith shops that dotted the area.

He pushed on the massive door till it swung open and then he entered the quiet, dark coolness that was the Rio Vista Supper Club at midday.

He walked through the dining area and turned right at a hallway. On the wall a small sign indicated the rest rooms were in that direction. Chances were that there was an office down the hallway as well.

Otis was half way down the hall when he heard some-one behind him.

"Hey! Where-the-hell do you think you're going?"

Otis turned to see a man coming down the hallway. The size of the man left no room for anyone else. He stood well over six feet tall and looked to weigh over two hundred pounds. His pounds were not the result of pastries. They were muscle. And he looked like he knew how to use them.

"Uh, I'm Otis Hightower. I have an appointment with..." Even though he had practiced the name, it was as lost to him at that moment as was the name of the first man killed in the War of 1812. He sat the sample case down and began to fumble in his coat pocket for the note pad he carried with the name on it.

"You looking for Mister Skinner?"

"Skinner? Yes, that's it. Joe Skinner. I have an appointment with him. He called my office and they sent me a letter." Otis realized that he was rambling. He stopped and took a deep breath. "My appointment was for ten am." He looked at his watch and saw he was two minutes early. "Is he here?"

"What kind of appointment did you have?" He looked Otis over, and then added, "You a salesman or something?"

Otis picked up his case. "Yes, I sell cards, dice, and punch boards for Saint Louis Games. We're the biggest—"

The man cut him off in mid-sentence. "Come with me. I'll take you to his office."

Together they walked down the carpeted hallway to another corner. This one led to the kitchen which was at the end of it. Just before the doors to the kitchen, was a small door on the left side of the hallway. There were no markings to indicate what was behind the door, but Otis's guide stopped and knocked.

"Mister Skinner, it's me, Victor. I got somebody out here who says he has an appointment with you." Even thought there was no response from the other side of the door, Victor turned to Otis. "Wait here. He'll open the door and let you in." He walked away without giving any indication of how long Otis was to wait.

Otis could hear kitchen noises as the cooks did the prep work for the upcoming evening meals. He knew the club served dinner from five pm until nine. Several months earlier, he and Virginia had dinner here with a friend. Dancing started at nine thirty and lasted until the place closed at one am. There were no hours set for what Otis knew went on downstairs. He'd never been there and had never sold them anything, but all of the salesmen in the company knew the place by reputation.

The air conditioning was another big draw for the Rio. Sitting in the cool comfort of a place like this sure beat having dinner at home with a fan blowing in your face to cool you off.

Otis was standing by the door when it opened. The man who opened it was about the same height as Otis but he looked leaner, almost like a fighter. He was wearing a white shirt, a pair of dark pants, maybe black or navy blue and was holding the last two inches of an unlit cigar in his hand. "You Otis?" He held out his hand. "I'm Joe Skinner." They shook hands and Skinner turned his back on Otis.

"Come on in my office. I got a place you can sit down." Skinner pointed to a large chair along the wall in the office. "Put your stuff down. Ain't no need to hold it all the time. You can trust me." Skinner turned to Otis. "Can I trust you?"

Before Otis could respond, Skinner laughed at his own joke and good-naturedly poked the salesman in the stomach with his fist. "Lighten up. That's a joke. You want a beer or something? I'll have one of the boys in the kitchen bring us a couple of bottles."

The office was well laid out. In addition to the chair where Otis sat, there was a large wooden desk and matching chair that he assumed belonged to Skinner. A wooden file cabinet stood in one corner behind his desk. Next to the chair where Otis sat was a small table. A larger work table sat along one wall. The table was covered with newspapers and magazines, none of which were readable from where Otis sat. The only picture on the walls was one of a younger Skinner in a Marine uniform with several other Marines holding a Japanese flag. On the opposite wall was a large calendar from a beer company. The calendar had a graphic of a near nude woman sitting on a bale of hay enjoying a bottle of beer. Skinner caught Otis looking at the photo. "You in the war?"

"Yeah, I was in the artillery. I made Normandy, first day." He nodded toward the photo. "Is that you?"

"First Marine Division. I made two landings and then

got my ass handed to me when a Jap mortar round went off about three feet from where I was standing." He stood and walked to the photo. "Three days after this picture was taken, only two of us were still alive. Now there's only me left." Both men were quiet for a moment as they both drifted back to their days under fire.

"But, hey, that was then and this is now. We all gotta move on. Right?" Skinner came back from the photo and took a seat behind his desk.

"How much you make a week lugging around all that shit?" Skinner pointed to the sample case and the treasure chest sitting on the edge of the chair.

"I do all right. I mean, I'm not getting rich, but—"

"That ain't what I meant. I don't care what you make. I just wanna know if you want to make more?

"Well, sure. I mean who doesn't want to make more." He leaned down to open his sample case. "That's why I brought my best selection of cards and dice for you to look at." Otis suddenly blanched. He realized he had mentioned the tools of the trade for the casino downstairs, but Skinner had not said anything about it or the reason Otis was there.

"I mean, I have a nice selection of…" He looked at the punchboard. "Of punch boards. They all have nice prizes. Here, take a look at this." He placed the wooden box with the soaps and powders on Skinner's desk. He was trying to cover his perceived mistake and was making a fool of himself.

"You been drinking already this morning?" Skinner leaned across the desk. "Cause, if you ain't been drinking, you need to see a doctor or something. You're as jumpy as a whore in church."

"No, I'm all right. It's just that I've been on the road a lot lately. I've got some new accounts and I'm trying to keep things running smoothly."

"That's okay. Just relax. This is a business call. Nothing more. Nothing less." Skinner hesitated, and then added. "You married?"

"Oh, yes. The same lovely woman for the last five years."

Skinner smiled remembering just how lovely Virginia was. "You're a lucky man. I can never seem to keep a woman for more than a year or so." He and Virginia had been having an affair behind Otis's back for a little over a year. Skinner knew her time was almost up, but this time the woman he was with was serving a purpose other than a bedmate.

"Now, Otis, let's see what kind of cards and dice you have. We need a new supplier."

This was what Otis lived for. Whenever he got the opportunity to open a new account, he had a five minute pitch that he used. It started with a few questions that no matter how the client answered, Otis had a response. Then he went into two minutes twenty seconds of product line description, another minute of questions and finally the thirty second close and ten seconds to ask for the order.

He had practiced it so many times that when he met other salesmen on the road, he sometimes was asked to give the presentation to them. "Listen and learn," he told them.

It started with him opening a notebook that described the number of people who played cards for fun and the number who played "more seriously" as he like to call it. Since gambling was illegal in each state in his territory, he never mentioned the word just in case he was talking to a police officer.

Before Otis could even tell Skinner how many people played cards for fun, he was interrupted.

"Tell me about your wife."

"Uh, my wife? What do you want to know? Her name's Virginia and she works—"

"Nah, that ain't what I mean. Does she want diamonds and furs and stuff like that? Things that you can't get her on what you make hustling punch boards to gas stations in Alabama?" Skinner stood, came around the desk and sat on the edge facing Otis. "You want to make her happy and keep her that way?"

Otis drew a blank. This sales pitch was not going the way he had planned. As he sat there, he realized nothing was going the way he had planned. "Well, yes, I suppose I do want those things for her. We've been saving to buy a television. We've got an old one I bought at a pawn shop in Memphis, but—"

"You ain't listening, Otis. You wanna do business with us, you gotta listen."

Otis sat back in the chair, and gave Skinner his undivided and quiet attention. "Okay, Mister Skinner. I'm listening."

"You know Mike Robinson? He works for Diamond Distributors. That's where we get our supplies."

Otis nodded. "I met him once or twice. We sometimes call on the same places when they first open. I haven't seen him in a long time. Are you thinking of changing suppliers? If you are—" He reached for his catalog, then stopped himself. "Sorry, old habits are heard to break."

"I've heard some good things about you. I want to give you some business." Skinner waited quietly for a second when he heard a knock at the door.

"Who is it?"

"It's me, Victor, Mister Skinner. There's a beer truck driver out here who says he needs to talk to you." Otis recognized the voice as the man he met when he first arrived.

"Tell him to see me next time he makes a delivery.

I'm busy talking to someone important right now." He smiled at Otis when he said it. He lowered his voice. "I ain't got time for no truck drivers today." He reached down and picked up a deck of cards from the open sample case. "How many decks you think we go through a week here?"

"I really don't know. I've never seen your operation, so I can't even guess."

"Hey, that's right. I'm talking to you like you've been here a thousand times. Let's go downstairs and you can see for yourself what kind of place we're running." Skinner stood and picked up a lighter. He flicked the top and touched the flame to the cigar he still held. He took one puff, blew out the smoke and looked at the glowing end. "This is a Cuban, Otis. The real thing."

The two men left Skinner's office and walked down the hallway toward the stairway leading to the lower level. As they passed the bar area, Otis saw someone in a deliveryman's uniform talking to the man he had met earlier. It was a heated conversation with lots of arm waving, but Otis knew instinctively that no amount of animation on the part of the driver was going to get him paid. As a fellow salesman he felt sorry for the man and hoped he was not going to be treated the same way.

At the bottom of the steps, Skinner pushed a buzzer and the door was opened by an old man who was pushing a vacuum cleaner across the carpeting. Once he opened the door, he went back to his cleaning and paid no attention to the two men as they walked around the room. The room was about five thousand square feet, with the gambling tables in the center and a large bar at one end. The bar was massive. The back bar had a series of mirrors in old frames. Each frame had the same style of hardware in each corner as did the front door leading to the Rio. A highly polished brass rail shined near the base of the bar.

If it was used as a footrest at night, there was no evidence of it when Otis saw it. Any marks on it had been polished away. At the bar area six tables and chairs surrounded a dance floor. The floor was made of an inlaid dark wood, probably mahogany and very expensive. Otis knew the Rio had a reputation as a place for high rollers. Now he could see why.

"We put this down here about three years ago. We got six tables not counting blackjack. We have three craps and three roulette and nine blackjack tables. We gotta have a few slots for the women who come down here with their husbands and boyfriends. If they ain't standing beside them at the table being a pain in the ass, they're over on the wall pulling handles. Either way: they're happy and that makes us happy." Skinner motioned with his hand as he described each game. "Here's what I want you to see. Come with me."

They walked to the far wall of the room where a combination cashier's cage and security stand was located. A woman sat inside the cage. She was placing chips in racks and getting ready for the night's business. "Open the door, Peggy."

The woman looked up when she heard her name. "Oh, Mister Skinner, how are you today?"

Before he responded, he turned to Otis. "Hold up your hands. Show her they're empty."

Otis had done the same thing several times in the past when he was taken into the cage or counting rooms in the various houses he serviced. He held his hands up, turning them to face her and then showed her their backs.

"He's unarmed and not trying to rob us, Peggy. You can let us in." Skinner stood by the door waiting for the woman to unlock it. He turned to Otis, "If you tried to get in there without showing her your hands, that little ole' lady would push a button and have half a dozen goons on you like stink on shit." He laughed. "But before they could get to you, she'd probably blow you away herself. She keeps a pistol in her lap whenever she's sitting down there at the cage. I never tested her, but they say she's damn good with it."

Peggy leaned to the right and pulled on the large handle, opening the door for them to enter her world. As Otis stepped inside, he noticed that she did, in fact, have a chrome plated revolver lying in her lap.

"We're going in the back room. Is that okay with you?" Skinner leaned over and gave Peggy a peck on the cheek.

Peggy was probably in her late fifties and could pass as the grandmother sitting at the end of the pew at church who volunteered to fix the chicken dinner for Sunday. Based on her job and what Skinner said, she'd probably shoot the chicken prior to cooking it.

"You can go back there, but don't you even think about messing around with anything. I've got it all laid out like I want it. You come in here and screw it up and then expect me to know where everything is at all times." She was smiling, but there was an edge to her voice that said she meant every word .

The cage was about six feet wide and eight feet long. It had a glass front that looked to be bulletproof. The glass was further protected by a steel grate with four by four spaces placed over the entire front. If anyone wanted to break in all he could get was what could be passed out of the cage through a four inch square hole. All things considered, it was probably easier to rob a bank.

A door at the back of the cage directly behind where Peggy sat led to another room. This is where Skinner took Otis.

"This is the supply room for down here." The room was not much bigger than a broom closet. There was not enough room for both men to stand in it at the same time. Skinner pointed at several boxes on shelves. "This is where we keep our cards and dice and other things we need for the floor."

Skinner was pointing at several cases of playing cards in individual packs and boxes of loose dice, but Otis Hightower only saw money. If he could turn this account, he'd have a goldmine, he thought as he counted the number of boxes on the shelves.

"Looks like a decent supply. How long you think this will last?" He tried not to let his voice give away his pleasure in being invited to the room. "You change decks on the tables when the customer calls for it, or do you do it on a regular basis?"

"Don't get ahead of yourself, Hightower. You ain't been in the place but thirty minutes and already you want to know how we do business." Skinner looked at him, and then broke into a grin. "Hey, I'm just pulling your joint. Relax." He placed an arm around Otis and led him back through the cage. "Let's go back upstairs. We need to talk about something."

On the way back to his office, Skinner opened the door to the kitchen and looked inside. Otis noticed that all the people working in there were Negroes. They were the men and women who got the food ready for the chef who came in later and took over. From the hallway, he could hear them laughing and talking but as soon as Skinner stepped inside the only noise that could be heard came from the pots, pans and other utensils they were using. No one said a word when they saw him.

"Hey Adam, bring us a pot of coffee and some cake or something to eat." Skinner spoke above the noise to an older man dressed in white pants and shirt. He had a chef's hat sitting on a head full of gray hair.

"Be right in, Mister Skinner. We gots a fresh pot and

Lucy made some of them little cake things you like. I'll have 'em in there for you and the other gentleman in ten minutes." The old man almost bowed when he spoke.

Without a response, Skinner closed the door and returned to his office.

Once inside, he took his seat behind the desk and motioned for Otis to sit in the chair where he had left his sample case. As soon as he sat, Otis leaned forward. "Mister Skinner, I can—"

Skinner held up his hand to silence him. "Let's get one thing straight. Right here and right now. You can't do shit for me, Hightower. I didn't bring you here to sell me anything. I brought you here so we can make some money. Together, you and me. You do like money, don't you?"

Otis gave a little nervous laugh. "Of course, I like money. Who doesn't?"

Now it was Skinner who leaned forward. "You ever been to Cuba?"

CHAPTER 12

By noon, Big Town was getting crowded. Most of the men were sitting around the wall in small groups clustered around a radio broadcasting a baseball game. The day games started between twelve and two. By the time they were over, the nighttime games were usually well underway. The men who didn't lose all their money on the earlier games stayed. Those who lost and could not come up with more money or credit either left or stayed and played pool for pocket change.

Johnny hardly ever bet on baseball. He'd play a football parlay card in the fall and he always got down on the triple-crown races. Last year he picked the winner of both the Kentucky Derby and the Preakness. He resisted the urge to place it all on the Belmont. The horse he wanted didn't even come close to finishing in the money. By winning both the Derby and the Preakness in a parlay he cleared over seventy dollars.

A thick haze of cigarette smoke hung over the group of men gathered around the radio broadcasting the Yankee's game. Whitey Ford was pitching; Billy Martin had made an incredible play at second base and hit a double and two singles. He and Mantle were swatting balls all over Yankee Stadium.

Johnny walked over to the radio where Henry was

booking the game. As he approached, Henry gave a nod
to acknowledge him and pulled a folded newspaper off
the chair next to him. Johnny took a seat and watched the
action.

A player named Slim tapped Henry on the shoulder
and said, "Three fly, two double."

Henry nodded, acknowledging that he was taking a bet
that Martin would either hit a fly ball or a double. If he
did, the bets would be paid off at a fifty percent return. If
Martin hit a ground ball that resulted in his reaching second base, Slim would be one dollar and fifty cents in the
hole. He'd make a dollar fifty on the two dollar bet on the
double but lose the three on the fly ball. If it was a fly
ball that got Martin to second base, he wins both bets for
a total of three dollars. Johnny knew that Henry had less
than a fifth grade education, but he kept up with the bets
placed with him before each batter came to the plate, paid
off the winners and figured the odds as he went.

The men heard the crack of the bat as the third pitch
was hit. For less than a heartbeat, the outcome of the bet
and the payoffs was in doubt. As soon as Mel Allen
spoke, Henry started his moves.

"It's a hard hit ball straight to the shortstop. He's going to grab it on one hop and fire it over to first. No way
Martin's going to beat this one. That makes it two outs
and nobody on." Mel went on to describe his favorite hair
tonic which just happened to be a sponsor of the game
that day.

Henry had dollar bills folded long ways stuck between
his fingers which he pulled out to pay off the two men
who won on Martin's ground out. All he had to do was
look around and the losers began to hand him the money
if they had not done so prior to his taking the bet. Very
few men were allowed to bet on credit or without actually
handing the bookie the money when they placed the bet.

As soon as the action on the field resulted in the end of a bet, all debts were paid. Losers handed their money to Henry first, and then he paid the winners. It was all an orderly progression perfected after years of daily practice for some of the men.

Each radio broadcasting a game had a similar group of men sitting around it. If there was not one single person booking the game, the action usually went to a single bet on the game as opposed to each batter.

Henry was in his sixties, always dressed in a brown suit with matching tie and wore a brown Stetson hat. He placed his hat on the radio prior to the game and everyone knew this was his area. The radios were territorial. Once claimed, it was reserved for the day.

Hockey Doc was cooking a new batch of hot dogs on the stream table when he glanced up at the large oval mirror hanging over the stairs. The oval mirror was placed in such a way that anyone entering the front door was immediately visible before they even got to the first step leading up to the second floor. As soon as he glanced up, his hand immediately went to one of three buttons beneath the bar. Buttons were placed at both ends and one in the middle for just such occasions. He quickly pressed the middle button and a red light started flashing over the bar and a bell sounded.

In seconds, Henry placed his hands in his pockets and stripped the money from his fingers. Men grabbed pool cues and began to shoot balls on the most convenient pool table.

By the time Detective Brewer got to the top of the steps all he found was a very busy pool room. He walked straight to the bar and stood in front of Hockey Doc.

"If you're on duty, don't even ask me for a beer. Even if you're paying—which I doubt—it'd be illegal to sell it to you, and I don't want to do anything to break the law."

Hockey Doc wiped the counter with a white towel as he spoke to Brewer.

"If I wanted a beer, I'd come back there and get it myself." Brewer placed his hand on the towel, stopping its back-and-forth action. "And while I was back there, I'd rip out all those wires to the bell and the light you push whenever a cop comes up here." He leaned closer. "And then I'd stuff the ends up your ass."

Both men knew there was a good-naturedness to their comments, but both knew there was a line not to be crossed, except on official business.

"How 'bout fixing me a chili dog and a Coke and bringing it over to me." Brewer looked around the seats on the walls. "I'll be over there." He nodded in the direction of where Johnny sat. "I'll be conducting an interview with a witness."

"This ain't curb service, you know. Since Thomas left, I got nobody to help me out here. You keep your eye on the bar. I'll set your stuff up here when it's ready." Hockey Doc began to swing the towel across the counter top again as a way to stall before preparing the food for Brewer.

Johnny sat on a stool beneath an overhead shelf. The shelf held a radio in a wooden cabinet. The radio cabinet was dark from years of smoke and hands turning it on and off and adjusting the placement so it could pick up the best signal. He was reading the morning newspaper and did not notice Brewer when he approached.

"Well, look who's here. It's Atlanta's very own Boston Blackie, Private Investigator. I figured the Dixie Detective would be out working on another charity case." Brewer pulled out a chair and took a seat.

"I don't do charity cases. I have to get paid for the work I do. Unlike some people, I don't have a cushy job for the city of Atlanta where they pay me to hang out in pool rooms." Johnny folded the paper and placed it on the chair beside him.

"Is pissing me off something you lay awake at night thinking about or does it just come natural to you?"

"Trust me, Brewer, I lay awake at night thinking about a lot of things, but you are never one of them."

Brewer was about to answer when he saw Hockey Doc place his chili dog and Coke on the counter and wave to him. The wave was his way of saying, "Here it is. If you want it come get it." It was now a battle of wills to see if Brewer broke and went to get it, or Hockey Doc relented and brought it to him. Brewer decided to wait.

"So, when's the last time you talked to Thomas?"

"You know the answer to that. He left here a few minutes before you came in. I've already told you that. I haven't seen him since that day."

Brewer was listening but he was watching his food. "Son of a bitch!" was all he said as he stood and walked to the counter.

The chili dog was in a paper container shaped like an open boat. The bun had been steamed and was so soft that with the chili on it, the entire concoction almost draped across his hand as he carried it back to his chair. He placed the Coke bottle on the floor beside his stool. He had to use the fork Hockey Doc handed him in order to eat from the container.

Brewer took a monstrous bite and started talking around his mouth full of food. "Your boy is in over his head on this one. This ain't a simple murder. It goes much deeper than that." He wiped his mouth with a paper napkin and took a long drink from the bottle.

"I could probably help him out if I knew where he was." He took the last bit of the chili dog and used the fork to scrape the residue from the container. "I gotta say, this is some good chili."

"I'm afraid I can't help you on this one. I haven't seen or talked to him since you were up here before." Johnny leaned back and placed his feet on the rail at the bottom of the chair.

"You see, here's the problem. First, I don't believe you. Second, I don't believe Thomas. So where does that leave me? I gotta turn someplace else to talk to someone I believe."

"And who is that?"

"See, that's another problem. I keep hearing from people I don't believe any more than I believe you or Thomas. The only thing I know for sure is that you don't want to get involved in this one."

"So what do you believe?"

"I want to believe Thomas didn't kill the guy, but I believe he saw who did. And if he did, he's in shit up to his neck if they know about it. These are out of town boys who play for keeps." Brewer pulled a handkerchief from his pocket and wiped his mouth. "You know anything about some action down in Havana?"

He now had Johnny's full attention. Action in Havana meant only one thing and one person. Meyer Lansky.

"The guy was involved with Lansky?"

"Not Lansky. This one was closer to home. He was doing some work for the locals here in Atlanta, coming and going through New Orleans. I'm sure you've heard of the Dixie Mafia. The dead guy was either a mule or a bag man for them. I ain't sure which one yet." Brewer tapped Johnny on the chest over his shirt pocket. "What're you smoking today?"

Without a comment, Johnny pulled out his pack and handed it to Brewer. "There's no reason on God's green earth for Thomas to be messed up with any of those groups."

"Alls I'm saying is if you talk to him, tell him I can

probably work out a deal if he turns himself in to me. Nobody else. Just me." Brewer stood to leave.

"Next time you take that high-yeller sister of his to Oakland Park to bang her, tell her that if she's hiding him and I have to come to her house, I'll probably not be such a nice guy as I am with you today."

As Brewer walked by the counter he turned to Hockey Doc. "Ring the bell or whatever you do when I leave. All those low-life's gotta get back to their ball games. They've already missed two innings." Even Johnny could hear him laugh as he walked down the stairs.

Brewer had not reached the sidewalk outside in all probability when the pay phone in the booth began to ring. Hockey Doc was pulling a beer out of the cooler beneath the bar, so he finished, walked over and answered it. "Big Town. All right, all right, slow down. I'll see if he's here." He held the phone up and motioned to Johnny without saying anything. This allowed Johnny to take the call or not and the person on the other end could not hear him turn it down if he called out to Hockey Doc.

Johnny slid off the chair and walked to the phone booth. He waited until Doc had stepped past him to enter the booth and pick up the phone. "This is Johnny."

A frantic female voice came over the other end. "You've got to help us. Please. If you don't they're gonna kill my Mama. You've got to..."

Johnny interrupted. "Rachel, is that you? What the hell is going on? Who's gonna get killed?"

"Some men came by here today and said if Mama didn't tell them where Thomas was, they would come back and kill her. They hit her and knocked her down in the kitchen. She lay there till a neighbor found her and had somebody call me at work. I came right home. You've got to help us." Her emotions were alternating between tears and anger. "I still have that money."

Johnny reached into his pack of Luckies and pulled out a cigarette. He tamped the end on the phone and stuck it in his mouth. By cradling the phone between his shoulder and his ear, he was able to pull his lighter out of his pocket and light the cigarette while he still spoke on the phone.

"Okay, slow down and tell me what happened. I want to know it all. Were they cops?"

"Mama said they didn't even try to pretend to be police."

Johnny noticed that, unlike Thomas and most of the other Negroes he knew, she did not pronounce the word as "*po*-lice."

"She said they just came in the house without knocking or anything. They asked her where Thomas was, and when she said she didn't know, one of them pushed her backward and she fell over a chair in the kitchen. They could have killed her, Johnny—" She caught herself and came back. "Uh, Mister Johnny. There was no need for them to do that to her." Her voice calmed as she talked.

"Is she all right? Anything broken or bleeding?"

"No, I helped her up and she can walk okay, but she's mighty stiff where she fell and then was left on the floor till our neighbor got there and found her."

Johnny usually went with his gut instincts. He credited those instincts for keeping him alive several times during the war.

He had a gut instinct now. It said hang up. This is not something you want to get involved with. He knew he was going against every survival instinct he had. But, he did it anyway.

"All right, do you know where the Zanzibar Club is?"

"On Decatur Street?"

"That's the one. Meet me there in one hour."

He put out his cigarette, left the phone booth, and

walked down the steps. He left Big Town and headed for
Decatur Street.

CHAPTER 13

Otis Hightower had never been so scared in his life. When he left Skinner's office it took all his strength and composure not to start shaking. He exited the Rio Vista through the front entrance, walked to his car and opened the driver's door. Once he was safely inside, it took him nearly a minute to fumble for and find his car keys. His hand was shaking so badly that he could hardly get the key into the slot near the bottom of the dashboard.

Otis turned the key to the right, pressed the clutch with his left foot and the gas pedal at the same time with his right foot extended so his toe pressed the starter. He waited for the engine to catch. Once it was cranked, he quickly pulled the gearshift into first and, with gravel spraying behind him, left the parking lot. He paid special attention to his rear-view mirror as he pulled out and drove across the parking lot to the road leading to the main highway back to Atlanta. He didn't think anyone was following him, but he constantly kept checking his rear-view mirror.

Later, he would reflect back and not remember leaving the driveway, crossing onto Bankhead Highway, and heading toward Atlanta. Otis was several miles down the highway when he finally gathered his composure and stopped at a little gas station just across the Fulton County line. He had stopped there many times. It was a place where he always sold a few punch boards. Selling something this time was the least of his concerns when he pulled off the highway. All he wanted was something cold to drink and a place to take a leak. He was afraid to look down at his pants fearing that he might have already done that.

Otis pulled up to the single gas pump. It stood by itself under the wooden overhang jutting out from the small combination grocery store and gas station. He knew the couple who owned the place had turned the front room of their house into the store when the highway became so busy. At first it was a store for the neighbors who lived along the many dirt roads that led off the highway. It became a place for others to stop when they added the gas pump. The old man was Bob and his wife was Gladys. Otis didn't know their last name.

Bob came out when he saw the car pull in. "Hey, Otis. Ain't seen you in a month or so. Thought you'd forgot about us." He pulled the hose off the gas pump and went to the gas cap on the car. "How much you want?"

"Two dollars' worth." Otis spoke over his shoulder as he disappeared inside the store.

The store consisted of what was once a large living room and bedroom. A wall had been taken out so the room was now approximately twenty feet wide and twelve feet deep. A long wooden counter stood on the right side wall. It was obviously hand made from the former wall since the wood on the counter matched the existing walls in color and age. Atop the counter was a wood-framed glass case where several types of cookies were kept in open boxes. Beside the cookies lay several rolls of dried sausage and two hams in white cloth bags. The meat was from hogs raised in the back of the business. Both the bags had large flies sitting on the cloth covering the delicacies inside. Since they couldn't get to the meat, they settled on attacking the cookies. Several dead companions of the ones on the cookies lay on the wooden bottom of the counter. At the end of the counter was a large drink machine filled with chunks of ice and enough water to cover the tops of the bottles. Otis pulled open the lid, reached into the near-freezing water and pulled out an RC Cola. He placed the end of the bottle beneath the opener on the side of the case and popped off the cap.

"You okay, Otis?" Gladys had watched him without comment so far. "You look kinda sickly." She pointed to a straight-backed wooden chair along the front wall. "You can set a spell if you want to."

"I'll be okay. I just needed something to drink." He placed a five cent piece on the counter and walked back outside.

Bob was still pumping, so Otis walked around back to the bathroom they had built for customers when they opened the store. He went inside, used the old commode, then splashed water on his face from the single spigot placed over a sink stained with rust halfway up the sides. He looked at his hands as he dried them on his handkerchief. They were no longer shaking, but he didn't know how long he could keep them still.

Otis regained as much composure as he could, left the bathroom and walked to where Bob was just hanging up the hose from the glass top pump.

He paid Bob two dollars for the gas and got back into his car. The three boxes of playing cards and dice on the seat beside him recalled Skinner's words.

"All you gotta do is deliver these cards and dice to the casino in Havana. We got a guy down there that's gonna put them into play. You're a card salesman, so nobody's gonna suspect you. You're supposed to be carrying stock. You take the stuff in, you bring some stuff out. You make the trip every month or so and you get a nice bonus to keep the Missus happy." Skinners eyes did not blink or show any emotion as he explained the deal to Otis.

"But, but, that's…that's…" Otis could not come up with the word.

"Cheating? Dishonest? Not nice? Pick one you like, and we'll use it. In the meantime, let's talk about how you're gonna be a part of something that's gonna make us all a lot of money." Skinner came around the desk and stood in front of Otis. If it was meant to be intimidating, it worked.

From his seat in the chair, all Otis could do was look up at the man. "Mister Skinner, I've worked a long time, almost since I got back from the war, for one company. I make good money. I'm not getting rich, but I do all right. I know some of the other men work some angles, but I never have. I—"

"Don't give me that goodie-goodie shit, Hightower. I've checked you out. I know more about you than you think I do. I know what you drive. What you smoke. I even know about that broad you see every time you go to New Orleans." Skinner poked his finger in Otis's chest as he spoke. "And now you know something about me."

Skinner stopped when there was a knock at the door. "Who is it?"

"It's me, Mister Skinner. I got you some coffee and those cakes you wanted." Otis recognized the man's voice from the kitchen.

"Set 'em down outside. I'm busy right now." Skinner lit another cigar and turned his attention back to Otis.

"I'll make it real simple for you. You work for us, and you get to keep doing what you do best." He waved his hand over the sample case and its contents. "You keep selling this shit all over the place, get laid every time you go to New Orleans, come home to a nice house and wife and fly to Cuba every month or so." He then leaned down so he was eye-to-eye with Otis.

"You decide you don't want to work for us, you walk out that door and we never see each other again." He paused, waiting for his offer to register.

Otis slid carefully from the chair. "I really appreciate the offer Mister Skinner, but I just don't think I can do it." He reached for his sample case, placed his hand on the handle and picked it up. Skinner was silent as he took his first step toward the door.

"Of course now you know something about me, don't you, Otis?" Skinner's voice was low and cold. "My old man used to say a *smart* man is a *quiet* man. Do you think I'm a *smart* man, Otis?"

"Uh, yes, yes I do. I mean just look around at this place. A man would have to be smart to be a part of this operation."

"But I just told you that I plan to take on one of the most powerful men in America, Otis. I'm going to hit him where it hurts. I'm going to take some of his money." His voice began to rise. "I'm going to *cheat* him, Otis! Is that a word you'd use? I'm going to *cheat* him. How do you think he's going to like that?"

"Oh, I don't know, Mister Skinner—"

"He ain't going to like it worth a damn, Otis. He's going to get mad. He's going to come looking for me. He'll probably want to kill me if he finds out." Skinner had started to raise his voice to the point the kitchen help knew he was not happy. "So that makes me a little concerned. Wouldn't you be concerned, Otis? Would you be frightened? How about scared shitless? I'll bet you'd be scared shitless, Otis if you knew Meyer Lansky wanted to kill you."

He walked to Otis and put his arm around his shoulder. Otis was shaking and he knew Skinner felt it.

"You know why he might do all those things to me, Otis? I'll tell you why. Because I asked you to do a job for me and you turned me down."

"Mister Skinner—"

"Shut up, Otis. Just shut the fuck up!" Skinner stopped his rant to regain his composure. "You see, if you deliver the merchandise like I want, then you have a vested interest." He smiled. "That term 'vested interest' means you got as much to lose as I do if Lansky finds out we've got some hot cards or shaved dice in one of his joints. Without no vested interest you don't give a damn if he finds me and strings me up by my balls before he strangles me with my dick. Suppose you're trying to impress your little squeeze down in New Orleans. You take her out one night for a drink, bring her home and just before you climb onboard, you say, 'Oh, did I happen to mention that Joe Skinner is running a deal on Meyer Lansky in Havana. He asked me to be a part of it, but I declined. I have no vested interest.' And then the next day she's working at the Woolworth's lunch counter and just happens to mention her traveling salesman boyfriend and what he said the night before."

Sweat was now bleeding from every pore on his body. Otis had no doubt that he would not leave the building alive.

"Are you with me Otis? Word spreads. Lansky hears about it and sends some goons to visit me. Hell, he may want to come ice me himself." Just like a switch was thrown, his voice and mannerisms calmed. "But there is a way out. There's always a way out, Otis. I'll bet you remember that from the war. No matter how bad it was, as long as you were still alive, there was a way out."

Otis nodded. "Yes, sir. There's always a way out."

"Good, so here's the deal. Now that I have confided in you, Mister Otis Hightower, you have a vested interest in the operation. I can't just let you walk out that door with the information you have. You have to be a part of it now or it won't work. And I want it to work. I want it real bad."

He motioned to the chair. "Have a seat. I'll bring in the coffee and stuff and we'll start over."

Without waiting, he opened the door where a tray was sitting on a small cart outside his door. He pulled the cart into his office and closed the door. Otis was sitting in the chair, his sample case by his side. "Fix yourself some coffee and have one of these cakes. They're really good. I think you'll like them." Skinner poured two mugs of coffee, picked one up and began to drink it. Your wife, I forgot her name, does she cook?" He took a bite of the cake.

"Virginia. She's a good cook. Nothing fancy, but she does real good with the basic stuff." Otis cautiously picked up the other mug of coffee. All he could do now was wait and listen. His fate was no longer in his hands.

"You keep your job with SLG, you keep traveling your same route—"

"Territory." Otis corrected him before he even thought about what he said.

"Okay, territory. You keep your same customers, you get laid when you go to New Orleans, and nothing changes as far as SLG knows. The only difference is when you go to Miami; you catch a plane, go to Havana and open a new account. It's all set up. They buy their cards and dice from SLG and you get the commission. The only difference is you ship them from this office. And for that you get paid. Could it be simpler?"

Skinner sat back and took a bite of the cake.

A thousand thoughts were running unchecked through Otis's mind. Why him? Where did Skinner learn so much about his personal life? How did he know about Alice in New Orleans? What if SLG found out? His mind was running so fast he didn't think he could verbalize an answer.

"But wouldn't they know, I mean how are you going to use the cards and dice?"

"Those are both good questions, Hightower, but they're none of your fucking business. You want Lansky to come looking for you, too?" Skinner had switched back to using his last name. Skinner stood and looked at Otis.

"Look, I got things to do. I want you to think my offer over. Maybe talk to your wife. Let me know." Skinner stuck out his hand.

Otis stood and shook it. "That makes me feel a lot better, Mister Skinner. I'll let you know when I get back from Miami next week." Otis had his hand on the door when Skinner spoke.

"You know, that's a really dangerous drive to Miami. You be careful. I don't want nothing to happen to you while you take a fucking week to think this over. So many cars out there you might have an accident just leaving the parking lot and I'd never know your thoughts on my business proposal."

When Skinner stopped talking it was so quiet in the room that Otis was sure he could hear his pores as they dripped sweat. He was certain his heart could be heard at least a mile away. He was trapped and did not even know he had been the prey until it was too late.

Otis stood with his back to Skinner. With quivering voice, he spoke without turning around. "When do you want me to send the first shipment down there?"

Skinner smiled. "Very good, Otis. I knew you were a reasonable man."

Otis turned and Skinner offered his hand which Otis

slowly took. Otis tried his best to smile as he began to walk toward the door again.

"Oh, Otis, there's one more thing I want you to do for me while you're in Havana."

CHAPTER 14

The Zanzibar was well known in several different circles in Atlanta. In the local community around its location on Decatur Street, it was a place to get a good noon-time meal of fried chicken, fresh vegetables and home-made pies and cakes. The clients were Negros who worked in the businesses on Decatur and the other streets in the neighborhood, or those who had no jobs. Occasionally a diner would see someone who was passing through Atlanta on his or her way into or out of trouble. The Z was set far enough back that the few customers who had cars could find a place to park, but it was still close enough to the street that a stranger in the neighborhood could find it when given the simplest of directions.

The Z as it was known to those who frequented it was also known to its white customers as a place to come if they wanted to hear blues and jazz the way it was meant to be played.

Upstairs, over the restaurant was a large night club. It was not unusual to see cardboard posters on telephone poles throughout the area announcing that Louis Armstrong, Cab Calloway or Count Basie were playing at the Zanzibar.

The Z had another secret. It was a place where couples

could dine, dance and drink together no matter what color they were.

Johnny pulled up in front of the building, parked his car and walked toward the front entrance. The street-level portion of the building had an old, red brick façade. Like many of the buildings in the area, it had been built in the 1920s when Atlanta started to expand outward from the railroad terminals at the city's center. Decatur was a workingman's street. Shops along the broad street sold work clothes, shoes, hardware and tools, feed, garden seeds and the other necessities of life for the men and women who kept the city alive. Many of the merchants were Jews who had emigrated from Europe earlier in the century. They had a special relationship with their patrons and it was not unusual for them to take small weekly payments on accounts. They built a base that lasted in some stores for many generations.

At one time, the Z had been a three story warehouse. The name of the former tenant was still visible in faded letters on the front of the second story. The building next door still served as a feed and seed store. As Johnny approached the entrance, two youths in overalls were working in a large open lot next door. The smell of the hay bales they were stacking drifted across the parking lot between the buildings. Johnny hesitated a moment and filled his lungs with the fresh, clean smell of the hay.

As he stepped inside the ground floor restaurant, he was immediately taken by the number of people who were seated at tables and at the counter. In most restaurants, the lunch crowd would have already cleared out. A man in a work shirt with so many patches it looked like a puzzle with no piece larger than a silver dollar sat at a table by himself. His plate was piled high with food; a quart-sized Mason jar filled with iced tea sat in easy reach of his right hand. He held a fork in his right fist and shoveled food into his mouth. For an instant Johnny wondered why his was the only table with just one person. Then he saw the man's left arm lying flat on the table and curled around the plate to protect his food. This was a practice learned while doing hard time in a Southern penitentiary. It may have been Reedsville, Georgia or Angola, Louisiana, but it was a fair bet that no man in the place could take a bite from his plate without having the fork embedded in their hand.

Johnny was still looking around when he caught a glance of a hand waving from the back of the room. It was barely perceptible, but he knew immediately that it was Rachel. As he made his way toward her, an older woman with both arms loaded with plates of food, eased by him.

"You find yoself a seat and get ready to have some real food." She dealt the plates out on a table like she was at a neighborhood poker game.

Rachel was sitting at the table, her back to the wall. "I got here early so's I could get a chair back here. I didn't know if you wanted too many people to see you."

The way the table was placed meant anywhere Johnny sat his back would be toward the majority of the people in the room.

"How about we change places? You can sit here." He pulled out a chair and waited for Rachel to stand. Once she was on her feet, he moved beside her and took her chair. From the seat, he nodded for her to sit to his right. In the center of the table was an ashtray filled with cigarette butts.

"How long you been here?" He pulled out a cigarette, lit a match from a small box sitting on the table, touched it to the end of the cigarette and then slid the ashtray across to her.

"Only about twenty minutes." She hesitated, lit a cigarette of her own and added, "I was afraid you wouldn't come."

Before he could respond, the old woman who had slid by him as he entered came to their table. "Y'all ready?" She had a white dish cloth in her hand which she used to wipe off the table. The cloth looked as if it had been in use since the first brick was laid for the building's foundation. "We got's some catfish today that's mighty good." She looked at Rachel. "I reckon you know what good catfish's supposed to taste like.

"How 'bout you, sir? What you gonna be eatin' today?"

Johnny and Rachel gave the woman their order and she returned to work the other tables in the room. Johnny looked around and then leaned toward Rachel. "Okay, what's going on?"

"I told you. Some men came to Mama's house today. They wanted to find Thomas and they pushed her down and then left her on the floor. If I hadn't come home—"

Johnny held up his hand to stop her. "I can only handle one of your family crises at a time. When's the last time you spoke to Thomas?"

"He called me at work. That day, you know…when you and him found that dead man."

"Tell me exactly what he said to you."

"He said he went to work at the pool room and started setting things up like he always does. After he fixed the coffee and got it going, he filled up the mop bucket and cleaned the office. Then he said he saw you." She stopped talking as plates of food were placed in front of each of them. The woman also sat a plate containing squares of corn bread. Johnny reached for a piece and cut it in half. With the steam rising from the still warm bread, he covered it in butter, placed the two pieces back together and gave his full attention back to Rachel.

"Did he say anything about seeing or hearing anyone else before he saw me?" He took a bite from the food on the plate and waited for her to answer. Even in the short time he had known her, he knew she was taking far too long to answer. "Look, I don't know what kind of game you think we're playing here, but let me give you my take on it. I don't think Thomas killed that man or anyone else. Even Brewer doesn't think he did it, but if Thomas knows who did or anything about who did it and doesn't come clean, he's as good as guilty himself. If Brewer can't find someone else, he'll track Thomas down and pin this on him. If that happens and you haven't leveled with me, then you're responsible."

He sat back and took a drink from the jar of iced tea. "Now." He paused and pulled out another cigarette, "You got something else you want to tell me?"

CHAPTER 15

The last time most people saw Charlie Dutton was when he stepped off the plane at the Atlanta airport. The people who saw him had no idea who he was or why he was on the plane. Charlie arrived on a flight from Miami. It was just after noon and he was hungry. He left Havana two nights earlier, flew to Miami, spent one night there and then caught a flight at seven that morning to Atlanta.

Charlie traveled light. All he had was a briefcase he carried and a small suitcase which was now in the belly of the airplane. The checked bag contained a shaving kit, a couple of pair of shorts and tee shirts, the now soiled shirts he had worn in Havana and Miami and a box of hand-made Madura cigars he picked up at the airport before leaving Cuba. Charlie wore a light beige suit, brown and white shoes, a shirt without a tie and a new hat he also picked up in Havana. Always a good dresser, Charlie had a gold pocket watch on a gold chain hanging from his belt on the right side. He wore a diamond pinkie ring and had another ring which he sometimes wore. That ring was made from gold he pried from the teeth of dead Japanese on an island in the Pacific. On the floor beneath his feet was his briefcase. Inside the briefcase was the reason for his trip.

Six months earlier Charlie had been a low level work-
er for the Dixie Mafia along the Gulf Coast in Alabama
and Mississippi. He collected money from juke boxes and
pin ball machines. Along the way he broke a few fingers
and an occasional larger bone if it was attached to a hand
that had been dipping into the nickels, dimes and quarters
he picked up on a weekly basis. Charlie knew if he did a
good job, his time would come. That time came when Joe
Skinner caught up with him at Brock's in Biloxi, Mississippi.

Brock's was a juke joint. It was just outside the main
gate of Keesler Air Base on Highway 90. It started during
the war as a cinder block building, but after a fire started
by a jealous soldier in 1945 when he found his girlfriend
with one of his buddies, it had been rebuilt as a much
larger structure. Large oak trees with beards of Spanish
moss dotted the parking lot. Each one looked like a veteran of its own war. With so many cars running into the
trees on the way into or out of the shale covered parking
lot, the trees were all missing most of the bark from the
base of the trunks up to fender level. The front of the
building was painted a dark brown with green trim. The
only outside light came from a single spot on a pole and a
large sign across the top of the building. Brock's was
spelled out in red letters that flashed twenty four hours a
day. The action inside and the flashing outside never
stopped.

Behind the main building sat three smaller cottages. If
there was any doubt as to what they were used for, all one
had to do was stand outside any time after dark. The
steady stream of men and women coming and going was
a dead giveaway.

The second generation owner of Brock's hired his own
muscle. He had two men posted outside after dark and
there were always at least three men inside. The inside

men doubled as bartenders when they were not tossing rowdy drunks, shipyard or oil field workers out the front door.

The only thing Brock's or any other joint on the Gulf Coast didn't control was the juke boxes and the pinball machines. Those belonged to Abe Salem. Joe Skinner came by on a regular basis to remind them of that fact and Charlie Dutton came by even more often to collect the money from them.

Brock's was shaped like a large letter "H" lying on its side with the bar in the center. The long leg closest to the highway had a dance floor at one end and a dozen tables at the opposite end where you could get the best Kansas City steak dinner for a hundred miles. There was a juke box near the edge of the dance floor. The sound was turned down on this one so it did not overpower the additional juke box Charlie had recently put on the opposite side of the building on the other leg of the "H."

That part of the building was where Charlie had the other juke box and seven pinball, shuffleboard and baseball machines. With a total of nine machines and two juke boxes in one location, this was Charlie's number one stop when he was on the road. It was also where he was to meet Joe Skinner.

Charlie parked his car in the shale-covered lot and walked to the front entrance. He had driven from his last stop in less than the normal hour that it took him in the past. The little beer joints along the coast that held his machines were deceiving if you didn't know how much business they generated. Most were cinder block rectangles with sharply peaked roofs. All except Brock's faced the Gulf of Mexico in case a hurricane decided to roar across the parking lot. That way, they presented the smallest target. Sitting parallel to the Gulf was a death wish, but Brock's had survived several storms.

Charlie was sitting at a table by himself when Skinner entered. There were two empty beer bottles on the table and Charlie was holding the third. Charlie stood when he saw Skinner as he walked past the bar and headed toward the sounds of the pinball machines.

"Hey, Mister Skinner. Over here." Charlie raised the bottle and used it as a baton to direct Skinner. "Can I get you a beer? Maybe something stronger?" He pulled out a chair for his boss.

"A beer to start. Maybe something else later on." He looked around the room. "Not a bad looking place. I haven't been here in six months. Maybe seven." A waitress wearing tight black pants and a white blouse brought his beer and sat it in front of him. She stood waiting for payment.

"Oh, hey, let me get that for you, Mister Skinner. My treat." Charlie slid a half dollar toward the waitress. "Keep the change." As the waitress turned away, Charlie slapped her on the ass and added, "And don't you forget who the big tippers are either, Sugar."

"How long you been working for us, Charlie?"

Charlie was quickly impressed. Skinner was getting right to the point and Charlie liked that. No table talk; no beating around the bush. *It's all business, so let's do business.* "Little over two years. I got out of the joint in 'fifty-one and came to work for you a couple of months later. One of my cellmates told me about—"

"I didn't ask for your life history, Charlie, I just wanted to know how long you'd been working for us." Skinner downed almost half the bottle of beer in one long gulp. "I was in one of our places back in Mobile last night. Little joint on the water called Fred's Crabs." He took another pull from the bottle. "Jeez, I went to the can in there, and the place was so dirty I was afraid to pull out my crank. I think that's where they got the name. Hadda be more crabs in the shitter than on the docks. If we ever pull out of that place, make sure you wash all the machines in Clorox before you take them someplace else."

"Yeah, that's a good, steady moneymaker. I got one juke box and a shuffleboard machine in there. I—"

"Why you telling me something I already know, Charlie? Didn't I just say I was in there last night? I seen the machines before the crabs ran me out. Don't tell me what I already know. Tell me you got a new place that wants five machines. Tell me about how some little shithole dive down the road suddenly got popular and we're doubling our take. Tell me something I can use." Skinner downed the remainder of the beer and motioned for another.

Before the waitress could return to the table, both Skinner and Charlie turned to the area with the pinball machines when a man began to bang on the side of a machine.

"Son of a bitch! This thing took my money and didn't let me play." The man banged on the face of the machine by the coin slot. "I put a quarter in there and it's supposed to let me play six games." He turned to another man standing next to him. Both were in their mid-twenties and dressed like they might have recently come from one of the many fishing boats that docked along the Mississippi coast. "Look up there on the counter. It's supposed to have a six on it and it ain't got a damn thing." He slammed his fist down on the glass top to emphasize his point.

Skinner stood and took the beer from the waitress's tray as she approached the table. He walked toward the man at the pinball machine. Charlie stood and walked beside him.

"Hey, squid go a little easy on the glass. There ain't no need to break it." Skinner was about an inch shorter than the other man. Unlike him, he wore dress pants, a long sleeved white shirt and black, wingtip shoes. If anything, he was overdressed for Brock's and that did not go unnoticed by the two men at the machine.

"Squid? Who you calling a fuckin' squid?" The man turned and gave his full attention to Skinner. "Looks to me like we maybe got ourselves a pimp out of a whorehouse down in New Orleans." He turned to his buddy for support as he laughed at his own joke.

"Yeah and he brought his punk with him." The second man nodded toward Charlie and laughed.

Before either of the men could regain their focus on Skinner and Charlie, the explosive sound of a breaking beer bottle echoed throughout the now quiet room when Skinner smacked the beer bottle against the edge of a nearby table. With the jagged neck of the bottle in his hand, he had a dangerous weapon. Broken glass crunched beneath his feet as Skinner crouched and moved toward the first man.

"Those are my pinball machines, asshole. I don't like it when people try to break 'em." He held the broken bottle by the neck; the sharp pointed end was at an up-angle toward the man's face.

All around them, the men and a few women were sizing up the situation and debating whether to take sides. Skinner knew he was in what for him would be hostile territory, so he angled himself with his back to the wall and Charlie between him and most of the other people in the place.

"You're making a real big mistake. I don't know who you are, but ain't nobody in here impressed by a broken beer bottle." The man was walking slowly backward, his hands held in front of him. "You drop that bottle or give me a chance to break one of my own and I'll show you how I make fish bait outta assholes like you."

The two men had the undivided attention of the crowd. Even some of the people from the other side of the bar had walked over to see what was going on. Charlie knew as soon as one of the bartenders came over and recognized him and Skinner, they would put a stop to the fight, but it didn't look they were coming any time soon.

"How 'bout I drop the bottle, and then it's just you and me, Sport?" Skinner dropped the bottle. As he did so, he knew his opponent's eyes would automatically follow the bottle to the ground for a fleeting second. That was all he needed. It was one fluid movement as the bottle dropped and his right foot shot out like a cobra attacking a mongoose. He connected with the point of his shoe in the man's groin and his opponent dropped like dead weight. With the man on the ground, Skinner stood over him. "Next time you decide you want to fight a man you don't know, you better be prepared for anything."

The crowd had moved in closer and as Skinner drew back to kick him again, he was hit from behind by a man who was wielding a full beer bottle. In less than a second, Joe Skinner lay on the floor beside his former opponent.

Skinner woke up while Charlie was placing him in the back seat of the Plymouth coupe he purchased when he got the job. It was a five-year-old, dark green two-door. He bought it from a car lot in Pensacola, Florida not far from the Greyhound bus station.

When he first started working he was afraid to tell Skinner he didn't have a car, so he rode the bus or hitchhiked to each of the joints. As a convicted felon, he was not supposed to own a gun, but he weighed the disadvantage of losing the money he collected against being caught. Jail for a weapons violation was better than facing Joe Skinner or, God forbid, Abe Salem and telling them he had lost their money, so he always kept a loaded .38 caliber pistol beneath the driver's seat.

"Hey, hey, what the hell you doing?" Skinner sat up as Charlie was placing his feet inside the car. "You let that asshole get the drop on me, you son of a bitch." He grabbed Charlie by the shirt front.

"No, no, it wasn't like that at all. Some guy came up behind us both and hit you with a beer bottle. I tried to push you out of the way, but—"

Skinner swung his feet out of the car and stood up. He wiped his head with his handkerchief, looked at it and did not find blood. "You can't let these guys mess with the machines like that. They cost money, and if they're broke they ain't making nobody no money." He turned toward Brock's. "Let's go back inside. I'm hungry."

The waitress sat them at a table as if nothing had happened. Fights in Brock's were a nightly occurrence and very few caused more than a broken table or a missed song on the jukebox.

"Let me have a steak, rare, a baked potato and another beer." Skinner looked at Charlie when he gave his order to the waitress. "He's buying."

In the middle of the meal, Charlie broached the subject Skinner had mentioned before. "Earlier tonight you wanted to know how long I've been with you, Mister Skinner." Charlie was hoping for a promotion. He could see himself as one of the bosses along the Gulf Coast. There were three men, including himself, who took care of the machines from Tampa, Florida to the Louisiana state line. Once you crossed into Louisiana, you crossed more than the state line. That was the dividing line between the upstart Dixie Mafia and the old line Mafia New Orleans family. Even Abe Salem did not cross that line.

Skinner cut into his steak and stabbed his fork into a piece. "Yeah, I had something for you, but that was when I thought you had some balls."

Charlie sat his beer down on the table. "Whadda you

mean? When you thought I had balls? You think I just let that guy hit you from behind?"

Skinner had a chunk of steak on the end of his fork and was about to put it in his mouth. Instead, he used it as a pointer as he spoke. "I think if you'd had any balls, you'd a'been watching my back and that never would have happened. I don't know if I trust somebody who works for me if he ain't got balls." He put the steak in his mouth and chewed as he maintained eye contact with Charlie.

Charlie and Skinner finished their meal in silence. After a final beer, Charlie paid and they left the bar.

Skinner was the first to notice the three men standing beneath a large, moss-draped tree at the edge of the parking lot. They were in position to watch the action and there was no doubt that, if necessary, they planned to become part of the action as well. "Looks like our friends have come back for more." Skinner spoke to Charlie as they continued to walk toward his car.

As they got closer, the largest of the three men stepped forward. He was wearing a ragged shirt, torn at the sleeves, revealing large muscular arms. "Which one of you bastards kicked my brother in the balls?" He took another step toward Skinner and Charlie.

"I think it was one of the whores that done it. She said he couldn't use them very good, anyways." Skinner turned slightly as he spoke. He whispered to Charlie. "You got a gun on you?"

"Not on me. It's under the seat of my car." Charlie looked at the men and knew he needed the gun. He glanced back toward the entrance, but the parking lot was around to the side, out of sight of the guards by the door, and those guys were concerned with security for inside Brock's and weren't likely to be any help for a fight in the parking lot.

"Ain't gonna do us any good in your car." Skinner continued to walk toward his car. "I left mine in my car 'cause I figured you'd have a piece on you."

"How about if I fix your balls so you don't need them anymore, wiseass?" Since the man had started to talk to Skinner, the other two men had gained enough courage to come stand behind their leader. "I believe I'm as good with a knife as you think you are with a broken beer bottle." The man had long arms burned to a deep brown by years on the water and muscles that he flexed as he talked.

"No need to get excited, boys, that was just a friendly little fight. Your brother was beating on one of my machines, and I beat on him. That sounds like a draw to me."

There was one light in the parking lot. It was on a telephone pole and was about thirty feet from where Skinner and Charlie were walking. The way it was positioned, they were in shadows and their opponents were in full light. The men were now in between Skinner and his car.

Skinner stopped, put his hands on his hips, and stared at the men. "If you wanna know the truth, it was my friend here who did the kicking." He placed his hands out in an expression of desperation. "I tried to stop him, but you know how some people are. They don't listen so they have to learn." He looked at the men. "My grandmother used to tell me that. Did your grandmother ever say anything like that?" Each word he spoke brought him closer to the men. Skinner dropped his hands, looked at Charlie, and then at the three men who were now less than a car length away.

"I'll tell you something else my grandmother used to say—" Before he finished the sentence, in one fluid movement, he reached into his back pocket, pulled out a switchblade knife, and hit the button to open it.

By the time the men saw it, the five inch blade had made its first contact. Blood flew from the long gash across the left cheek of the leader. He grabbed his face and screamed in agony.

A second flash through the air and he was cut from wrist to elbow along his left arm. He immediately started backpedaling in the parking lot. Three steps backward and he fell. As soon as he hit the ground, he began to scramble to his knees.

By that time, both of the other men had lost much of their bravado. Much, but not all. Charlie saw the glint of a knife as one of the men pulled it from a small leather holster on his belt. During the day time it was probably a filet knife used on the docks. The filet of choice in the parking lot was now Charlie. The man held it in his right hand as he came toward Charlie.

Charlie blocked the first lunge and then turned sideways as he came at him again. The man slipped on the loose shale parking lot and gave Charlie just enough of an advantage to let him grab the arm with the knife.

With the third man helping the profusely bleeding man on the ground and no longer a threat, Skinner watched as Charlie twisted the man's arm and wrestled him against the car. Charlie was using his head to force his opponent's head to the side, so it was Skinner who immediately recognized the look on the man's face when his knife entered his own body. For a second, they remained locked in combat and then Charlie felt the man go limp. He stepped back and watched as the man fell dead on the ground.

"Get the knife, Charlie. Your prints may be on it." Skinner began to walk backward toward his car. He kept an eye on the two men on the ground who had not yet realized their companion was dead.

"Oh, fuck! I can't go back to the joint. Not in Mississippi. No fuckin' way." Charlie pulled the knife and walked toward Skinner. "What do I do now?"

"Don't worry. I can make all of this go away. All you got to do is get to the airport in Miami. There'll be a ticket waiting for you to Havana. You go down there and pick up something for me. By the time you get back, all of this will be over for you." He pulled a piece of paper from his pocket and wrote on it. "This is the name of the place you should go to in Havana. And it has a man's name on it. Call me from Miami. If you get stopped by the cops, you eat this piece of paper. You got it?"

"Yes, sir. I do. I'll do a good job for you, you'll see. And you can't ever say I don't have balls after tonight, Mister Skinner." Charlie was almost running when he left for his car.

"I'm gonna make all of this disappear, just you wait, Charlie." Skinner spoke aloud as he watched Charlie's car kick up gravel as it sped across the parking lot.

Nine days later, Charlie lay dead on a pool table at Big Town.

CHAPTER 16

Johnny drove through town, picking up Marietta Street and then University Avenue. At University he skirted the construction for the new four lane highway that locals were calling "the expressway." Atlanta, everyone said, needed a four lane highway like a cat needed a side pocket. There were perfectly good highways leading into and out of the city. You could take State Highway 85 to Columbus, Georgia's second largest city. North on 41 for couple of hours and you were in Chattanooga. Where else would a person want to go?

Johnny wanted to go south about twenty miles into Clayton County. He took the new expressway to where it ended at the edge of the city and drove to a golf course just outside the country town of Jonesboro. The city had been the site of one of the major battles during the Atlanta Campaign when Sherman was doing his best to burn the state to the ground. That had been ninety years earlier and the city still had no concept of forgive and forget.

Anyone driving through the county with a car tag from any state not represented by a star on the Confederate Flag was considered a carpetbagger and was fair game for the police. It was not uncommon for a tourist or traveling businessman to be arrested for no reason, and if he did not have enough money to post bail he was relieved of his spare tire, his suitcase or watch. Fortunately the golf course where Johnny was going was not in the city limits, so he didn't have to worry about meeting a cop who might not like encountering a stranger from Atlanta.

Johnny tried playing golf one time about two years ago. He had a job following a woman whose husband said she was having an affair with a neighbor. He thought they met two or three times a week when he was at work. He had slipped home several times trying to catch her, but never could. The husband had even asked a cousin to watch his wife for him. When the cousin reported nothing out of the ordinary, he hired Johnny through one of the attorneys who frequented Big Town. After two weeks of following her, Johnny found out several interesting things to report to the husband. First, his wife was taking golf lessons to surprise him so she could play with him on the weekends. In order to verify what he had been told, John- ny had to rent clubs and follow her on a golf course one day to see if she was really serious or just using the les- sons as an excuse to meet someone.

When Johnny rented the clubs he had to purchase balls. He bought five of them. By the sixth hole he was down to only one ball and he lost that one on his second shot on the twelfth fairway when he tried to clear a water hazard. He finished the round just walking and keeping out of sight as he discovered the second interesting thing about the wife.

The reason the cousin did not report anything to the husband was to save himself from self-incrimination. As soon as the round of golf was over and three other times that week, the wife met her husband's cousin for at least two hours in a motel on the north side of town.

Johnny turned in the photos and expenses to the law- yer at the pool room.

"What the hell is this charge for golf clubs and five

golf balls?" The lawyer asked when he opened the invoice.

"I had to have clubs when I followed your client's wife on the golf course. I don't play, so I had to rent them." Johnny was sitting in one of the tall chairs along the wall watching two men play a game of bank pool.

"Okay, I understand the clubs, but you still got the balls. Use 'em next time you have to follow someone on the golf course." The lawyer stood in front of Johnny, partially blocking his view of the table.

"The balls are a cost of doing business. I don't have them anymore." Johnny leaned so he could see.

"Don't have them? What'd you do, give them away?" As he was arguing about the balls, it suddenly dawned on the lawyer what happened. "You followed her to Grovetown, didn't you? You lost the balls. Where? In the rough or in the water?" Now he was smiling.

"Both."

The lawyer folded the invoice and put it in his jacket pocket. "No problem, I'll see you get paid all your expenses." He was laughing when he left Johnny and headed for the steps.

Johnny didn't have playing on his mind when he got into his car and headed south to Flat Rock Golf Course.

Flat Rock was an eighteen hole-course and the last one between Atlanta and Columbus. As soon as he pulled off the main road and into the dirt drive leading up to the club house, his car was assaulted by several young boys, both white and Negro who jumped on the running boards on both sides.

"You need me to caddy for you, sir? I'm the best out here," a young Negro boy about twelve years old yelled from the passenger's side of the car.

"Don't listen to him. He ain't as strong as me. He can't carry but nine holes. You want to play eighteen today." Another boy, this one white, hung onto the mirror on the driver's side.

"Hey, hey, mister. I got some good golf balls for sale too, Titleist and Dunlap's. You know they's the best."

Johnny ignored both boys and the others who simply ran beside the car. He pulled into a parking space with the boys still hanging on.

"Awright, get off the car, so I can get out," he said to the one on his side.

"Okay, I'll come on around to the trunk. That's where you got your clubs ain't it?" The boy stepped down and started toward the back.

"Not today, boys, I'll let you caddy next time." Johnny started toward the club house.

"How 'bout some balls? Dime apiece for the Titleist and a nickel for the Dunlaps. Ain't nobody else got any that cheap. And none of mine got no cuts. They's almost new." The boy from the other side of the car fell in step beside him.

"If I pull out a ball I bought from you, I'd have half the men on the course coming after me swearing I stole the balls right out of their bags," Johnny said, tapping the boy on the shoulder as they walked.

"Oh, no. They ain't stole. I fount ever one of 'em in the rough. You can ax anybody. They'll tell you that Roscoe don't steal." The boy stopped and spoke with his hands on his hips.

"Tell you what, Roscoe, next time I come down here and need a caddy, I'll ask for you." Satisfied, Roscoe ran off to join a group of boys heading for another car just turning into the parking lot.

The clubhouse for the course was a long, low, green wooden building. One end was a screened area where several men sat at tables drinking beer, replaying their game in animated conversation or engaged in a poker game. Outside the building several teenage boys and older men sat on benches waiting to be selected as caddies by their regulars. Those about to go out were busy at a ball washing machine.

One man in his late twenties was busily turning the handle on the washer as he watched a ball turn from a dirt covered, dingy brown color to almost white as the soapy water did its work.

Johnny walked through the open doorway into the clubhouse. Two men stood behind the wooden counter just inside the door. One was busy ringing up a purchase for an older man and the other was handing out an order of soft drinks and crackers to two men who had just finished the course. Neither paid any attention to Johnny. He looked around and found a sign that said locker room. Beneath that was the sign he was looking for. It indicated the men's room was also in the locker room.

The locker room was hot and smelled like the gym where he changed when he played high school football so many years ago. As he stood and looked around he realized that he had not been in a locker room since his last football game in high school. Nothing had changed. The benches looked the same, the lockers looked the same and the place smelled the same.

He finished, left his journey down memory lane and went back outside the clubhouse.

Outside, he noticed a Negro man standing beside the building. Johnny recognized the look on the man's face. He was looking for someone, but he didn't expect them to be carrying a golf bag. He had a white tee in his mouth and alternately chewed on it and rolled it from side-to-side as he scanned the parking lot and the men who got out of the cars. He was about Johnny's age, but built heavier. He had a nose that said he had been on the wrong end of too many fists. He wore a pair of pants that had at one time been the bottom half of an expensive suit. Now the cuffs were frayed and the seat was slick. Even with that, the man wore them with dignity.

Johnny waited until a party of four golfers left the clubhouse and headed to the first tee. As soon as they were out of range, he walked to the man.

"I think you're looking for me." He pulled out a pack of cigarettes and let one drop into his hand. He hesitated a second, then offered one to the man.

"Depends. You need a caddy?" He took the cigarette and held it without placing it in his mouth.

"If I did, his name would be Thomas. Sound familiar?"

"You got to do better than that, Mister. Half the mens down here named Thomas." He reached into his shirt pocket and pulled out a wooden kitchen match. He flicked the end with a hard yellow nail and watched as the flame caught. He touched it to the end of the cigarette in his mouth, looked over the end of it at Johnny and then blew the smoke out.

"This one's got a high-yeller sister named Rachel. Does that narrow it down some?"

Without responding, the man turned and walked toward the end of the clubhouse. Johnny followed.

At the end of the clubhouse was the eighteenth green. Beyond that stood two small buildings. One was a shed where an old green tractor was sitting waiting for the next time the fairways needed cutting. The other building was an equipment shed. It was situated so that it could not be seen from the clubhouse. Only those players making their approach shot to the eighteenth green had a clear view of two sides of the building. Johnny's guide led him to the side that was further protected by a small stand of peach trees.

As soon as they got beside the building, the man said,

"Stay here," and walked toward the tree line on the fairway. In the distance, Johnny saw a farm tractor with a large mower attached cutting the fairways. Even from this distance the smell of gasoline fumes mixed with fresh cut grass drifted across the landscape and settled into the trees where he waited.

In less than five minutes, Johnny saw the man returning with Thomas. With them was another man he had not seen before.

"Mister Johnny." Thomas seemed almost breathless. "Rachel called me and said she had talked to you. Said you was gonna help me. You know I never kilt that man. But somebody thinks I did, else why they come to Mama's house and do those things to her?" Thomas walked to the edge of the shack, turned and came back. "I don't know what I gonna do. I can't go back—"

"Start from the beginning. Pretend I'm Detective Brewer. Tell me everything you know and don't leave out anything." Johnny looked at the two men standing on either side of Thomas. "And you can tell these two boys to back off." He looked from one to the other. The second man who came up with Thomas was the same age as Johnny and the other man. He was dressed only slightly better. His shoes were black with black electrical tape wrapped across the toe of the left shoe to either patch a hole in the top or keep the sole from falling off. He had on a white shirt and a bow tie. He wore a brown cap that reminded Johnny of a gangster from the thirties.

"These are my cousins. This is Broadway." He pointed to the man with the cap. "And that's Heavy. He's a prize fighter." Both men gave a slight nod but did not say anything. "I'm staying with them."

"Okay, now that we have your living arrangements out of the way, let's talk about a dead man. What do you know about him that I don't?"

Thomas looked at his two cousins, took a deep breath and began. "I came in at the same time I always does. When I tried to open the do', my key didn't work. I tried it two more times and then I pulled on the do' and it opened by itself. I looked and seen some paper in the little hole where the lock goes."

"Sounds like somebody got there before you did, Thomas," Heavy observed.

"They ain't got there first; they fixed it befo' they left the night befo'," said Broadway.

"I don't know who did it, but it was open when I got there. I went upstairs like I always do, but I was careful, 'cause I knowed something was bad wrong. Mister Hockey Doc, he don't never get there befo' I does, so I knowed it ain't him up there."

"You heard somebody?"

"I slid down real little so's I can't be seen over the top of the steps and when I got to the top, I snuck between the tables all the way back to the room where I keeps my mop and bucket."

"You always was a sneaky little devil, Thomas." Broadway said with what sounded like pride.

"Thomas, get to the point, did you see or hear anyone up there?"

"Yes sir, Mister Johnny, I did."

"Did what, Thomas? Did you see somebody or did you hear them?"

"I done both. I seen some mens and I heard 'em too."

"Start with what you heard. Did you hear them call each other by name or say anything you remember?"

Thomas began to walk again. He looked at Heavy. "You sure can't nobody see us here?"

"Ain't nobody gonna see us if you stop walking around like you got all the room in the world. Stand still, boy!" Thomas stopped and looked across the green, freshly cut fairway. For him, the image he dredged from his memory was as sharp and as deadly as the spinning blades leveling the grass and weeds behind the tractor. He kept his eyes on the open expanses of the golf course as he continued. "I heard them arguing. They was three of them. One of the men had the other one by the arm and he had it pulled up behind his back. I knowed that had to hurt."

Johnny pulled out his cigarettes and this time did not hesitate as he offered one to Broadway and to Heavy. He knew Thomas did not smoke so he nodded for him to continue while they lit up.

"By that time I was in my little room and watching them from behind the do'. That's when it happened."

"Happened? What happened?"

"That's when I heard that gun go off. I swear it sounded like a cannon to me."

"You heard them shoot him?"

"I heard it, and I seen it too. I seen them hold that gun on that po man and then pull that trigger when he was begging them to let him live." Thomas turned to his cousins. "I ain't never heard nothing so pitiful in my life. Even the Germans wasn't that bad. At least you had a gun and you could shoot back when we was over there. This po man didn't have a chance. They just shot that man like he was a dog. Then they picked him up and laid him on a table." He looked at Johnny and for the first time, he locked eye contact with him. "You believe what I'm saying, don't you Mister Johnny?"

In those eyes, Johnny saw the same look he saw when he got to Japan. A whole nation of people whose eyes had no life, no purpose. They had witnessed a horror beyond the ability of human words to describe. When the first Atomic Bomb vaporized the city, the people, the life that had been a thriving, though an enemy city, the ones who survived it could never describe the horror in sufficient terms to convince the world not to do it again. Johnny patrolled the streets and found burned, stiffened bodies still sitting as if they were about to have a meal. The problem was that there was no meal, no table and no house. It had become a part of the atmosphere and was gone forever. Those who survived were relegated to living like they were only two generations from writing on cave walls. There is a point in each person where he has to dig deep to come back to the living. Thomas was reaching for that spot as he continued to talk to Johnny.

Johnny knew how it felt to watch a man die and he knew instinctively that Thomas, like he, had managed to live his life to this point after the war without experiencing it again. He placed his hand on the man's shoulder. "It's okay Thomas. I know it's hard to think back over what you saw, but I believe you. I don't believe you killed that man or anyone else. We've just got to convince a few other people. Now, think about it and tell me if you heard any names."

Thomas was silent for a while as he thought. "I didn't have to hear no names for the man who was shot. I knowed who he was."

"But you did hear a name, didn't you?"

"The only name I heard was what he called the man they shot. That dead man. Everbody called him Charlie." He turned to Broadway and Heavy. "Y'all remember him. He used to caddy down here sometimes. I tol' you about him."

He turned back to Johnny. "That man kept saying something 'bout you got my suitcase and I want it back. You don't give it back, you gonna die. Right here and right now." He took a long breath. "I tell you it was awful 'cause I knowed that man wasn't gonna give them others nothing. I could just tell."

"The other man. The one who wanted the suitcase. Did you see him? What was his name, Thomas? What did Charlie call him?"

"All I heard him do was beg for them not to kill him. He said he done what they wanted. Something 'bout killing a man in Mississippi and going to Cuber to get some money. He was saying 'Please, don't kill me.' I won't never forget him saying that."

"But you did see him, didn't you?"

"Oh, I seen him all right. And I ain't never gonna forget that face. It was like I was looking at the devil himself. No sir, Mister Johnny, I'll never forget that face. It was pure evil." Maybe Thomas had not yet reached the depth of his memory for that day.

When Johnny returned to his car, he realized Thomas had answered several questions but he had left even more unanswered.

Who was the man Thomas had seen?

What was in the little suitcase that was worth killing Charlie for?

Why did he care?

Why was he going to let himself stay involved?

He knew the answer but couldn't let himself say it.

CHAPTER 17

Sunday night Johnny went to a little place down Ponce de Leon Avenue from where he lived for dinner. It was two doors down from the Emerald. The sign said they had been there since 1939 and he had no reason to doubt it. Several months earlier, he had dated one of the waitresses a couple of times. She wanted to get married and let Johnny know it on the third date. He asked her out once more after that, and she took it to mean he was as interested in marriage as she. By the middle of the date while they were eating a hamburger after seeing a movie, he explained his position on marriage, and she asked to be taken home. They never dated again, and soon she was gone from the restaurant.

Johnny didn't let that incident dissuade him from continuing to eat at the restaurant. It was an easy walk on a good night, and Johnny needed a good walk. He was getting more involved with Thomas and the murder than he had originally expected. He thought he'd find Thomas, and he'd tell him enough to get Brewer off his back. Thomas was going to remain the number one suspect until Brewer found him or Johnny gave him sufficient reason to look elsewhere. At the moment, he was unable to do that, so he just wanted a good meal.

He walked from the boarding house along Ponce de

Leon Avenue. The Sunday evening crowd was different than any other night. People were walking to local churches for their evening services, some caught busses for a movie downtown and some just walked. Few passed him without exchanging a greeting. It took less than fifteen minutes to get to the restaurant.

"Just sit anyplace you want to. We're not too busy tonight." Nick, the owner, a Greek with a good handle on the English language stood by the door when Johnny came in.

"I'll take a place over there." Johnny pointed to a booth along the wall.

"Never with your back to the door." Nick waved his finger at Johnny. "I notice these things. You don't know that I do, but I see everything in my place." Nick waved to the bartender. "A drink for my friend who never trusts anyone." He turned to Johnny. "Will you trust me to have a drink with me?"

"Of course, Nick. I trust you with my life every time I eat a meal in here, don't I?"

The waiter brought two small glasses of Ouzo, the fiery strong native drink that all Greeks, or at least all that Johnny had ever met, drank like Atlantans drank Coca Cola.

Nick and Johnny touched glasses and downed the shot in one drink. "Now you can eat a good meal and it will sit well on your stomach." Nick laughed and went to greet a couple who had stepped inside from the street.

Johnny had his dinner, and against his better judgment, accepted Nick's prodding to have dessert with the final cup of coffee. By nine thirty, a quarter moon barely lit the night sky as Johnny left the restaurant for the five-block walk home.

At the corner of Ponce de Leon and Kennesaw Avenue, Johnny stopped beneath a street light and pulled a cigarette from a pack in his shirt pocket. He placed it between his lips, pulled out his lighter and spun the wheel after flipping the lid open. He barely bent his head to meet the flame when he caught a fleeting glimpse of movement to his right. His natural instinct took over and he pivoted to face it. Had there only been movement on the right side that instinct would have been correct.

As Johnny spun toward the man to his right, a second man he did not initially see came up on his blind side. That was the man who hit him first. He drove his fist deep into Johnny's kidney, dropping him to his knees. With lights, unlike anything he had seen since an artillery barrage at night during the war, flashing in his eyes, Johnny knew he was in trouble. He rolled to his side just as the man to his right aimed a kick at his face. The kick missed and the man had enough force behind it to throw him off balance when he did not connect.

That was just enough time to let Johnny make an agonizing rise to his feet and reach into the shoulder holster beneath his left arm and pull out his pistol. His first target was the man who had initially attacked him with the fist to the kidney. Johnny felt bone break as swung the flat side of his .45 caliber and it connected with the man's cheek. With his right arm already outstretched, he swung around just in time to see the second man pull his own pistol and level it toward Johnny. The loud boom of the .45 automatic echoed along the quiet street as Johnny fired two times at the man with the gun. By the time he turned back to face the other man, that one had staggered to a car which was speeding away.

So much for loyalty, thought Johnny as he looked at the man at his feet.

The sound of the gunfire caused several residents to raise their windows and peer out. One called out to Johnny. "I got a phone. You want me to call the cops?"

Johnny hesitated and called up to the man. "Yeah, call and ask for Detective Brewer."

A man holding a shotgun stood on the front steps of an old home about fifty feet from where the man lay bleeding. "You need any help down there? I know there was two of them that jumped you."

"No, thanks. I'm okay. You didn't happen to get the tag number of the car the other guy jumped in, did you?" Johnny stood over the body and looked down at it.

"Nah, he was hauling ass as soon as he seen that you wasn't going to give up your wallet."

Robbery? Now there was a different take on the last few minutes. That possibility never crossed his mind, thought Johnny. He was thinking about that when he heard the distant sound of a siren. As it grew closer, the neighbors who had been watching slowly closed their windows and left Johnny to tend to the business on the sidewalk on his own. Even the man with the shotgun returned inside as the first car rolled to a stop.

As soon as the first officer stepped out of his patrol car, Johnny raised his hand to identify himself. "I'm armed, officer, and I have a permit." He slowly peeled back his lightweight sports coat to reveal the re-holstered weapon.

"Just don't make any quick moves, Mister. Hand me the piece and your papers. Real slow." The officer placed his right hand loosely on his own weapon as he approached Johnny.

Johnny pulled the automatic from the holster with his left hand. He spun the weapon around and dropped the magazine into his right hand. He held the barrel toward the night sky and said, "I'm going to clear it now. There's a round in the chamber." Before the officer could respond, Johnny quickly pulled the slide back and watched as a short, fat .45 caliber slug flew through the air and dropped to the ground. Without saying anything, he stooped and picked it up.

Just as he was standing erect again, he heard another car door slam. "Well, well, look who's shooting up the neighborhood. I thought you only did that in pool rooms." Brewer walked to where Johnny stood. He looked down at the body.

"Friend of yours?"

"Never seen him before. He and another man jumped me when I stopped to light a cigarette.

"Maybe they just wanted to bum a light. You ever think about that?" Brewer leaned down and pulled a handkerchief from his back pocket. He picked up the gun lying on the ground by the dead man. "I'll bet you're gonna tell me he pulled this on you and tried to shoot you."

"I think that was what he had in mind."

While Johnny and Brewer talked on the sidewalk, the patrol officer was interviewing the one person who had stayed outside when the sirens broke the stillness of the night air. He finished talking to the old man and came to Brewer.

"Detective, can I speak to you for a minute?" He held a small notebook in his hand.

"Don't go nowhere. I ain't through talking to you, yet Morocco." Brewer walked away with the patrolman.

Johnny looked at the man who lay in his own blood on the sidewalk. Around him the night air was filled with the smell of flowers and budding fruit trees. Someone had cut grass that day and the green smell of freshly cut grass drifted across the sidewalk when the wind came from the right direction. The smells of new life mingled with the odor of the spilled blood marking fresh death.

Brewer came back to Johnny. "My officer said the witness saw you being hassled by two men." He looked around. "Except I don't see but one body. Where's the other guy?"

"He jumped into a car and left. I think it was waiting for them. It happened really fast, so I didn't have a lot of time to spend on each one of these bums."

Brewer was looking at the dead man. "I don't know who this guy is but I know who he ain't. He ain't a bum. Look at those shoes. Alligator." He bent down and looked closer. "And he's got a belt to match." He stood up and turned toward the ambulance which was pulling to the side of the street in front of them. "I'll bet you a chili dog, he's clean. No driver's license, no identification at all. Wanna bet?"

Before Johnny could answer the back door of the ambulance was opened and the long gurney pulled out. The two men wrestling the gurney to the ground looked at the victim. The driver stood by the victim's head and spoke to Brewer. "You want us to take him now or wait till you get some pictures?"

"Wait a few minutes. We got a photographer on the way. He ain't gonna get no deader." He looked at Johnny. "You got a cigarette. I'm fresh out."

❧❧❧

Otis Hightower drove to Miami with only one stop. He spent the night in Lake City, Florida at a small tourist court that had five cabins. He stayed there on occasion when he drove from Atlanta to Miami. It was about half way and just outside the city. Next door was an American Legion Hall that had a poker game three nights a week. He kept them supplied with playing cards and punch boards. Twice a year they had a Monte Carlo night and always ordered several extra boxes of cards and a couple dozen pair of dice. Another reason the liked to stop there was the bartender. She was a blonde who reminded him of Veronica Lake, the way she wore her hair. He'd talk to her every time he came in and once even took her to dinner when he came by on a night when she wasn't working.

Otis checked into his cabin about seven. The room was the same, no matter the number of the cabin. The bed had a metal frame and a decent mattress. There were two tables, one on either side of the bed. A lamp sat on one of the tables beside the bed. The table on the other side had a radio, but if this room was like the others he had stayed at in the past, the only thing the radio picked up was static. The closest decent station was in Valdosta but that was over sixty five miles away. The little radio was just not strong enough to pick up any programs.

Once he got to the room, he didn't want to leave, even for dinner. He usually carried a loaf of bread and some sandwich meat or a banana or two so he could make sandwiches at night. Otis sliced a banana and placed it on a piece of bread, placed another slice of bread on top of it and sat on the edge of the bed as he ate.

He finished the sandwich and pulled a Police Gazette out of his suitcase. This one had a picture of Rita Hayworth on the front cover and promised a juicy story about her love life on the inside.

The tabloid was a guilty pleasure for Otis. He didn't exactly have to hide them from Virginia, but he knew it was best to keep them out of sight. Virginia was sensitive to photos like they sometimes had in this one and in Confidential.

"Maybe I should just go over and check out the bar at the Legion Hall," he said aloud to himself.

An hour later, Otis returned to his room alone.

Otis slept that night thinking about Veronica Lake and not about what he had in front of him the next day.

The drive from Lake City to Miami took all day. By the time Otis got there, he was worn out just from the drive. He drove straight to the airport and grabbed a room at a hotel just off NW Thirty-/sixth Street. Once he got to the hotel, he unloaded his car and put the boxes of cards and dice in his room. He paced the room for over an hour wondering what would happen if he just didn't catch the plane the next day. He had the two hundred dollars Joe Skinner had given him. Two hundred dollars! He could call Virginia and tell her to catch a Greyhound and meet him in Miami. With two hundred cash, they could almost start over. He could get a job doing something and Virginia could always get a job in a bank like she had in Atlanta or be a waitress or something. Even as he tried to determine how to do it, he knew he was stuck. He was headed for Havana and he had no alternative.

CHAPTER 18

Abe Salem was not a man you wanted to be around when he was mad, and he was very mad when Joe Skinner sat across from him at the table in Abe's office. "What the fuck do you mean, 'He's dead'? If he didn't give you my money before he died he better hope he's dead or I'll kill the son of a bitch myself." Abe picked up the heavy coffee mug sitting in front on him on the table and hurled it across the room. It was half filled with coffee and the black stain ran down the wall when it hit. "You do have my money, don't you Joe?" He leaned across the table before his lieutenant could answer. "Don't fucking tell me you don't have it, Joe! I don't want to hear that you let him get killed before you got my money." His dark eyes bored holes in Joe as he waited for an answer.

"All's I know is I got a call from one of the players down at Big Town. They said the cops were all over the place. When the porter came in to clean up that morning, he found Charlie dead on a pool table. The cops didn't ID him right away, but my guy recognized him just before they bagged him and took him out." Joe tried to maintain eye contact but it was impossible when Abe was upset. It was like a starring contest with the devil.

"The guy was dead. Maybe it was somebody different.

You don't look the same dead as you do alive. Could'a been a mistake." Abe stood and walked to a bar in the corner of his office. He poured himself a drink and downed it in one gulp. Abe then poured a second one and looked at Joe. Joe motioned for him to pour one for him as well.

"Tell me again when this guy left Havana and what he did up to the point he was using a pool table for a morgue slab." Abe demanded.

"My guy says he left Havana with the money on schedule. He flew straight into Miami, had a couple of hours between planes then caught one to Atlanta. He got to the airport at about noon. Charlie had a car so he probably left it out there someplace and went straight to it when he got back. I know he was on the plane because Sam Church, down in Miami, met him when he came in from Havana and watched him get on the plane to Atlanta." Joe poured himself a second drink. "After that, Poof! Nobody sees him till he's on the table."

"Somebody seen him. They seen him and they took my money." Abe Salem's business card said Salem Real Estate. As a convicted felon, he couldn't hold a license himself, but his wife, Delores could and did. She fronted the business and all of the money Abe claimed on his annual income tax form was from property she sold and he claimed. As a prominent real estate broker, he had to dress the part. Abe usually wore a hand tailored suit, white shirts and white-on-white silk ties. He had a tailor who did hard time at the same place as Abe. The tailor's crime was grand theft auto. Abe's was murder, reduced to manslaughter. Anyone who knew Abe realized the time he spent in prison was for the one time he got caught. They knew there were many others who had crossed him and had disappeared forever and for which he had never served a day.

Abe paced the room as he spoke. "This is not acceptable, Joe. Whoever killed him has my money, and if that person doesn't walk in my door in the next few hours, he will never walk again when I find him. You put the word on the street. I want..." He stopped pacing and hesitated as if it all became clear. "Wait a minute. You said somebody found the body before the cops got there?"

"Yeah, they got a nigger that mops the floor first thing in the morning and then works as a rack boy. He's a gimp. I've seen him a couple of times when I was there. He's probably long gone by now, though."

"He's got my money! Find him and you find the money. He's either got it or knows who does. Find him, Joe. I don't give a shit what you have to do, but you find him and you find my money." Abe took his coat off the wooden rack in his office, put it on and left without another word.

ᏓᏛᏓ

Red was walking by the phone at Big Town when it began to ring. He grabbed the handset on the second ring. "Big Town. Whoever you want ain't here...Oh, yes, sir, I think he may be. Hang on and I'll get him...okay, okay...I'll tell him. Yes, I got it. You think I'm deaf or stupid? Yeah, you, too." An angry Red slammed the receiver back on the phone box and yelled across the room.

"Johnny, your best friend, Detective Sergeant Brewer, wants your ass in his office within the next thirty minutes or he's gonna send a black and white to pick you up." He turned to Hockey Doc. "And he said he's gonna send the Vice Squad up here along with them."

Hockey Doc came from behind the bar. "Johnny! Get your ass in gear. I don't need a repeat performance of the police checking out my place."

"I'm on my way. Don't worry, I'll be there in plenty of time to cool him off.

Johnny drove down Decatur Street and found a parking place on the street across from the Atlanta City Jail. He pulled into the space, got out of the car, placed a nickel in the parking meter, and walked across to the landmark building everyone knew by reputation, location or by having been an inmate. In two minutes he was sitting in Brewer's office.

"Look around you, Johnny, this ain't no pool room. This is my office. I'm a real Atlanta Police Detective, and you spend most of your life pretending you'd like to be me when you grow up."

The office was on the left side of the hallway leading from the Chief of Detective's office to the holding pens at the end of the long corridor. Johnny saw several men being placed in the pens when he and Brewer walked by them. Brewer's second floor office had one window facing the outside world. Brewer was not big on decorations or personalizing his work space. There were no pictures of family or associates. No children, no promotion parties, no fishing trips, no commendation certificated. For him, it was a work space and nothing more. The room was dominated by a large wooden desk and an office chair that looked like it came from a second hand shop. Johnny sat on the only other piece of furniture, a single wooden chair that was placed across the desk from Brewer. On the desk top between them were several large black and white photos of a dead man. It was the one Johnny had shot.

"You see, I don't even mind you killing this guy. My gut says he was up to no good here, and sooner or later he's gonna do something bad and make trouble for me. You just stepped in and took away his opportunity." Brewer opened the drawer in the center of the desk and rummaged around for a moment then looked up at Johnny. Without his having to ask, Johnny reached into his pocket and pulled out his pack of Luckies.

He tapped the pack on his extended left index finger and pulled out a cigarette for himself and passed the pack to Brewer.

After lighting it and blowing out a large plume of smoke, Brewer continued. "All I want to know is who he is, or was, and why he wanted to kill you." He sat quietly and looked at Johnny. "We both agree that he and his partner were trying to kill you, don't we?"

"Sounds reasonable, but I don't know why." Johnny shook his head to emphasize his confusion.

"It pains me to ask, and I hate to even use the word, but were you working on a case?"

"Nothing that would require that kind of muscle to get me off it."

"Let me decide how much muscle these two guys were. What were you working on?" Brewer stood when he saw another detective standing in his office doorway. "Notice I said 'were working on,' 'cause whatever it was, you've stopped working on it." He nodded to the man in the doorway.

The detective handed a piece of paper to Brewer. "Here's the initial report on the fingerprints."

Brewer looked at the information for a quiet moment. "Our boy's got a rap sheet here in Atlanta. Couple of arrests for A and B. He did some time in Reedsville. Says here he usually works with a partner. You think that might have been the other guy?" The smile on Brewer's face was as phony as it was wide. His smile disappeared when he slammed his fist down on his desk and almost screamed. "If you ever expect to walk out of here again, you tell me why I find you standing over a dead body every time I've seen you for the last week! I wanna know and I wanna know right-fucking-now." He slammed his fist down again for emphasis. Even with the door closed, Johnny saw several other detectives react to the noise. "You think you skated on this guy—" He threw down a photo of the body lying on the pool table at Big Town. "—but this one ain't over yet, either. Both of these guys were killed with a .45 slug and that's what you carry. In my book, that's too much of a coincidence to let pass. We both know you killed the second one, so now let's talk about..." Brewer opened the first page of another file. "Let's talk about Charlie Dutton." He closed the file. "And then we'll talk about Thomas Johnson and his sister Rachel. You go first."

Johnny sat back in the chair and crossed his arms. It was a short stall for time, but even he wasn't sure why he felt he needed it. He picked up the photo and held it. "You know more about this guy Charlie than I do. Some of the guys at Big Town said they knew him. Said he came in sometimes and played pool and during football season he played a parlay card sometimes. I think I may have seen him but I'm not sure." He leaned forward in the chair. "You know I shot the second man. And you know I didn't shoot the first one. You've already fired my piece to check ballistics, so you know they're not a match on Charlie. I don't know what else I can tell you. I don't know the men who jumped me, and I don't have any idea why they did it." Johnny stood. He was taking a chance and they both knew it. "If I find out who shot Charlie or why I was jumped, you'll be the first one to know." He took his time as he lit another cigarette. "So, if you don't have any more questions, I need to get back to my place. My land-lady said we're going to have meatloaf tonight."

It was a classic stand-off. They stood on either side of the desk like two bull elephants each waiting for the other to blink so the charge could begin.

"Okay, sit down. Let's talk." Brewer went to the door and called for another officer to bring them two cups of coffee. "Maybe we can work together on this." He returned to the chair on his side of the desk. "And by work together, I mean, you tell me everything you know and what you learn in the future. You do that, and I don't come up with some bullshit charge just so I can lock you up for investigation."

"I've already told you everything."

"Now don't start yanking my crank the first time I give you a chance to work with a real detective."

The junior grade detective tapped the door open with his foot and placed two white paper cups on the corner of the desk. "Do you gentlemen need anything else?" he inquired with a not-too-subtle sarcastic tone. Brewer dismissed him with a wave of his hand and ignored the comment.

"Tell me what you know about where Thomas is or where he went when he left Big Town. I know you been asking around about him." He took a drink from the cup. "You doing it because somebody's paying you or because you enjoy dipping your wick in that high-yeller sister of his?"

Johnny knew he had to be very careful how he answered Brewer. On the surface he might appear to be a bumbling incompetent, but that was how he caught many people in lies and other traps. Although Johnny had not done anything that could be considered illegal, he did possess some information he did not plan to share with Brewer. At least not now.

"You know as well as I do that Thomas didn't kill anyone. Look at the difference in size alone. This guy, Charlie was several inches taller and had fifty pounds on Thomas. Even if Thomas had shot him, do you think he could have lifted his body onto the pool table?"

"Maybe he had some help. All them coloreds stick together. You know that."

"Sure, Thomas and one of his friends kills Charlie, lays him on the pool table, the other guy hauls ass and Thomas sticks around to mop the floors and do his normal opening of Big Town. I think with all he's been through in his life, Thomas has learned to be a little smarter than that."

"Okay, let's say he didn't kill Charlie. Try this one on for size." Brewer opened the folder again. "Charlie works for Abe Salem. That name ring a bell with you?"

"Dixie Mafia?"

"One and the same. So, Charlie works for them picking up nickels, dime and quarters from juke boxes and pinball machines in gambling houses and beer joints all along the Gulf Coast. Suddenly Charlie decided he wants to go to Cuba." He flips several pages in the folder. "Any idea why he goes to Havana?"

"To work on his tan?"

Brewer looked up from the folder. "Don't be a smart ass, I'm trying to let you help me work my way through this. Anyway, he only stays one day and then he heads back to Miami and then lands here in Atlanta. Near as I can figure he winds up dead the next morning." He closed the folder. "You got anything to add to that?"

Johnny shook his head. "All of that is news to me. But now you're at the point I came in, right?"

"Good guess. Did you learn that in Private Investigator school or are some of my skills beginning to rub off on you?" Brewer hesitated. "The way I hear it on the street is that the late Mister Charlie Dutton may have left Havana with a lot of money. If that's true, when he turned up dead, he didn't have it." Brewer stood and walked to the window. "At least when I got to the scene, he didn't have it." He cast an accusing eye at Johnny then looked out into the street below. "I also hear that some very bad people are looking for that money. The way I see it is they probably think you got it or know where it is. You may or may not, but if you do you're not inclined to share that information with the bad guys. They don't know you as well as I do, so they think all they gotta do is knock you around a bit and you'll tell them anything they want to know. See, I know you're not gonna roll over that easy, and that's why I got another stiff on ice downstairs."

Brewer came back and sat down. "What I need to know is why Charlie suddenly went from nickels and dimes to the big time as a bag man. No stops in between. One day he's in some shithole town in Mississippi and the next day he's got a bag full of money and is flying all over the place. And then I want to know what happened to the money he was carrying."

Johnny finished drinking his coffee. "I noticed you don't seem concerned about who killed him.'

"The 'who' ain't that important. If I find out the why, then the who will be there too. You know, money makes people do some strange things to each other. I seen a mother kill her own daughter for a week's pay about a year ago. The old woman said her daughter owed her six dollars for food she ate at her house and wouldn't pay her. From what I hear, Charlie was carrying enough money to get himself killed several times."

Johnny realized that Brewer knew about the missing money when he talked to him at Big Town. He didn't mention how much was missing and may not have known at the time but he seemed to know now.

"So what do you want from me?"

"I told you, I want Thomas. Just to talk at first. If he convinces me he didn't kill Charlie, then he walks." Brewer smiled. "On the murder charge. But there's that little matter of the missing money I'd like to talk to him about."

"How much money is missing?"

"How does seventy-five thousand sound?"

Johnny immediately thought that half the people both he and Brewer knew would kill their immediate family for that kind of money. But Thomas wasn't one of them.

CHAPTER 19

Otis Hightower didn't like to fly, but unless he wanted to take a boat he had no other way to get from Miami to Havana. Cubana Airlines had flights that were almost like the busses that ran between Atlanta and Birmingham. One time Otis had to catch a bus to Birmingham, and all he had to do was go to the bus station and wait for less than an hour. Like the bus station, he was in the Miami airport less than an hour before he was able to leave for Havana.

As soon as he got inside the terminal, he did just what Joe Skinner had told him to do. Go to Cubana Airlines, buy the two-day excursion package and enjoy the flight.

"Have you been to Cuba before?" the woman behind the counter asked Otis as he walked up. She had an accent that he guessed was Cuban, but since he was not entirely sure he had ever actually met anyone from Cuba, he wasn't certain what she was supposed to sound like.

"No, this is my first time." He placed three of the twenty dollar bills Skinner gave him on the counter. He looked at the remaining seven in his wallet. "Have you been there? Cuba, I mean." He stammered.

"I was born there, and I go back about once a month. You will like it this time of year." She smiled a very friendly smile at him. She reminded him of a movie star.

He couldn't remember which one, but he knew it would come to him. "Is your trip business or pleasure?"

"What? Oh, it's pleasure. I mean business, but it will be a pleasure to get to see Havana." Otis shook his head knowing he had sounded like a schoolboy as he stammered through the conversation.

"I'm sure you will find many things to like in Havana. It is an exciting city if you like the nightlife. If not, there is plenty to do during the daytime." She smiled as she continued to write his ticket. "There are many museums you can visit and the citadel is a most interesting place." She placed the ticket in an envelope and handed it to him. "Don't forget to have a Mojito at one of the many outdoor cafés. If you have never had one, you will find it the most exciting drink you have ever had."

Otis took the ticket and walked to a nearby gate area where a sign indicated the next flight to Havana was leaving in less than an hour. He stood at the end of a row of seats beside a man who was dressed in an off-white, linen suit and a pair of brown leather sandals.

"Is anyone sitting there?" Otis pointed at the seat next to the man.

"No, it is open for anyone."

Otis took a seat and noticed a newspaper lying on the next seat. He picked it up, opened it and immediately realized it was printed in Spanish. As he folded it, his seatmate noticed. "No se habla Espaňiole, eh?"

"I'm sorry. I don't understand you." Otis turned to the man.

"That's what I said. You don't speak Spanish." The man's accent was even more noticeable than that of the ticket agent.

"No, I don't. I'm sorry."

"You probably won't have a hard time in Havana. Many of the residents speak English. We learn your lan-

guage, but very few of us get to come to the United States
and use it. You, on the other hand, don't learn Spanish
but you come to Cuba in droves." The man reached into
an inside pocket of his jacket and pulled out a long thin
cigar. He took his time as he clipped the end with a small
cutter and then struck a match to the end of the cigar. He
spoke to Otis as he rolled the cigar in his mouth to make
sure the flame of the match touched every part of the end.

"Do you like a good cigar? I can tell you where to find
the best ones in Havana. All hand-made. Some of the
men who work there have been rolling cigars for fifty
years or more. They are true craftsmen." He took the cigar out of his mouth and looked at it admiringly.

Before Otis could answer, the gate agent announced
that the flight to Havana would be loading in ten minutes.
He then left the counter and walked outside. Otis stood
and followed him to the doorway.

Sitting on the tarmac less than one hundred feet from
the building was a twin engine DC-3 airplane. Otis recognized it as the same type used in the European Theater
of Operations during WWII. On D-Day he had seen hundreds of them as they dropped airborne troops and then
later as they were able to land and evacuate the wounded.
He watched as the pilot opened the window and leaned
out to say something to one of the men on the ground.

The man gave the pilot a "thumb's up" signal and
walked to the door where Otis stood.

The gate agent returned to the counter. He checked a
few papers and then nodded at Otis. "We'll be loading
now. The pilot is ready." He held a small clip board with
a list of names on it. He reached beneath the counter and
picked up the microphone.

He spoke into the handset in what Otis took to be
Spanish. As he spoke, several people stood and made their
way to the exit. The agent looked around and seemed to

be satisfied that those who spoke Spanish had responded to the announcement. He then spoke in English.

"Ladies and gentlemen, Cubana Airlines announces the immediate loading and departure of Flight Nine-Oh-Three to Havana. Please have your tickets out so I can see them." He placed the microphone back on its holder and walked to the door where the line was already forming.

Otis took his place in line behind a women and her young daughter. The woman looked to be in her mid-thirties. She had hair the color of the inside of a coal mine hanging loosely on her shoulders. Long silver ear rings dangled from each ear. He watched as they became tangled in her hair as she moved her head in her animated conversation with the young girl. Their conversation was entirely in Spanish, so Otis could only stand and listen.

Once on the plane, Otis took an aisle seat next to a woman who held a small baby in her arms. Otis's first thought was that he hoped the baby slept all the way to Havana. His hopes were dashed when the pilot fired up the engine on the right side of the plane. It caught with a loud backfire and a white plume of smoke as the alcohol fuel injection burned off and the engine cranked. The backfire was loud enough to awaken the baby who began to cry.

As soon as she secured the door, the stewardess came to the seat and leaned across Otis to speak to the woman. "Can I bring you something for the baby? Do you have milk?"

The woman looked at the stewardess and shook her head, "No hablo Inglés." Even without a translation, Otis knew the woman did not speak English. Without missing a beat, the stewardess spoke to her again, this time in Spanish as she gently rubbed the baby's arm to soothe it.

The plane was probably purchased surplus after the war, Otis thought as he noticed what he recognized as a patched-over bullet hole in the floorboard beneath his seat. As the plane rolled down the runway, it began to even out when the tail section lifted from the single wheel and became level with the two wheels in front. In less than a minute, he felt the plane break free from the ground and begin its wide circle over the city to gain altitude before heading east over the Atlantic and then south to Cuba.

The seats were cloth covered and the arm rest between Otis and his companion was covered in a brown plastic. There were two small cigarette burns beside the ashtray where a careless smoker had missed putting the lighted end of their smoke in the tiny tray.

The pilot made an announcement, first in Spanish and then in English that the flight was going to be smooth and that any passenger who wanted one could get a complementary Cuba Libra from the stewardess who would be serving them shortly.

Otis released the seatback and leaned back to both enjoy the trip and to contemplate what he had gotten himself into. He closed his eyes and was asleep before he could take advantage of the free drink.

The pilot's announcement of their impending arrival in Havana awakened him.

⌒⌒

Joe Skinner was furious. He stood in front of the car and paced. The man standing across from him had three inches and about fifty pounds on Skinner but that didn't matter. Skinner was the boss.

They met at a small park just off Bankhead Highway. The two cars were parked in an area where families usually pulled in on the weekends, unloaded their picnic baskets or sports equipment and had a pleasant day. The park was surrounded by tall pines, a few oak trees and thick mats of honeysuckle vines that were in full and sweet, fragrant bloom. If Skinner had to kill the second man, this was as good of a place as any.

"What the fuck do you mean, Victor, 'he hit me' and then he got away?"

"Honest, Mister Skinner, I didn't see no bulge or nothing to show that he was packing. If I did I would—"

"You would probably have gotten yourself killed just like your sorry-ass partner did, that's what you would have done." Skinner paced some more. "I can't believe you. I send two of you to grab this guy and bring him to me and what happens? Your partner...Rufus, Roscoe—"

"Robert. His name's Robert."

"I don't give a shit if his name is Roosevelt, you let some two-bit PI pop his ass and break half the bones in your face." He turned to face the man. "I oughta break the other half myself."

Victor's face was a painter's palate of colors from his hairline down to his chin. His lip was split on the edge and his left ear looked as if it was missing a small piece. Even though Victor was talking, it was muffled because his jaw was not functioning as it should. The flat side of a well-placed .45 automatic covers a lot of face.

Skinner stopped pacing. He came back and stood almost nose-to-nose with Victor. "Okay, here's what you're gonna do. You go back to that pool room where we found Charlie. Talk to everyone in there and find out where that rack boy is hiding. And then you find his ass. You find the boy, you find the money. Charlie had it on him when he left Miami and when he landed in Atlanta. Someplace between the airport and the pool room he hid it. If it was in the pool room that nigger knows where it was. Since he ain't been seen since you popped Charlie, I'm going to go out on a limb and say he has it." Skinner's voice dropped lower the longer he spoke to Victor.

He walked around a few times, almost in circles as he focused his thoughts. This time he emphasized what he said by tapping Victor in the chest with his finger.

"You know that half-assed PI Morocco's been trying to find him too, so let's just pretend Morocco is better at this than you and found the nigger and the money. If that's the case, now you got to find HIM and get my money. Either way, you find my money or you will be taking up grave yard space next to your partner." He began to drive his point home by poking his finger harder into the man's chest. "And if you mention a word of this conversation to anyone, and I mean anyone, I'll kill you myself. Do I make myself clear?"

Victor did not respond.

He did not have to.

CHAPTER 20

The Tropicana was one of the most opulent casinos in Havana. The first thing most people noticed when they entered was that the patrons dressed to match their surroundings. Otis walked in from the street and was immediately struck by the stark difference between the gambling houses and illegal casinos he called on as a sales representative and the operation spread before him. Tables abounded with craps, roulette and blackjack games in progress all over the main floor. He walked to the first craps table he came to and took a place beside a man in a tuxedo who had the dice.

"Come on, come on, little dicey, make me some more money." Tuxedo man held the dice in his open right hand and rolled them around. He leaned across the table and tossed chips to the stick man. "Double the six and eight and give me all the hard ways." Without comment, the chips were collected and placed on the felt.

From the other end of the table a tall, red-haired woman in a blue dress called out to him. "Okay, Tony, make us some numbers. I've got this month's alimony riding on this next roll."

People around her laughed as Tony responded. "If I don't, does that mean you'll actually have to find a job and go to work?"

"Not on your life, sweetheart. I said this month's alimony, not every month's." She smiled and motioned for a waitress to brink her another drink.

Satisfied that all the bets were down, the stick man called out, "The point is nine" and nodded toward the shooter.

Tony closed his hand, cocked his arm to the side of his head and fired the dice down the table. They bounced against the far wall, and rolled to the center of the play area. Each die had a three showing when they stopped spinning.

A roar came from many of the men and women at the table, not the least of which was Tony. Otis recognized the chips being slid to him as five hundred dollar denominations. On one roll of the dice, Tony had won almost ten thousand dollars. The stakes in this casino were far beyond anything Otis had ever seen.

"Would you care for a drink, señor?" A dark eyed beauty stood beside Otis. She held a cocktail tray.

"Uh, no. Not right now. I want to look around a little first." He smiled and walked toward the blackjack tables.

There were seven tables in the section where he stood. Five of the tables had six players each and the other two had at least four people playing. It was difficult to determine who was playing and who was watching on several of the tables.

The tables were almost exactly like the ones used in casinos and gambling houses in his territory. The only noticeable difference was some of the designs representing the casino were tropical in nature. Dealers used single decks of cards and dealt as fast as the players and action allowed. Otis watched to see if there was sufficient time for a mechanic to deal seconds or false shuffle without being caught by either the players or the pit bosses. Otis moved from table to table as he timed the hands. He wanted to see how long they played with one deck of cards. He watched to see if the dealer changed decks when they rotated or if a player could call for a new deck.

Otis was standing by the second table when a tall man in a black suit came and stood beside him. The man spoke without looking at Otis. "You are a player, señor?"

"Oh, I, uh I will be. Later. I'm just watching now."

"I have also been watching, señor. I have been watching you watching our dealers. Is that how you pick out a table? By the dealers? Is that your system?"

"No, this is my first trip to Havana, and I was just curious, that's all."

"What is your game? Blackjack or craps?"

"I really don't have a favorite. I play a little at both of them."

"Then please enjoy yourself here at the Tropicana. If I can be of assistance to you, please don't hesitate to ask. You'll find me..." He hesitated and looked at Otis. "You'll find me everywhere." He pulled a cigar from his jacket pocket and walked away.

Otis had a prepaid room at the Tropicana as a part of the package Skinner told him to purchase. He looked around and found the lobby area for the hotel and walked to the desk to check in.

"I have reservations. My name is Hightower, Otis Hightower." He placed the ticket envelope on the counter.

The reservationists opened it and extracted the receipt for the room. "Yes sir, Mister Hightower, we have a very nice room for you. Do you have luggage with you or is it being delivered by Cubana Air?"

"It will be delivered."

"Very good, let me have someone show you to your room." He rang a small bell on the counter and a young man in bellman's uniform stepped up and took the key from the man's hand.

"Please follow me, señor and I'll show you to your room."

Otis reached for his key. "There's no need to take me. Just tell me where the room's located and I'll find it."

"Oh, I'm sorry, señor, but in Havana we must escort each guest to their room. It's a law." The young man turned and walked toward an elevator.

Once inside the room Otis reached into his pocket for a tip.

"Uh, all I have is American money. Can you take that?"

"No problem sir. We use both American dollars and Cuban pesos here in Cuba. I'll be happy to take American money." He smiled and held out his hand.

Otis handed him a fifty cent piece and watched as the man left in disappointment.

Otis went to the bed and lay across it. Firm, but not too firm, so he would get a good night's sleep if nothing else. He took his jacket off and hung it in the closet. The room was nicely furnished. Otis thought that Virginia would like a room like this one. It had a big bed with two pillows on each side. There was a table next to the bed with a clock and a radio. Beneath the window was a long dresser. Sitting on the dresser was a round mirror about the size of a dinner plate on a stand. Otis fingered the mirror and found that it turned over to reveal a magnifying mirror on the opposite side. He flipped it over several times just to see the different image he got.

On the opposite side of the room was a small table just right for two people to use for a dinner table if they didn't want to eat at the hotel restaurant. Otis hardly ever had room service unless he was with Virginia. She liked to have breakfast sent to the room, and then Otis would serve her in bed. He did that once in New Orleans with his lady friend down there. She seemed much more appreciative than Virginia ever was when he did it.

The bathroom was small. The tub was one of the new ones without the four feet on it. It sat flush with the floor and had a shower attachment at the end hanging on the wall. A plastic curtain hung on a rod over the tub ready to be slid over it to keep the water confined.

Otis looked at his watch when he left the bathroom. It was twenty minutes after seven. He had an appointment to meet his contact at nine. His solitude was interrupted by a knock at the door.

"Be right there. Hang on." He opened the door and the bellman stood in the hallway with the suitcase that had been delivered by the airline.

"Your suitcase, Senior. Will there be anything else you need tonight?" The bellman stood, waiting for his tip.

"No, that's all." Otis placed two quarters in his hand. "Thanks," he said as he took the suitcase and closed the door.

Once he had the case, he placed it on the bed and opened it. All the boxes he had packed were still in there and none had been opened. Otis took the five boxes of decks of cards and the two boxes of dice from the brown leather suitcase and placed them on the table. Each box contained twenty decks of cards or twenty pair of dice.

The cards had to be marked, but without opening them, he could not tell how they had been engineered. Like the cards, the dice were in a sealed box, but about the only way they could work the dice was by substituting them for what was known as "six/eight flats." In the hands of a person who knew what he, or possibly she, was doing, the dice would roll sixes or eights. Either number had better odds when bets were placed on them on the numbers line.

A couple of rolls at the right time and you could walk away a big winner. If you walked away at all. That was the problem. Get caught in a roadhouse in Georgia or Tennessee and you'd probably get a few broken bones. Get caught down here and you would never be seen again.

"At least I don't have to use them. All I have to do is deliver the stuff and get the hell out of here tomorrow," he said to himself as he closed the suitcase and headed downstairs to meet his contact.

Otis went to the restaurant as he was told.

"May I assist you, sir?" The maitre'd' had a thick accent, but Otis liked the sound of it. The man was dressed in black pants with a black silk stripe down each leg, a white shirt with puffy white sleeves and a black bow tie. He reminded Otis of something out of a Carmen Miranda movie.

"I'm meeting someone here. His name is Miguel Hernandez."

"Oh, yes, he's already here and awaiting your arrival. Please, come this way." Without waiting, the maitre'd' walked between several tables and stopped at one along a back wall. He immediately pulled out a chair and motioned for Otis to sit.

"Your waiter will be with you very shortly, gentlemen. May I send someone to take your drink orders while you wait?"

Otis took his chair and looked at his dinner companion who spoke to the maitre'd' in Spanish. Like most of the men in the room, he was wearing a tuxedo. Unlike the other men, his looked as if it had been worn many times already. Perhaps this was a work uniform for him, he thought as he waited for them to be alone at the table.

Otis spoke first. "I'm Otis Hightower." He reached across the table to shake the other man's hand.

"Miguel Hernandez. Mucho gusto." He extended his hand.

"I'm sorry, I don't speak Spanish."

"I said I was glad to meet you." He hesitated, "I am glad to meet you, am I not?"

"I certainly hope so. If not, I have made a very long trip for nothing." Otis leaned back and relaxed for the first time since leaving Miami. "Actually, I'm not exactly certain why I'm here. Other than to deliver a package."

"And that you will do as soon as we enjoy a very nice dinner. Do you like Cuban food?"

"The only thing I know about Cuba is that I'm supposed to order a Mojito and I don't even know what that is."

"I took the liberty of ordering one for us when you were seated. I think you will like it, and since you are not familiar with our cuisine, if you don't mind I will order for us." Without waiting for a response, Miguel held his hand in the air and caught the attention of a waiter.

"My friend and I would like Achiote Chicken, Moros y Cristianos and pan Cubano."

"Si, señor. Right away." The waiter closed his pad and disappeared into the kitchen.

Soon they were enjoying their second Mojito and a meal of spicy chicken, black beans and rice and Cuban bread.

As they finished, Miguel spoke to the waiter in Spanish once again. He quickly reappeared with a wooden box which he opened to reveal a selection of cigars. Each was meticulously handmade and they represented all styles, shapes and sizes.

"No meal is complete without a good cigar." Miguel selected a panatela from the middle of the box.

The waiter held the box in front of Otis. "And for you, sir?"

Otis rarely smoked but he did not want to offend his dinner partner. "I'll have this one," he said as he selected the short, stubby Robusto in the middle of the box.

Later when they returned to his room, Otis felt slightly dizzy from the effects of the cigar and the drinks. It was not enough to keep him from delivering the cards and dice which Miguel took without examination or comment.

As Miguel walked to the door to leave the room he stopped. "I will meet you tomorrow morning at seven. We will be at the same table where we had dinner. I will have something for you." Without further explanation, he left the room.

Otis waited an hour and then went down to the casino. He went to the roulette wheel and watched for a few minutes then dropped one of the twenty dollar bills Skinner had given him on the felt.

"Give me twenty in chips, please." Since Miguel had taken care of dinner, he had a little extra money he didn't mind playing with.

He placed one chip on the number thirteen and another on seventeen. The dealer spun the wheel and gave the ball a spin in the opposite direction. As it slowed its revolutions, he waved his hand over the layout indicating there could be no more bets placed on this round.

A woman sitting next to Otis began calling for her number. "Come on seven. Seven. Seven. I need a seven."

The ball bounced several times and landed on twenty three where a short man with a very large stack of chips in front of him had placed three five dollar chips.

"YES!" he yelled as the ball settled into the slot.

"Why does he have to win? Look at all the money he has already." The lady spoke to Otis. "I'll bet he has a system."

"Maybe it's just luck. I don't think systems work as well as some people would have you believe."

The woman was in her mid-thirties and dressed in a tight skirt that came to mid-calf. She wore a small hat that had a veil pulled to the side. From what Otis could see, she was attractive and seemed to be very friendly.

"My name's Otis. I'm from Atlanta," he said as he leaned over the table to place his chips on the same numbers as before.

"Hi, I'm Janet. From Columbus."

"Georgia?"

"Georgia? No, silly from Columbus, Ohio. I came on a cruise ship from Miami. I've been saving for this trip for two years." She placed a chip on top of his covering thirteen. "Maybe you're a lucky man Otis." She placed her hand on his arm as the wheel spun and the ball began to bounce.

For the next hour Otis and Janet watched, at first, their individual stacks of chips rise and fall with each spin of the wheel. Ultimately they placed them together. Two drinks and a short run of good luck on the wheel and it was Janet who suggested they celebrate the victory in her room. Otis readily agreed.

❧❧❧

Otis looked at the clock beside the bed when he awoke. All he wanted to do was open his eyes and not move. If he was laying in the right direction he could see the clock. When he focused on the dial, it said it was a little after three. Otis looked down to make sure he was not dreaming.

Janet lay beside him, his arm resting gently between her bare breasts. He slipped as easily as he could from the bed and quietly dressed. In the few hours they had spent together the night before, Janet had made it clear to him that they would enjoy only one night together. She was leaving at four in the afternoon for the next stop on her cruise. They didn't exchange phone numbers, addresses or last names. He took one last look at her nearly nude form and left the room.

Her room was two floors above his and he only passed one other person as he made his way down the hallway and into the elevator. Otis tried to make himself presentable prior to leaving her room but the best he could do was to make sure he had on shirt, pants and shoes. He hung his jacket over his shoulder and put his tie in his pocket.

On the elevator the one other early riser spoke to him in Spanish and he didn't even try to respond that he didn't speak the local language. All he wanted was to get to his room, shower, change and meet his breakfast companion.

"Good morning. I trust you had an interesting evening." Miguel was seated when Otis came to the table.

"One of the best I've had in a long time."

Miguel signaled for a waiter. "I hope you don't mind, but I have matters to attend to and I will not be able to linger this morning. Please enjoy your breakfast. Order what you wish as I have already taken care of the bill."

The waiter poured Otis a cup of strong Cuban coffee. The steam rose from it and he leaned forward to smell the aroma. "I wish I could get this coffee at home."

"I will make sure you have some the next time you visit."

Otis put his cup down. "The next time—"

"But in the meantime, I have something for you to take back to our mutual friend." Miguel opened a long thin velvet covered jewelry case and handed it to Otis. "Do you like it?"

"It's very nice. But I want to ask you about what you said. That I'd be coming back—"

"And here is the case for him." Miguel closed the box and placed a leather brief case on the table. "Do not let this out of your sight. Our friend does not want to lose another one." With that Miguel stood, picked up his coffee cup and took one last drink before leaving.

Otis placed the velvet box in his inside jacket pocket, picked up the case and left the restaurant for the airport.

By this time, he had a good idea what he had gotten himself into.

CHAPTER 21

For fifteen minutes every day the world came to a stand-still for Hockey Doc. No matter what else was going on, he tuned the radio behind the bar to his favorite soap opera, Ma Perkins. He could be in the middle of a winning streak on a ball game, or preparing a lunch order for fifty, it didn't matter. Everything stopped. The announcer was giving the wrap up for that day's episode and his pitch for Oxydol Soap Flakes when Johnny slipped up to the bar.

"I need to ask you a question, Hockey Doc."

"Hang on. I'll be there in a minute." He pulled a clean bar rag from the stack beneath the counter and wiped away some beer that had been spilled when a player knocked over a bottle.

As soon as the bar was dry, he stood across from Johnny. "What can I do for you?"

"Remember when Charlie Dutton was found on the table that morning?"

"How the hell can I forget it? Of course I remember. What kind of question is that?"

"You know I saw Thomas in here and he left before the cops arrived. I was just thinking over the conversation we had. He said the door was open when he got here."

"Couldn'ta been. He's got a key and I got one. Ain't

nobody else got one." Hockey Doc reached into the beer cooler and pulled out two bottles, stuck the end into the opener on the case and handed one to Johnny. Johnny watched the foam spill from the top and run down the side of the bottle. He picked it up and took a sip.

"Thanks. Do you remember who locked up the night before?"

"Course I do. It was me. It's always me. I'm the last one out of here every night."

"What about if you want to take a night off. Who locks up then?"

"That don't hardly ever happen, but when it does, I get Slim to do it. He's been coming in here since before I bought the place. Most of the time if I need him to lock up, he just spends the night. He sleeps on the floor back in that little room behind the office." He used his beer bottle and pointed toward the rear of the room.

"He wasn't here that night was he?"

"No, the cops asked me the same thing about me closing up. I locked the door when I left and Thomas opened it the next morning like he always does. Somebody must have picked the lock or something if it was open."

"You never lost a key or anything?"

"Never, but now I've already called a locksmith to get my locks changed. I didn't get my key back from Thomas and I want locks that ain't so easy to pick this time."

Johnny finished his beer and left Big Town. He went down the street to a diner and walked in.

The diner had a curved front that wrapped around the corner so it fronted on two streets. The entrance was dead center where the two streets came together. Inside there was a long counter with low metal stools. Perched atop each was a red plastic seat that spun around. Five booths nestled along the back wall. Johnny chose a booth in the middle and took a seat.

Before he settled in, a waitress was standing beside
him. "Coffee?"

"No, let me have a Coke and a cheeseburger."

"Fries?"

Johnny shook his head and she left to hand the order
to the cook. As she did, he noticed the daily newspaper
was on the seat beside him. He picked it up and began to
scan the sports section. The first thing that caught his eye
was a story about the upcoming Master's Tournament at
Augusta. It took him a minute to understand why he was
interested.

As soon as the waitress placed the food in front of
him, Johnny reached around and pulled his wallet out of
his pocket. Inside the first fold was the piece of paper he
had taken from Charlie's pocket when he first found him
dead on the pool table. He unfolded the paper and looked
at it.

The paper was half of a scorecard from Flat Rock Golf
Course. That was the course where Johnny spoke to
Thomas. It was also where Broadway and Heavy said
Charlie had caddied sometimes. There were four names
on the card and scores for all of them. Only one had shot
a decent game. Flat Rock was an eighteen-hole course
with a par of seventy two.

According to the card, a player named JR had shot a
seventy three, one over par. All of the other were in the
high eighty's or low ninety's. All entries were in the
same penciled handwriting.

On the back of the card was the number twenty seven.
Other than that, there was nothing unusual about the card.

It was probably one that Charlie had kept when he
caddied for one or two of the players. Johnny folded it
again and put it back in his wallet. He finished eating his
lunch and left a fifty cent piece on the table.

Just outside the door was a phone booth. Johnny

stepped inside and pulled the door shut. It was time to talk to Thomas again.

Johnny dropped a dime in the slot and dialed a number. He let it ring three times and then it was answered.

"Grady Hospital."

"Laundry, please."

"One moment and I'll connect you."

He waited for the call to be switched to the laundry room. He had never been there but he could picture it in his mind. All of the sheets, towels, pillowcases and clothing for the patients and staff at the largest hospital in Atlanta went through there. Each piece was washed, dried and ironed. It had to be like working in Hell with the constant heat. The mental picture of the men and women who worked there was going through his mind when the phone was answered.

"Laundry."

"Can I speak to Rachel?"

"Which one? We got three of 'em?" The man's voice was short and to the point. He was probably the supervisor and did not like having his employees called away.

"Rachel..." Johnny wasn't sure if she used the same last name as Thomas or not, but since they claimed to be brother and sister, it was a place to start. "Rachel Johnson?"

"Hang on; I'll see if I can find her."

He heard the man yell her name several times even though he had covered the mouthpiece with his hand. It was probably necessary to yell to be heard over the equipment.

"She coming." The man spoke into the phone. He removed his hand and left it off because he could hear him as he continued talking to Rachel. "It's a man. Sounds like a white man to me."

"Hello?"

"Rachel, it's Johnny Morocco. I need to talk to Thomas. Do you know where he is?"

"I—I think I do. He's out at that place where I told you he was before."

"Plunkett Town?"

"Yes, but if you're going out there, you won't be able—"

"I know. You need to go with me and show me where to find him." Johnny hesitated. "Okay, look. I need to talk to him. This thing is getting much more serious than I first thought. What time do you get off?"

"Five-thirty tonight. I came in at six this morning."

A large truck rumbled down the street beside the phone booth making so much noise Johnny could not hear.

"Say that again. What time?"

"Five tonight. I can meet you—"

"What time do you get home?"

"I'm home by six, but if I'm going with you I need to change clothes. It's so hot in here that—"

A man was standing outside the booth now. He was pacing and looking at Johnny as if he was in the only phone booth in the city of Atlanta.

"Give me your address and I'll pick you up at seven. Make sure you get in touch with Thomas. Tell him to stay out of sight and for him to stay someplace we can find him tonight."

Rachel gave him her address and he wrote it on the back of a page he tore from the phone book hanging from a chain beneath the phone. He stepped from the booth and looked at the man. "All yours."

As he walked back toward Big Town he did not see the man watching him from across the street. Had he looked, he would have noticed him immediately.

It was hard to miss a man with a black, blue, purple, and green face.

cscs

Johnny left Big Town a little after six. He walked across Edgewood Avenue to the parking lot and got into his car. After pulling out of the lot, he turned right on Edgewood then took Courtland to Decatur. Traffic was not bad, and he followed a trolley down Decatur to the intersection where it became DeKalb Avenue. Running parallel to him was the railroad tracks which carried freight and passengers out of the city to the north. By the time he got to the western edge of Cabbage Town where it merged into Reynoldstown it was getting dark.

These and many other communities were settled by slaves freed during the Civil War who suddenly realized that with freedom came the reality that they had no place to live. Those who stayed in the South banded together, mostly for security, and many of the communities they established still existed though they had changed to meet the economics of the city over the years.

Cabbage Town was now one of the housing villages that served the workers at Fulton Bag Cotton Mill. As an incentive to work for slave wages in inhuman conditions for their entire life, workers were allowed to live in a house owned by the mill. Even under those conditions, the workers paid a few dollars a week for the house. Nothing was free for them, and there was no way out for the majority. Cabbage Town was a place you did not want to be after dark unless you had a reason to be there. Johnny went into Cabbage Town looking for the place where Rachel lived.

Johnny drove down DeKalb Avenue, turned right, crossed the railroad tracks and headed into an area he was completely unfamiliar with. He had gotten the address from Rachel, so he had a reasonable expectation of finding the house. At least here the houses had numbers, and most were on streets with names. When he slowed to find Savannah Street, he did not notice the car behind him drop back also.

A wooden sign on a telephone pole said this was the right street, so Johnny pulled up in front of the second house on the right. The neighborhood was as he expected. Kids ran through the yards. Some of the kids had bicycles and a few were on skates in the middle of the streets in the waning light. Old women sat on front porches. They had wash pans, balanced on apron-covered laps, filled with beans or peas which they deftly shelled. He remembered his own grandmother as she sat on a similar porch. She would hold a butterbean fresh from her garden in her hand and run her thumb up the length of the seam which popped open under her gentle, firm pressure. If the bean was the long green type, it was stripped of its ends and snapped into equal pieces in seconds. It looked like the women on the porches had learned the craft from the same person who taught his grandmother.

The house in front of him was a clapboard constructed dogtrot style. It had a small front porch with a screen door in the center. He knew if he walked into the house he would be standing in a long hallway leading all the way to the back of the structure. On either side of the hallway would be the rooms, with the kitchen at the far end by the rear exit. If there was an indoor bathroom, it would also be toward the back end of the house. He took one last look around and stepped up on the porch.

The front door was partially closed behind the screen door. From several yards away, he could smell the aroma of cooking meat. Many of the people still cooked outside, so he could not tell if the smell came from Rachel's house or a neighbor's. As soon as he stepped on the porch a dog began to bark from inside the house. His barking alerted several other dogs, both inside and outside neighbor houses that also began barking.

"Hesh up, dog." A strong female voice came from inside the house. "You better hesh up, 'fo I throw you out."

Johnny watched as the dog slunk away from the door, turned and barked once more and then disappeared into the home's darkness.

"You Mister Morronoco?" An old lady in a blue patterned dress stood in the doorway. The broom she held in one hand looked more like a weapon than an instrument for cleaning.

"Morocco." He corrected her, "Like the country." Without waiting for an invitation, he tugged at the handle on the screen door.

"Come on in. Rachel be ready in a few minutes. She always wanna take a bath 'fo she go out at night." She turned and walked into the room to the left which served as the main room. "Y'all have a seat and I'll get you some cold water if you want it."

"That won't be necessary. I won't be here long." Johnny took a seat facing the back of the house. He had a full view of the hallway and the kitchen. The old woman came back and took a seat across from him. She sat without speaking.

Johnny reached into his pocket and pulled out a pack of cigarettes. He glanced at the woman as he tamped one out.

"Ain't no smoking in my house. I don't let my chil'rens do it, and I don't let nobody else do it neither," she said without emotion or apology.

Johnny heard a noise from the rear of the house and glanced down the hallway. As he did so, Rachel emerged from the bathroom and entered a doorway down the hallway. Just like the woman said, she had been taking a bath. She was wrapped in a towel that barely covered her breasts and stopped well short of mid-thigh. She entered the room and with the door only half closed and her back to Johnny, she dropped the towel. For a second she stood completely still. In spite of himself, Johnny could not take his eyes from the naked woman who stood for his inspection. Whether it was intentional or not, Johnny knew she was playing with fire, and he felt like a bulldog measuring the strength of his chain.

Less than ten minutes later, she emerged and walked to the front room.

"Mama, this is the man I told you about. He's going to help Thomas."

"Thass who I figured he was," was her only acknowl-edgement of the comment.

"We're going to Aunt Emma's house to see if he's there. I called the store today and told them to send somebody over to her house and tell him not to leave if he was still there." She kissed the older woman on the cheek and opened the screen door.

Together, Johnny and Rachel walked to his car.

If someone had bet him as he walked toward the car that he was the only white man on the street Johnny would have taken the bet and given good odds.

Unfortunately, he would have lost.

CHAPTER 22

When Johnny and Rachel left the house, he noticed several young men watching them. "Friends of yours?" he asked as they walked across the street to get into his car.

"They want to be more than just friends with me, but it's not going to happen." Rachel took her time as she opened the car door. It was a slow deliberate move designed to let the ones watching her know she was leaving with Johnny.

"That's probably not a smart thing to do, you know."

"And why's that?" Rachel settled into the seat and opened her purse to get a cigarette.

"You have to live here. I don't. They might not like you rubbing this in their noses."

"By 'this' do you mean my going out with a white man?"

Johnny pulled out of the side street and headed back toward Atlanta. By now it was completely dark and the city was coming to life with a different feel to it. Atlanta at night became the oasis of activity in a desert of lethargy. Conventions had started holding their meetings in the city. Tourists came for the food. There were night clubs where you could have dinner, get a drink and listen to music until well after midnight. Ten miles in any direction from any of these and you were in the South that most people thought they knew from books like *Gone With the Wind* and *Tobacco Road.*

The plantations no longer existed, but the cotton and tobacco fields as well as the share-croppers who worked them did.

"I mean this is not some northern city where you can come and go and do as you please. And we are not 'going out.' You're taking me to find Thomas."

She touched the flame from a lighter to her cigarette. "I heard Mama tell you not to smoke in her house."

"I imagine your mother, or whoever she is, has a lot of rules that you break."

"Oh, I break a lot of 'em. Some I do by myself, and some I have help with." She blew out the smoke. "What kind of rules do you break, Mister Johnny?"

Johnny remained quiet for most of the drive. It was an easy route from where she lived to Stewart Avenue and then straight south from there. Once they got to the edge of Hapeville, he knew he had to ask her for directions.

"All right, it's up to you now. Where do I go?"

Rachel guided him into the community known as Plunkett Town. As soon as he crossed the railroad tracks, any semblance of pavement disappeared. The red clay roads were pitted and had deep ruts. It had not rained in weeks which was a mixed blessing. Had the roads been wet, the clay would have become so slick that driving was almost impossible. With no rain, the dust raised was thick enough to coat everything in the community. Soon, the inside of the car had a fine sheen of red on it.

"Roll the window up. I don't want everything in here to turn red." Johnny rolled his window to within an inch of the top. "Leave just enough so we don't die from the heat."

"If I do, I won't be able to see the house." Rachel

looked out the window. "Slow down, I think you turn up here."

"You think? You mean you don't know where he is?"

"Most of the time when I come out here I take the bus. I hardly ever come in from this direction." She pointed. "Over there. That's it. Turn down that little street."

The houses on both sided of the street were mostly made of weathered wood. They had a front porch and a tin roof. Windows were covered with shutters made of wood or tin. Most of the windows were propped open with a stick or pole that ran between the edge of the open shutter and the window sill. Almost every house was sitting on a foundation of flat round river rocks stacked at all the corners and several places in the middle. From the gentle soft flicker of the lights he could see, it appeared that most of the interiors were lit with candles or lanterns. Few houses had the steady glow of electric lights. Plunket Town was not high on the list of places that received city services.

Occasionally he saw a shadow dart between the houses. The movement triggered a chorus of barking dogs. A few residents sat on the porches and some children were playing in the dark streets, but for the most part Plunkett Town was not open for business. He had driven down several streets and had seen the headlights of only one other car.

"Pull up and stop here." Rachel pointed to a house sitting on a slight rise. "That's my aunt's house. If Thomas got my message, he'll be there." She opened the door. "I think you better stay here until I find out if he's in there." Rachel walked around the car. When she got even with Johnny's window, she leaned down. "This is not some city where you can come and go and do as you please." Even in the dark he could see the half smile, half smirk on her face.

Rachel walked to the house. She had played there as a

child when her mother left and she had been shifted from
relative-to-relative for almost two years. The smell of
creosote hung in the air from the wood stacked in the
back yards of many of the houses. With the railroad so
close by, discarded creosote coated wooden ties were collected and brought home to be used as fire wood. Rachel
knew that the glow from within the house did not come
from electric lights. As she stepped on the stones leading
up the first step, she sensed someone watching her from
within the house.

"Rachel? That you?" A voice came from behind the
open front door.

Rachel did not immediately answer, but took several
more steps and got on the porch. She felt a board give
slightly under her foot. "Yes, it's Rachel. Is that you Daniel?" She stepped closer and peered into the darkness in
front of her.

The entrance to the house was covered with a screen
door. Several cotton balls were tied to the door with
strings. Each time the door was opened or closed any
flies, mosquitoes or other insects that happened to make a
rest stop on the screen were whisked away as the balls
bounced around from the action of the door.

"Who's that out there in the car? He one of yo' boyfriends?"

"Don't you start that nonsense with me Daniel. You
just get back out of the way and let me in. I came here to
talk to my brother, not to have arguments with the likes
of you." She placed her hand on the leather strap hanging
from the edge of the door and pulled it open. Before she
stepped inside, she turned and looked at Johnny.

Once inside, Rachel immediately recognized the smell
of fresh hot cornbread coming from the kitchen. She by-
passed Daniel and went directly to the room that held
some of the best memories of her childhood. It was here

that Aunt Emma spent most of her time. She and Thomas, and sometimes their older cousin Daniel, were tasked with bringing in wood for the stove upon which Aunt Emma worked her magic. As Rachel looked around, she realized things had not changed much for the old woman.

The black, iron wood-burning stove dominated the center of the room just as it had since her earliest memories. A large round pipe ran from the top of the stove through the ceiling and out the roof of the house. On one wall was a long wooden shelf that was waist high on the old woman. This was where Aunt Emma often sat Rachael when the young girl watched the old woman cook. The shelf was where all of the preparation for any meal was done. A smaller shelf just above the prep area held a variety of cans and jars. Most of them were in their second use as containers for salt, flour, spices and herbs. The wooden ice box still sat beneath the single window in the room, and hams and bags of dried sausage hung from hooks in the ceiling over the ice box.

The ice box was about four feet tall and two feet wide. The door was hinged in brass and a tin pan sat on the floor underneath the case to collect water from the melting ice inside. Rachel knew if she opened the door, she would find a pitcher of sweet tea, some buttermilk and the fresh vegetables Aunt Emma planned to use in the next day or two. It might also hold a piece of meat or fish that she had purchased with money she got from selling the eggs collected daily from her chickens.

A ham, smoked in one of the neighbors' smoke houses was wrapped in cheesecloth. Rachel could see that the ham had provided many breakfast meals for Aunt Emma. Hanging next to the ham were several flat bags approximately eight by twelve inches. The smell of sage and other spices was good for an instant flashback to days when she and Thomas turned the hand-cranked meat grinder for

Aunt Emma when she made the sausage and then patted it out into thin rectangles in the bags.

She didn't get to the house very often any more, but when she did Rachel let the pleasant memories wash over her as she stood in the middle of the room. Her aunt was placing a large black cast iron pan on a metal rack so it could cool. She spoke to Rachel without turning around.

"You just pull up a chair, child, I'll hug you when I get this cornbread out of the skillet." Aunt Emma tapped the pan firmly on the edge of the shelf and the crisp, round treasure fell gently to the rack.

"Come here and give me a hug." She held out her arms for Rachel.

"Aunt Emma, it's been so long since I was here." At her height of five feet six inches, Rachel towered over the tiny, white-haired woman. Her flower patterned dress was probably made from the cloth of the feed or flour sacks she used. Rachel noticed for the first time that she was using a cane to assist her. "Here, let me help you." She took the heavy skillet, wiped it out, and hung it on a hook on the wall.

"Now don't you go worrying 'bout me. You got plenty troubles of your own. He's setting right inside that room." She pointed with her cane. "Right yonder."

Rachel didn't have to ask if Thomas was the one she was referring to as he came out as soon as he heard the two of them talking.

"I got your message. Is he wit' you?"

"He's in his car out front. He wants to talk to you. He says he can help."

Daniel walked in and stood beside Thomas. "Ain't no white man gonna help a colored man when they think he done kilt a white man." He had an open bottle of beer in his hand.

"You don't know nothing 'bout Johnny Morocco, Daniel. He said he'd help Thomas and I believe him."

Daniel took a long look at his cousin. "Well, looka here. Sounds like little Miss better-than-the-rest-of-us done found herself something special."

Before Rachel could respond, Aunt Emma hit Daniel on the leg with her cane. "Don't you be talking to family that way, Daniel. I won't have it in my house." She walked past them. "I'm going to my room now. It's time to read the Good Book and then go to bed." She gave Rachel a kiss on the cheek and disappeared into her room.

"I want to bring him inside so he can talk to you Thomas. I'm going to go get him now." Rachel walked toward the door.

"You sure he ain't the po-lice, Thomas?" Daniel asked.

"I'm sure."

"Okay, go get him. I'll be in the kitchen," Daniel said as he walked away.

Johnny was smoking his second cigarette when he saw the door open and Rachel emerge. He noticed her take a quick look around and then walk to the car. She came to the driver's side and spoke to Johnny.

"Thomas is inside. He said he'd talk to you."

Johnny opened the door and stepped outside.

"My cousin Daniel is in there too, but he's going to stay in the kitchen. I don't think he'll give you any trouble."

"Trouble? What kind of trouble does he want to give me? I'm out here in…in…"

Rachel interrupted. "You can say it, everybody else does. It's Niggertown. That's what you were going to call it, wasn't it?" She walked toward the house without waiting for Johnny.

The door slammed behind her, bounced once on the

springs, and Johnny caught it prior to it hitting again. He opened it and stepped inside.

"Thomas, we need to talk about what you saw. Again."

Before Thomas could respond, the door opened again and the doorway was filled with another man. This one was well over six feet tall, weighed about two hundred fifty pounds, and was holding a gun.

Two people in the room had seen Victor before. Thomas recognized him as one of the men in the pool room the morning Charlie was killed. Johnny recognized the discoloration on the side of Victor's face and knew it was the man he had hit with his automatic.

Before Johnny could reach for his pistol, Victor did it for him. He pulled the automatic from its holster and now had a gun in each hand.

Victor looked at the group. "Which one of you niggers got Joe Skinner's money?

CHAPTER 23

Abe Salem walked through the casino portion of the Rio. Almost everyone there stopped what they were doing as he passed and greeted him. He was a king walking through his domain. He stopped when he got to the table where Joe stood with Virginia.

"You look nervous tonight, Joe. Something wrong?"

"No, just trying to keep track of everything. You know how it is." Skinner could hardly keep eye contact with his boss.

Joe turned to Virginia who stood by his side. "What do you think? Is Joe up to par tonight?"

Their relationship was no secret within the walls of the Rio. She had been there many times with Joe and Abe had seen her almost every time. On several occasions she and Joe had dinner at the same table with Abe and his girlfriend. Virginia knew Abe was married and had even seen his wife one night when he brought her to the Rio.

"I always think Joe is up to par, Mister Salem." Virginia smiled as she spoke.

"Joe, you better keep this one. She's as full of crap as you are."

Abe continued his walk through the casino, leaving Joe and Virginia by themselves.

"I didn't want to say anything, honey, but I agree with

Mister Salem. You don't seem right tonight. Is something wrong?"

"Nothing's wrong! What the hell's wrong with you two? I feel like a monkey on a string. I'm supposed to dance every time you pull the fucking cord?" Joe snapped at her.

"Joe, you know I don't like it when you get upset. Let me go get you a drink. That'll make you feel better." Without waiting for a response, she walked to the bar and ordered a fresh drink for both of them.

Joe looked at his watch and then turned to a player standing by one of the craps tables.

"What time you got?

"I'm a little slow, but my watch says it's twenty till eleven."

Joe looked at his watch again. "You sure you're right? I got quarter till."

"Hey, I said I was a little slow. What difference does it make, twenty till or fifteen till?" The man attempted to turn back to the table.

Joe grabbed him and spun him around. The player was about Joe's height and had a few pounds on him. From the suit and tie he wore it was impossible to even guess at his occupation. He could have been an executive or a house painter out for a night of fun.

It didn't matter to Joe, who got in the man's face. "Who the fuck you think you're talking to, you asshole?"

For a fleeting second, the man was caught off-guard, but that second quickly passed. He quickly sat down the drink he was holding and stepped back ready to defend himself.

"You got a problem, buddy, let's take it outside."

Before Joe could respond, two bouncers stepped between the two men. One faced Joe and the other his opponent.

"It's okay, Mister Skinner. We'll take care of this." He held his hands up, palms facing Skinner. "We got everything under control."

"Just get that asshole out of here and make sure he never comes back."

The other bouncer spun the man around and held him in a bear hug. "I got him. We're going to take him out, and you won't see him in here again."

The man was struggling even though the bouncer held his feet off the floor. "Let me go, you big son of a bitch. This is between him and me if he has the balls to do anything without his two pet gorillas."

He was still making noises when they carried him from the casino floor. Some of the players had stopped to watch the action, but those around Skinner knew that if he was involved it would not last long, and he would be the winner.

That group continued to play.

"Jeez, honey, I leave to get you a drink and look what happens. Maybe we need to go someplace else tonight." Virginia handed him his drink. "You know just you and me."

Skinner took his drink, downed half of it and handed her the glass. "You stay here. I got to check out something in my office."

During the time the casino was open, both Joe and Abe had a person sit in their office in order to answer the phone and run errands if needed. Joe had Doris, an elderly lady who had once been a madam in a brothel in Chattanooga. She drank straight scotch and chain-smoked Camels. Her voice sounded like it began in her toes and was filtered through a gallon of pebbles in her throat on the way out. She had worked for Joe for almost ten years and knew most of his secrets.

Joe opened the door to his office and stepped inside.

"Doris, have I had any calls tonight? I'm waiting for one from a man named Victor."

She was reading a movie magazine when he came in. "If you did, I would have come and found you. That's what you pay me for, isn't it?" She picked up her glass and took a drink. "You want a drink? I just opened a fresh bottle of scotch. It's in the cabinet."

"I don't need a drink. I need a phone call."

"I can't make the phone ring, but I can pour the Scotch." She got up and went to the bar where she pulled out the bottle and a fresh glass. She poured a drink and handed it to Joe. "Here, this'll make you feel better. And if it don't, you won't feel any worse."

He took the glass and took a seat in the chair in front of his desk.

"No offense, Joe, but you look like hell. That broad not taking care of you?"

"Nah, it ain't that. I just got a lot on my mind." He took a drink from the glass.

"It's always women or money. If it's not one it's the other. I can't help if your problem is money, but if it's women, I do have some experience in that business. I can make a couple of phone calls to some of my girls and—"

"I appreciate it, Doris, but that's not the kind of phone call I need." He downed the remainder of his drink, sat the empty glass on the edge of the desk and returned to the casino floor.

೧೫೧

"I seen you in Big Town. You was the one what—" Thomas didn't get to finish his thought before the man drew back and hit him with the pistol he held in his right hand.

"See how you like your nigger friend getting hit in the

head," Victor said to Johnny as he watched Thomas stagger and fall against a chair.

Rachel and Daniel tried to grab Thomas to break his fall, but Victor stopped them. "Don't neither one of you move a muscle unless I say it's okay. I didn't come all the way out here to play games. I came to get Mister Skinner's money and that's what I'm going to do no matter what it takes."

Victor looked at Rachel. "If you look as good in the daylight as you do in this shit-hole house, I may just take you back with me." He reached out and ran the end of the pistol down the side of her face. Victor spoke to Johnny without looking at him. "I don't blame you for keeping this one for yourself. She's one of the best looking high yellas I ever seen."

"Why don't you put the guns down and you and I can get the money and split it?" Johnny slowly reached into his pocket and pulled out a cigarette.

"Split it? After you killed Robert? I'm supposed to split something with you?" Victor turned back toward Johnny.

Thomas had slid down and was propped on the edge of an overstuffed chair. The intruder waved one of the pistols at Rachel. "Help him sit down and then don't make a move. I don't want to do it, but if I have to, I'll blow your ass away just like I'm gonna do these others."

Johnny flicked a match and lit the cigarette. "Let's talk about Joe's money. Did he tell you how much was missing?"

"Don't matter. He said you or the gimp had it. That's all I need to know. I get it from you and take it back to him and we all live happily ever after." Victor laughed at his own joke. "Or at least, me and him do. I haven't decided about the rest of you yet."

For the first time, Daniel spoke up. "Man, you better

take a look around. You walk out that door and you'll be
the only white face within a mile in any direction. If you
think you can just come into this neighborhood and shoot
somebody and walk away, then you 'bout the dumbest
white man God done ever made." Daniel shook his head
and then turned to assist Rachel with Thomas.

"I guess that leaves you and me to work this out,
doesn't it?" Johnny smiled as he spoke.

A voice came from behind Victor that no one in the
room expected. "I guess y'all forgot about me." It was
Aunt Emma.

Before he could turn around, Victor felt a hard jab in
his back. "If you even think 'bout hurting another one of
my children, this shotgun I got in yore back is gonna go
off. Now I know it's gonna mess up my house, but it'll be
worth it." She nodded toward Johnny. "I reckon you better take them guns outta his hands 'fo he hurts somebody
else, and I have ta shoot him."

Johnny took both the weapons. He handed Victor's
pistol to Daniel. "Here, I'll bet you can use this."

"You bastards better shoot me now, 'cause I ain't never gonna forget this." Victor turned to look at Johnny.
There was a darkness in his eyes unlike anything Johnny
had ever seen. "Ain't nobody in the world ever got but
one chance to kill me. This is your second time. If you
blow it again, you'll regret it till the day I watch you die."

He felt another sharp jab in the back. "Who you calling a bastard? I don't know about this gentleman, but
ain't none of my family falls in that category." Aunt
Emma poked him again. "How 'bout you apologize."

"How 'bout you pull the trigger and get it over with
before I take it away from you and shove the barrel up
your—"

Before he could tell the old woman where he wanted
to shove the barrel, Daniel drove his fist into Victor's

midsection. Under normal conditions it might not have made much impact on a man his size; however Daniel was holding the .45 automatic and the barrel dug deep into Victor's stomach. As Victor doubled over, he spun around and reached for what he thought was the shotgun in his back. His hands wrapped tightly around the walking cane held by Aunt Emma. With him on one end of the cane and her holding the other, it was a tug of war for only a second.

He spun around with the cane and hit Daniel across the side of the face. The force of the blow broke the cane and knocked Daniel across the chair where Thomas was still being tended by Rachel. When Daniel fell, he dropped the gun. Victor immediately dove for the weapon. As he hit the floor, Johnny fired one round from the pistol he held in his hands.

Victor scrambled to avoid the next shots. In the process, he knocked over the table next to the chair where Thomas was trying to stand. The table held a glass lamp filled with kerosene. In the center of the two-piece lamp was a cloth wick. A yellow flame streamed upward into a clear glass chimney. Both Rachel and Johnny saw the lamp as it tipped over and spilled its liquid on the old chair and the floor beneath it.

Johnny immediately recognized the smell of the kerosene and knew that if the flame reached the now soaked chair or floor, there would be a fire of catastrophic proportions. Even as Victor found the gun and grabbed it, Johnny dove for the lamp in a futile attempt to catch the upper portion before the wick touched the flammable liquid and the entire place burst into flames.

The sound of the round being fired in his direction was so close and so loud it made Johnny's ears ring.

"I'm gonna kill every one of you people. And then I'm gonna cut your guts out," Victor yelled.

Around them the flames were searching out fuel. The fire spread across the floor like a flood, covering everything in its wake.

"Rachel, get your aunt out of here." Johnny fired another round in the direction of where Victor's voice came from. From the corner of his eye, he saw Rachel as she half crawled and half dragged the old woman across to the front door. By the time they reached it, the room was in serious flames.

As soon as the door opened, Victor fired two more shots. One went through the open door and disappeared in the darkness. The second dug into the doorframe and sprinkled Aunt Emma with wooden splinters. Rachel hugged her aunt and covered her body with hers. "Don't worry, Aunt Emma, I won't let him hurt you."

As they crawled onto the wooden porch on the front of the house, Aunt Emma said, "I think you better tell that to the man in there that's shooting at us."

Inside the house, Johnny knew he only had seconds to make it out or he would not make it out at all. He dropped to the floor, and with the oily, black smoke curling all around him, he followed the fresh air just inches off the floor that was coming to him from the front door.

Once he made it out, he lay on the porch and caught his breath. From down the street, Johnny could hear neighbors shouting as they questioned the gunfire and came to assist with the house fire. He saw several carrying rifles or shotguns as they ran.

"Rachel, tell these people not to come up here. There's no telling what Victor may do to them if he gets a chance," Johnny yelled across to the far side of the porch where Rachel sat on the ground holding Aunt Emma's head in her lap. When he saw they were safely out of the fire's reach, he added, "Can anyone here call the fire department?"

Before Rachel could respond, he heard a voice he recognized. "Ain't no use to call 'em. They won't come here for no fire. They just let the house burn and hope it don't cross the railroad tracks. If it do, it might burn down some white folk's houses and that'd be a real tragedy." Broadway was standing beside Johnny. He had an old shotgun in his hands. "You need some help here, or you got things working like you want 'em?" He continued to stand and stare at the fire.

"It depends on what happens to the man inside. He's not going to be real happy to see any of us if he gets out. He was trying to kill—" Before Johnny could finish, they heard shouts coming from the back of the house.

"There he goes!"

"That's the man was shooting at Aunt Emma."

"Sounds like he found the back door. Let's go." Broadway held the shotgun with the barrel pointed toward the back of the totally engulfed house.

All around them, neighbors were forming a bucket brigade and tossing buckets of water on the house. Each house, Johnny noticed as he watched the men and women still moving toward the fire, had large wooden rain barrels positioned beneath a corner of the roof or under a downspout. This caught rainwater which was always available when the fire department was not.

As they rounded the corner of the house, a neighbor pointed. "Y'all looking for a big white man?"

"Yeah, which way did he go?" Broadway responded.

"He's ducking down and running toward the railroad tracks. Just listen to the dogs, they's got a good fix on him. They'll tell you which way he's going."

Broadway motioned for Johnny to follow him. "If we stay close to him, he won't be able to double back and get his car. He'll have to walk out of here and he just might not make it." He stopped and looked at Johnny. "You stay real close to me. Ain't no good reason for a white man to be running around here in Plunkett Town at night. We get separated; somebody might not know you're one of the good ones." He turned toward the tracks.

Several neighbors gathered around Rachel and Aunt Emma. "I'm okay. I got my chil'rens out of there. Don't nothing else matter. We're all alive." The old woman motioned for several of them to help her sit up. "I need to stand up. If I don't, I'll catch my death of cold on this ground. I don't want to live through all that shooting and burning and then catch a cold that kills me." She was helped to her feet and she took Rachel by the arm and led her toward the dirt street and away from the fire.

"Aunt Emma, I'm so sorry about all this. I never meant for it to happen." Rachel began to cry.

"Now you just dry them tears up, Rachel. Ain't none of this your fault." Aunt Emma looked back at the house and watched as it began to collapse in on itself. The neighbors were now concentrating on saving a house nearby on one side. They tossed bucket after bucket of water on the side of the house to make it too wet to burn.

"But Aunt Emma, everything you own is gone." Rachel held the old woman's hand in hers.

"Everything in that house is stuff that I bought or was given to me. Ain't none of it important. As long as we all got out, I'm happy." For the first time she looked around. "Where's Daniel and Thomas? Oh, my sweet Jesus, they still in the house?" She pulled her hand from Rachel's and started toward the charred remains of her house.

A neighbor stopped her. "No, they ain't, Miss Emma. I seen both of them run out the back about the time I seen the first flames. I don't know where they went, but I know they got out."

CHAPTER 24

Otis held the case in his lap all the way from Havana to Miami. He hadn't eaten since morning so when they got to the terminal in Miami, he went to a coffee shop and bought a cup of coffee and a piece of pie. He placed both on a small metal tray, and as he carried the tray with one hand, another traveler bumped into him. He tried to keep the tray level but with the case in his other hand, he was unable to do so, and the pie slid across the tray and fell to the floor.

"How about watching where you're going." Otis stood over the pie as the spoke to the other person.

"I said I was sorry. What else you want me to do?" The man who had jostled him gave Otis a look that left no doubt that he had gotten all he was going to get.

"Don't worry." A young woman with a mop had already come from behind the counter. "I saw him knock it off your tray, so just go have a seat, and I'll bring you another piece as soon as I clean it up."

"You should make him do it," Otis said over his shoulder as he walked to a table and sat his coffee down.

He waited with the coffee until the woman brought him another piece of pie. Otis took his time eating. He had a long drive ahead of him, and he didn't look forward to it. He planned to hit the road as soon as he got his suit-case from the airline.

The sun was just beginning to set when Otis walked down the steps and crossed the terminal to a door leading to the parking lot. By the time he got his car and returned to the terminal he knew his bag would be there. All he had to do was pull up in front of the baggage rack, grab his bag and he'd be gone in less than a minute. As he drove to the rack he wondered if he should leave the case in the car or hold it when he got out. He erred to caution and picked up his suitcase in one hand as he held the smaller case in the other.

Otis usually called Virginia once a week when he was on the road. Since he had spent two days in Cuba, and she didn't know he was there, he thought it best not to mention it when he called her.

Virginia answered the phone on the second ring. Because Otis was a salesman and sometimes got orders from his customers on the telephone, he and Virginia paid the extra fifty cents per month so they could have a phone that was only a two-party line. The ring for Otis and Virginia was two long rings in succession. The other person on the line had one short and one long ring.

"Virginia, it's me." Otis put sixty five cents in the phone when the operator connected him to his home line.

"Oh, hi, Otis. Where are you?"

"I'm in Miami, but I'm coming home. I—I'm leaving tonight."

Virginia looked at the watch he had given her for her birthday two years earlier. It was a small Bulova with a nice black band. "But it's too late to leave tonight. You're not going to drive all night, are you? I don't like it when you sleep in the car. You know it makes your back hurt."

Virginia stood by the phone in a half slip and bra. She had just gotten out of the tub and was putting on her make-up when the phone interrupted her. She had plans for the next two nights, and those plans did not include Otis coming home.

"I'll be okay. I'll drive till I get really tired, and then I'll stop. Maybe I'll get in the back seat. It's more comfortable. Anyway, I want to be home as soon as possible. I've got some business in Atlanta I need to take care of."

While he talked, Otis looked to the east and watched as a line of thunder storms rolled in from the ocean. He could see the rain coming down in a line parallel to the shoreline of Miami Beach. A few flashes of lightning danced from the dark clouds to the water. Along the shore on Collins Drive many of the hotels and businesses had shuttered their doors. A few of them remained open and two had small game rooms in what had been the hotel lobby during the heydays of the twenties, but those days were behind them now. Miami Beach, for the most part was a ghost town. A lightning strike and the resulting fire would be welcomed by most landlords.

"Okay, but call me at the bank tomorrow and tell me where you are and when you'll get home." She checked herself in the mirror. "I worry about you, baby." Virginia placed the phone on the cradle and finished dressing.

As soon as she finished, she was going out to the street where she caught the bus that took her to the Rich's Department Store in downtown Atlanta and a reference place for directions second only to Five Points. It was the biggest store in Atlanta and probably the South, so Virginia heard at work. There was a bus stop in front of the main entrance where half of the commuters in Atlanta stood at some point while they waited for transportation to work or home. Joe always picked her up there. He said he didn't want to take a chance on anyone seeing him come to her house, and she believed him.

He pulled his car up on Whitehall Street and blew the

horn. Virginia knew immediately who it was and stepped toward the car as it slowed for her.

"I thought I was going to be late." Virginia slid across the seat and gave Joe a kiss on the cheek.

He placed his hand on her leg and squeezed. "I woulda circled the block once for you, baby."

They drove through the early evening traffic leaving the city and went directly to the Rio Vista.

Joe was in an especially good mood. He had received a call during the day from Otis. He was on the way back to Atlanta and was due in town by five the next afternoon. That gave Joe plenty of time to be with Virginia. He was so happy, he had already gotten a room at a little tourist cabin not far from the Rio.

Joe and Virginia spent the entire night there, and he got her back in time to go to work the next morning. After he dropped her off, he'd meet Otis and pick up the money. He'd take his cut, and after that he'd take the money to the Rio and give it to Abe. Joe had the best of both worlds. If asked, he would be hard-pressed to find something that could go wrong.

***

Johnny was at Big Town by ten the next morning.

After he and Broadway spent thirty minutes looking for Victor the night before, he went back to Aunt Emma's house. She and Rachel had gone across the street to a neighbor's house and were sitting on the porch. Johnny and Broadway had to walk through a street of mud because of all the water spilled enroute to and on the previous night's fire.

"What are you going to do now?" Johnny bent down and spoke to the old woman. She was sitting in a rocking chair. In her hands she held a small tin box. It was smoke smudged and Johnny assumed it had been rescued from the fire or the ashes afterward.

"I appreciate your concern, Mister, but I've started over so many times in my life, this is nothing new." She spoke without looking at him. Her eyes were focused across the street at where her house once sat. They were locked in on a point unseen to anyone but her.

He looked at Rachel. "Do you want me to take you back home or are you staying here tonight?" Both Rachel and Aunt Emma laughed at the irony of what he said. "I mean, do you have a place you want to go?" He stood up and looked around. "I don't think I'll be able to talk to Thomas tonight, so I'm heading back."

Rachel kissed Aunt Emma good-by and left with Johnny. They hardly spoke on the drive back to Rachel's house. When they arrived, she sat without speaking for the time it took her to find a cigarette and light it. When she finally opened the car door and left, Johnny felt the sweat as it rolled down his neck. It left a track of fire he had not felt in a long time.

As he pulled away from the house, he knew there were more eyes on him than he could see. One of the young men he had seen across the street was watching and Johnny couldn't blame him. If the tables were reversed and a colored man drove through a white neighborhood and let a white woman out of his car, he might not make it to the corner.

On the drive back to his boarding house, Johnny tried to put things in perspective. He had a good idea of what had happened to Charlie and why, but there were still a few pieces of the puzzle he didn't have. The one thing he did have was an idea of where the missing pieces fit.

The next morning Hockey Doc pulled the handle on the old coffee urn and held his cup beneath it as the first cup of the day was ready.

"Hey, Hockey Doc, when you gonna get another rack boy. You know Thomas ain't never coming back." Slim Hardin walked toward the counter. "You need to find somebody that can make a decent cup of coffee. This stuff you brew makes me want to join the Army again just to get a good cup of coffee." He blew across his fingertips as he spoke. Slim had been in the Philippines when the war started and had survived the Bataan Death March. When he was liberated he weighed less than one hundred pounds and was near death. Before he was captured by the Japanese, he had been a radio operator for the Army. During interrogation at the Prisoner of War camp they found out his previous duty. For several months he was tortured by having bamboo slivers stuck beneath his fingernails and set aflame. Since that time he constantly blew on his fingertips.

"You find me one and I'll hire him. In the meantime, if you don't like my coffee, don't drink it." Hockey Doc took his coffee and went to the far end of the bar.

Johnny pulled a cup and took a seat. He had just unfolded the morning paper when he looked over the top of it and saw Detective Brewer walking toward him.

"You picked a winner this time, Johnny. Yes, sir, you hit the Derby, the Series and the Irish Sweepstakes." He was still smiling when he took a seat next to him.

"If I hit so many winners, where's my money?" Johnny folded the paper.

"Oh, there's money in it all right, it just belongs to someone else."

"Somehow I think there's a story here that you're going to tell me."

Brewer placed a piece of paper on Johnny's folded newspaper. "Take a look at that and tell me what you think."

It was a photo and a rap sheet. "That's most of what

we know about the bad guy you killed. Any of it look familiar?"

Johnny took his time and read the sheet. It started with his release from jail in Florida as a juvenile when the man was eighteen. From there he began a career that took him through petty theft, burglary, grand theft auto, and one charge of attempted murder. From that charge it seemed he changed his career path to that of professional muscle, or Tush Hog, as they were known. Men like him were always available to break bones, intimidate witnesses, and generally be the enforcement end of any enterprise.

"So why'd he get so interested in me?"

"See, that's what I don't understand. Not completely." Brewer picked up the rap sheet. "You got a cigarette? Anyway, this guy's working as a Tush Hog for some very bad people in Miami with ties to Atlanta. I think he and his partner or his employer, who by the way is still on the streets and still looking for you, so I'm told, are probably the ones who killed Dutton up here."

Johnny handed him his pack of Luckies after taking one for himself.

"I think ol' Charlie was a bag man for Meyer Lansky out of Miami. He was bringing some cash here for cleaning or a payoff. Somebody got wind of it and relieved him of it. What I don't understand is how he wound up here at this dump. I know as soon as I find the money— and I will find the money—that I'll get the answer to that one, too." Brewer took a long pull from the cigarette and exhaled. "You got any thought on that?"

Slim picked a rack off the floor beneath the table in front of them, placed it on the table and began to fill it with balls. Another man stood beside the table. He held a cue and chalked the tip as he watched Slim place the balls in number rotation for a game of eight ball. As Slim's hands deftly placed one even numbered and one odd numbered ball in rotation, he blew on his nails.

"You keep thinking I have some money or know where it is. If I did, do you think I'd still be hanging around a pool room?"

After a coin toss, Slim won the break. Brewer was momentarily distracted as he watched Slim fire the cue ball down the table and into the number one ball. The balls scattered, rolling all over the table and there was the solid thunk as a ball fell into the leather pocket. Slim checked, found that he had sunk an even numbered ball, and lined up his next shot.

"Yeah, I think you would. You know why I think you'd still be here? Because you're a loser just like every other bum in this place. You're all losers and you need each other. Look at Slim. Who else is gonna let a bum like that work around them all day while he blows on his fingernails? He'd give a normal person the creeps. You guys just let him do it and don't think nothing of it."

Brewer stood and crushed the cigarette beneath his foot on the wooden floor. He leaned close to Johnny and held the rap sheet as he spoke. "Here's the deal. I don't give a shit who killed Dutton. I don't give a shit that you shot this guy. I don't even give a shit that you're porking that high yeller. What I do give a shit about is the money. And there's lots of it out there that don't really belong to nobody. I'm going to find it, and if you get in my way…" He stood up. "Well, let's just say if you get in my way, you won't never get in my way again."

As he left, Johnny realized he had taken his matches with him. He tried his lighter and it was out of fluid.

"Hey, Slim, you got a light?"

"Sure, here." He tossed a book of matches to Johnny. He pulled one out, drug it across the sandpaper surface and watched it burst into a flame. As he held the matchbook he noticed the advertisement. It was for the Rio

Vista Supper Club. It had a printed invitation to join them for dinner and dancing. It was from the host: Joe Skinner. Johnny smiled as he slipped them into his pocket.

CHAPTER 25

The first time Johnny got into a real fight was when he was a young boy. It was the summer after the fifth grade. He was playing second base on a team with only five players on each side. Johnny, like the second baseman on the other team, covered second, short and third. The other players were the pitcher, two fielders, and a first baseman. The catcher was a member of the opposing team when they were at bat.

It was a mid-summer day when the only thing to do was play ball or go to the beach. The boys had caught a ride on a truck the day before and it took them within half a mile of the ocean. They walked the rest of the way, spent the day swimming in their pants with the legs rolled up and then walked most of the way home wet.

The fight the next day began as a result of a line drive. A skinny kid who could run better than he could hit, slammed it up the middle of the infield. It came in waist-high on Johnny and he grabbed it in flight making the out. The runner on first had a good lead, but when he saw Johnny catch the ball, he spun in the dirt and headed back to first. Johnny pulled the ball from the center of the ancient leather glove he got from his older cousin and fired the ball down the line toward the first baseman for the out.

His accuracy was good and he would have made the double play if the runner, a boy a year older than Johnny but still in the same grade, hadn't stood from his crouch for the last few feet of the run. The ball hit him in the back of the head, bounced up and into the glove of the waiting first baseman.

Without a word, the runner turned, ran toward Johnny, and hit him square in the mouth. Too brave to cry and too afraid to run away, Johnny stood his ground and exchanged blows with the other boy. After a few more punches landed on Johnny, several of the other boys separated them and the game ended.

That night, Johnny had to explain to his father why he had a busted and bleeding lip. Rather than the reaction he expected, Johnny's father told him to go back the next day and challenge the boy to fight him again. His reasoning was that most bullies used up all the guts they have the first time they do something. If you challenge them, it puts you above them and they can't handle it. It worked for Johnny the next day as he openly challenged the other boy, who backed down. They remained friends for years until the boy left home at sixteen and was never seen again. That was the summer Johnny got interested in boxing. The YMCA in West Palm Beach taught the fundamentals and, as he got more and more interested and better at it with weight gain, he was encouraged to enter into some Golden Gloves competitions. By the time he was in the Army, he was an above average boxer who knew how to box and fight.

Johnny thought about that on the drive to the Rio Vista. He also thought about his two meetings with Victor. He did not consider them to be fair fights. If his hunch was right, tonight he would even the score a little.

He drove out just as the sun was dropping behind the western skies. He had about an hour of time between the last ray of the late spring sun and the full darkness of the night. Johnny wanted to take that time to make sure that Victor was at the Rio.

Once he selected an empty parking space at the edge of the lot, he pulled in and cut the engine. He sat in the car for a few minutes to see if there were any workers or guards on the outside of the building.

The river side of the parking lot was thick with honey-suckle vines. The gentle sweet smell of them filled the air as he sat with his windows rolled down. Bees landed on each bloom and, when they were loaded with pollen, flew to the next pale yellow blossom. Johnny smiled as he re-membered he and his friends pulling the blossoms and sucking the same sweet nectar from them when he was a kid.

As he watched the building, Johnny saw several gar-deners. They were working on the front walkway leading to the entrance. The garden was in full bloom with roses of all colors. Johnny paused when he recognized one of the men pushing a wheelbarrow. The man would push for a minute, then stop, take off his gloves for a second, re-place them and move on. The windows on the outside of the building had large wooden shutters on the edges with some type of green vine growing in them. Johnny smiled hoping it might be kudzu and it would someday take over the entire building and smother it to the point that people no longer could find it.

Ten minutes after full darkness set in, he opened the door and stepped from his car.

Johnny quickly walked across the parking lot. On the way he met one couple who he assumed were out for a mid-week dinner. He reached the door and pushed it open. Just above the handle was a large placard announc-ing that the inside was cooled with air conditioning. Once inside, he immediately felt the chill as his shirt, which had grown wet with sweat on the drive, grew cold on his back.

He was greeted by a man in a tuxedo and a bad toupee as soon as he entered. "Will you be having dinner with us tonight, sir?" The man was about Johnny's age and looked like this was second or perhaps third job for the day. His eyes were puffy and his hands shook as he held the menu.

"Uh, yeah. I think so." Johnny looked around. He spotted a table near the back of the room. "How about that table over there?" He pointed.

"I have a much better one closer to the band stand. We have a very nice group playing tonight." He tried to steer Johnny to the better table in hopes of a better tip.

"That one." Johnny pointed.

"Right this way, sir." He led Johnny to the table. "I'll have someone come by for your drink order in just a minute." He started to walk off when Johnny stopped him.

"A friend of mine said this was Joe Skinner's place. I knew a guy in Florida with that name. I wonder if it's the same one? My guy was big. Maybe three hundred pounds. Red hair." Johnny was laying it on.

"Oh, no, that's not him. Mister Skinner is nothing like that. The ladies think he's quite a man. He's..." He hesitated and turned toward the stairway leading to the casino downstairs. "As a matter of fact, there he is now. He's standing over there with the lady." He pointed toward Joe who stood with a very attractive red-haired woman on his arm.

"No, not the same guy. Thanks." Johnny took his seat and kept his eye on Joe. He was still watching him when a familiar face showed up. Joe was talking to another man when Victor came from the stairway and whispered something in Joe's ear. Joe hardly paid any attention to him and dismissed him and what he had to say with a wave of his hand. The entire time Joe spoke to the other man Johnny noticed he played the consummate host. He greeted most of the diners by name, shook hands with the men and kissed the ladies on the cheek. Occasionally after they were seated, Joe reappeared with a flower for the lady. It was always a rose and probably freshly clipped from those growing outside.

Johnny was on his second drink and awaiting his dinner when Joe's hosting duties came to an abrupt end.

The man walking into the dining room looked to Johnny to be no different than any of the other men who sat with their ladies at tables throughout the room. He had on an off-the-rack, brown suit that had too many miles and too many cleanings. Even from his seat in the corner, Johnny could tell the pants were getting slick from sliding in and out of a car all day or sitting in an office chair. Either way, he looked like he barely had enough money to afford dinner and certainly not enough to go downstairs and gamble.

He walked in and looked around. He did not see Joe as quickly as Joe saw him. Even before he began to walk toward him, Joe dropped the woman's hand and turned toward the hallway leading from the room.

Halfway across the room, the man yelled, "Joe Skinner, you can't run from me."

By that time Joe had disappeared down the hallway. Several of the diners quickly left their tables and headed for the door. This was not a place to be when trouble started. Although Johnny did not know personally a single person in the dining room, he knew the Rio Vista was a favorite of some of Atlanta's political leaders when they wanted a night out. The problem was that many of them took a night out with guests other than their wives.

One tall, gray-haired man Johnny recognized as a judge grabbed a woman young enough to be his granddaughter and headed for the door. He was followed by several others.

Johnny quickly dropped several dollars on the table and walked in the same direction as the man. He had hardly gotten to the doorway leading down the hall when he saw Victor cut between Joe and the man.

He had a false smile on his face as he walked toward the intruder. "You don't want to make a scene, Mister. Let's you and me go outside and talk this over. Mister Skinner is too busy tonight to—'

Before he could finish, the man whipped a leather covered sap through the air and slammed it against Victor's head. Even Johnny felt pain for him as it connected and dropped the larger man like a stone.

From down the hallway, Johnny heard another voice. "Hey, you're the card salesman. Otis something or another, right? What the hell's going on?" Johnny didn't have to even guess who that was. He could tell from the scars on his face that it was Abe Salem. "Look what you did to one of my men. Are you crazy, coming in here like that?" He looked around. "Where's Joe?"

"I'm Otis Hightower and I'm here to see Joe. Not you or anybody else. So let me go in there and talk to him. Just me and him. Alone." Otis had the beginnings of a tear rolling down his cheek and his voice was quivering.

A small crowd had gathered and Johnny managed to stand behind several people and still observe the action in the hallway. Someone had pulled Victor to a sitting position and had put a cloth filled with ice from the kitchen on his bleeding and bruised head.

Otis pointed to the door leading to Joe's office. "I'm going in there, Mister Salem. Don't try to stop me. This has nothing to do with you. It's between me and him." Otis pushed open the door. He had changed hands with the sap and now held it in his left hand. As soon as he turned the doorknob, he reached into his jacket pocket and pulled out an automatic pistol. He held the pistol in front of him as he entered the office.

"Otis, are you nuts? I told you never to come here at night." Joe saw the pistol in Otis's hand. "Okay, partner, just put the gun down and we can talk about whatever it is that's got you so hopped up." He stepped slightly toward him as if he wanted to reach out and take the gun. The door was still open, so Johnny had a good view of the action inside the office.

"I did what you wanted me to do. I knew it was wrong but I did it anyways. I went to Havana, met Miguel and left the cards and dice like you said."

"So what's the problem? You did what you were supposed to do and I paid you. You think you deserve more?" Joe's arrogance was beginning to show. "You think you're the only guy I can get to work for me?"

By this time, Abe had come to stand in the doorway. "Joe, what the fuck is going on? I don't like this shit in my place. Take care of it." He turned to Otis. "And what's your problem, anyway? You get some bad pork in Havana? You didn't get laid while you were there? That's not our fault. We just paid you to deliver cards and dice. Nothing more."

Joe was clearly sweating now. In the hallway, the waiters were trying to get the patrons to return to their seats. They were circulating with open bottles of Champagne and glasses which they filled and handed to the guests.

Otis leveled the gun on Joe. "What about the gift I had to bring back for you, Joe. You want to tell me where it's at?"

"Gift? What gift. I don't know what you're talking about."

"Oh, I think you do. It was in the case with the money—" Before he could finish what he was about to say, Joe lunged for him. Otis quickly backed up and Joe stumbled over a small table beside the chair in his office.

"Money? What money? What's he talking about, Joe?" Abe was now fully inside the room.

"Don't listen to him, Abe, he's nuts." Joe was picking himself up from the floor.

"No, I want to listen to him when he talks about money." Abe turned to Otis. "Tell me about the case with the money."

"I got it just like Joe said. I met Miguel—"

"Miguel? You let this guy go to Miguel?"

"Abe, listen—"

"I am listening. To him." He turned back to Otis. "So what happened after that? After you met Miguel?"

"He gave me a case. Told me not to open it."

"But you did, didn't you Otis?"

"Yeah, I learned how to pick locks in the Army, so I picked the case."

Now only three people were in the hallway, Johnny and two men who looked like they could be police on Abe's payroll. Victor had been moved to the kitchen floor where he still lay unconscious.

"And what did you see in the case, Otis?" Abe was talking to Otis but his eyes were locked onto Joe.

"There was seventy thousand dollars in it."

Abe went ballistic. 'Seventy thousand dollars!" He grabbed Joe by the shirt front. "You got seventy grand and just how much did I get out of that little case that Otis brought back from Havana?" Even Joe didn't see the fist coming when it smashed into his face. "I got sixty. Unless our little friend Otis can't count, you owe me ten grand." Abe hit Joe again and then turned to Otis.

"Wait a minute, why the fuck do you care how much

he stole from me? I'm the one that should be holding the gun."

"It's not the money, it's the lizard."

"Lizard?" He still held Joe by the shirt. "Lizard? What the fuck is this nut talking about, Joe?"

Otis answered before Joe could think of anything to say. "Miguel gave me a gift for Joe. It was a lizard pin. It had red eyes like maybe they were rubies or something. It was a really nice pin."

"What's that got to do with anything?"

"When my wife, Virginia, came home from work today she was wearing it. Now I know where she's been getting all her new clothes."

Abe pushed Joe away, and he crashed into the sofa. "You son of a bitch, I should kill you myself. You been skimming from me and Lansky. You can't do that and live, Joe, it can't be done."

Joe looked at Otis. "Virginia was a whore anyways. I picked her up at a bar one night when you were out of town. We—"

Joe never got to finish what he was saying. Otis fired three shots in rapid succession. The force threw Joe back on the sofa and he began to bleed out as soon as his back hit the cushions.

The sound brought everyone in the building to their feet. Those in the dining room who had ignored the commotion in the hallway quickly forgot about dinner and headed for the door.

Downstairs it was a different story. The front of the cashier's cage was immediately slammed shut and a very large man stood in front of it with a shotgun in his hands. The tables were shut down and all money was secured in lock boxes beneath the playing area. Players grabbed their money or chips and stuffed them into their pockets. One player on a roulette wheel tried to grab any loose chips and a dealer almost broke his arm when he grabbed him across the layout. By the time the third shot stopped echoing, the downstairs casino was almost empty.

Johnny ran to the door of Joe's office when he heard the shots.

"Are you crazy? Shooting Joe in my club?" Abe looked at his friend who was sprawled across the sofa. His head was laying back on the top of the piece, his feet splayed out at the bottom. Abe went to the obviously dying man and leaned down to speak to him.

"Joe? Joe? Listen to me. Is this the guy that brought the last shipment out of Havana? Does he have my money?" He grabbed his head and held it in both hands, turning his face to him. "Joe, the money you scammed, where is it?"

Joe was only able to moan.

Abe looked at Otis. "You killed Joe over some broad?"

"She's not some broad. She's my wife. And I love her. That's why I had to shoot her too."

"You killed your wife and Joe?" Abe looked around the room. "Where the hell is Victor? Somebody's got to get this cleaned up." Abe reached beneath Joes coat and pulled his pistol from the shoulder holster. He leveled it toward Otis. "Did you bring back a delivery from Havana last month?"

"No, I only went last week. That gave Joe a whole week with Virginia. She told me they spent two nights together." Otis had tears now freely flowing on his cheeks.

"Son of a bitch!" Abe looked at Joe and at Otis. "I should shoot you myself for all the trouble you're going to cause me." Before he could finish, one of the bodyguards from downstairs grabbed Otis from behind and his gun went flying from his hands.

"What do you want me to do with him, Mr. Salem?" Otis dangled in the bigger man's arms. His feet were almost a foot off the floor.

"Get him out of here. Out back and wait for me. Where the hell is Victor? I need somebody to get Joe out of here." Abe looked around and for the first time, noticed Johnny. "Who the hell are you?"

"Nobody you need to know tonight. You got enough troubles." Johnny turned to walk away.

"Wait, what's that supposed to mean? Do I know you?"

Johnny ignored Abe and walked down the hallway toward the entrance. As he walked, he did not notice the kitchen doors open behind him. Victor stood in the open doorway, bracing himself in the jam, as he tried to get his balance.

Johnny walked to his car in the parking lot and tried to place the final pieces in the puzzle he had going in his head. Joe was obviously skimming money being paid to Abe which was coming in from Lansky's operation in Havana. The dead man from Big Town had probably decided to take it all and had gotten himself killed for his greed. It would have been a calculated risk on his part. He had to figure Joe couldn't say anything to Abe about the money being missing because if he did, he'd have to mention the amount he was looking for. If it was more than the usual payoff, he'd know Joe was skimming. Losing one courier and sleeping with the wife of another was too much even for Joe.

As Johnny walked across the asphalt he got a glimpse of Otis in the shadow of the one light burning in the parking lot. He was still being carried by the muscle. He was not moving, so he may have been out cold or already dead. Soon it wouldn't matter either way to Otis as he was being carried to the edge of the parking lot that ended with a sheer drop to the Chattahoochee River below.

With Johnny's attention drawn to Otis, he did not see Victor until it was almost too late.

"Okay, asshole, it's just you and me this time." Victor swung a fist the size of a canned ham at Johnny's head. He barely managed to duck under it and caught most of the blow on his shoulder. Even so, it knocked him against the car.

Johnny remembered his father's words and the reason he had come to the Rio Vista in the first place that night. "You got the drop on me once. Sucker punched me on the street. I don't like that, so I want to see if you are as tough as you think you are." Johnny walked back a step and stopped. His words drew Victor off-guard for the slight second he needed to get inside the bigger man. This was not a time for him to be a boxer. Now he needed to be a fighter.

Johnny moved forward quickly and drove his fist into Victor's belly. Having caught him off-guard, Johnny knew he had only seconds if he was to beat the man now doubled over in front of him. He placed both hands on Victors bowed head and in one fluid motion brought his right knee up and his hands down. He felt the sickening crunch as Victor's nose cartilage was crushed on his knee. At the same time, he knew he had broken several of Victor's teeth when they hit the boney part of his knee.

Victor crumbled at his feet. He was barely conscious. He was in extreme pain from the last blow to the head he got inside the Rio and now this. Johnny's best bet would be to drag him to the river's edge and send him on his way downriver just as he assumed had happened to Otis, but he couldn't bring himself to do it.

As he stood over the bleeding man, he looked down. "I know I'll see you again someday. You're not the kind to let this pass."

As Johnny got into his car, he saw two men carry a large bundle out the kitchen door of the Rio Vista. The bundle was wrapped in what appeared to be a dark curtain of some sort. It had to be Joe Skinner and the men who carried him were headed for the part of the parking lot that ended at the river's edge.

CHAPTER 26

Johnny called Detective Brewer from the pay phone at Big Town. He answered on the third ring.

"Detective Brewer here."

"How many chili dogs can you eat?"

Brewer recognized Johnny's voice. "You paying?"

"If you bring your own cigarettes, I might."

"Is this a social call? If so, you can buy the beer too, but if I'm working, I gotta stick to that rot-gut coffee that Hockey Doc makes. Which is it?"

Johnny pulled his lighter from his pocket, opened the top and spun the wheel to get a flame. He touched the flame to the cigarette in his mouth. "Tell you what, you come down here at lunch and we'll trade some information. You got something I want, I got something you want."

"You find the money?"

"I wish. But I think you'll like what I do have for you. See you in an hour." He hung up the phone and walked to the chairs along the wall.

On the newly covered table number seven two regulars were playing a game of bank pool. He watched as Chappy and Red handled their cues like a concert violinist would his bow.

Chappy won the break and gently rolled the cue ball

down the table to the rack. It hit head-on with the number one ball with just enough force to break loose the two and three balls at opposite corners of the rack.

Red came off the back rail with right English and banked the two ball into the center of the table. Each succeeding shot required the target ball to be banked into a rail before it could go into a pocket. Both men were masters at the game. After several more banks into the still-massed balls from the rack, Red put four balls in pockets in succession. Two were cross table banks going from one side rail across the table to where the ball dropped into the leather pouch on the opposite side.

Chappy made the last two money balls and Red dropped a fifty cent piece on the table.

Johnny was reading the paper when Brewer arrived. Johnny sat beneath a sign that cautioned the players that there was to be no gambling, spitting on the floor or masse' shots on any table. None of the rules were enforced.

"So, it's Bulldog Drummond himself. Or are you Boston Blackie this week. I can't keep up with which detective you're pretending to be." Brewer picked up the newspaper Johnny had been placing on the chair as he read a section and tossed it on the floor.

"I think I liked it better when you called me the Dixie Detective." Johnny was dressed in a pair of dark gray pants, a white shirt and black wingtip shoes. "You know, I feel good today—so good that I'm not going to let you ruin it for me."

"So you're the Dixie Detective." Brewer hitched his pants up and heaved himself up on the stool. "Whatever you call yourself, this better be good."

"I called you up here to give you some information that might even get you a promotion. If you want to be an asshole about it, go ahead. It's not going to bother me at all." Johnny slipped off the stool, reached down, picked up the newspaper again and began to read it.

"Okay, okay, you know I like to bust your balls sometimes. Hey, I'll tell you what. I'll buy the dogs today. Whadda you say?" He slapped Johnny good naturedly on the back as he got up and walked to the counter.

As he walked by the table where Chappy and Red were into another game, he asked, "You boys ain't gambling are you? I'd hate to run you in and mess up the game."

Chappy, who was lining up a shot spoke without looking up. "Don't you see all those signs on the wall? Nothing up here but good, law-abiding citizens." He took the shot and missed. He turned to Red. "See what happens when I get close to a cop."

Brewer returned with a tray. On it were four chili dogs and two bottles of beer. Brewer sat them on a chair and pulled it up in front of them as a table. "Okay, what am I doing up here?"

Johnny took his time and explained the last few days' activities to Brewer. He did not leave out much, but what he told him was tailored in the way Johnny wanted it to come across to the detective. He told him about finding Thomas and then losing him again after Victor sat the house on fire. When he got to the previous night's activities at the Rio Vista, he stopped. "Here's where it gets a little hairy." Johnny took a bite of his chili dog, washed it down with almost half the beer and continued. "I thought I had a good idea of what was going on, but when I got there, it turned sour on me."

"That happens when you deal with the criminal element. Especially when you don't know what you're doing." Brewer finished the first dog and reached for his second.

Johnny ignored the sarcasm. "I went to see the connection between Joe Skinner and Victor—"

"The goon who tried to kill you?"

"Yeah. Twice. Once near my house and again when he followed me to Plunkett Town to find Thomas. I wanted to see how he was connected to Skinner and then see if he wanted to take me on again."

Down the row of chairs from them one of the men turned on a radio and began listening to a Chicago Cubs baseball game. A Milwaukee Braves game was already in progress and the players gathered around the radio kept shooting glances over to Brewer to see if he noticed the money being handled. As soon as he heard the second game being broadcast he stood up.

"Okay, you bums, listen to me 'cause I'm only gonna say this one time. I'm here having lunch. I'm technically off duty until I finish eating and that may take a while, so unless you kill each other or burn the place down, I don't give a shit what you do. Just don't make it so obvious." He sat back down, and turned back to Johnny. "You think they understood?"

"I think you made yourself quite clear."

"So go ahead and tell me what happened."

Johnny told Brewer everything that happened at the Rio Vista. "If you look down around Columbus in a week or so, you may find a body. Abe said he was a card salesman, and the guy said his name was Otis. I know he went into the river, and I imagine Skinner did too."

The players let out a roar when Dee Fondy hit a triple which resulted in two runs crossing the plate to put the Cubs up two to nothing in the second inning.

"Okay, let me get this straight. This card salesman kills his wife then knocks off Joe Skinner? Do you know how much he couldda got paid for a hit like that if the word got out he was gonna do it? So, I guess we got a stiff named Virginia waiting to go ripe so some neighbor can call us and let us know where to find her." Brewer reached into his own pocket and pulled out a cigarette. He fired it up without offering one to Johnny.

"And the money. You can forget it. I think Joe killed Charlie and took it. They did it up here because they had an insider who had a key. This was a safe place to meet; only it turned out to be more than a meeting place for Charlie."

"Who's working for them in this place? They trying to grab a piece of this penny ante gambling that's going on?"

"No, not even that." Johnny handed the matches he got from Slim to Brewer. "I saw him working outside at the Rio planting bushes and stuff. I think he was just convenient."

"So what makes you think I need to give up on finding the money?"

"Because Joe has it. Or rather he had it. If you find it now, you've got to do it from where he was stashing it. Thomas was just in the wrong place at the wrong time of day. I don't think they even knew he was here. He's going to be running for the rest of his life for something he didn't do and doesn't know who did." Johnny put a half-eaten chili dog on the paper plate and wiped his mouth with a napkin. "There should be enough there to raid a gambling house, and solve three murders."

"Three?"

"Yes. Charlie's. Joe did it or had Victor do it for him. Either way he was responsible. Otis the card salesman shot his wife, who you have to find and Joe who you may also have to find. The only body you have is Charlie's."

"Murders without bodies do not go over well with my lieutenant."

"Find the bodies and then solve the crime. You'll look

like a genus. You have all the information you need."
Johnny stood up. "It's been a long day for me. I'm going
to catch an afternoon movie at the Roxy. You should try
it sometimes. Nice and cool inside. Get to see a double
feature and a cartoon. You do laugh sometimes don't
you?"

Johnny left Big Town with Brewer sitting beneath a
NO GAMBLING sign.

CHAPTER 27

Johnny could hear the noise in the background. He was standing at a pay phone in the lobby of the Roxy Theater and had dialed the number for the laundry at the Grady Hospital.

"Hang on. I'll see can I find her."

He heard the phone hand piece bounce when it was dropped. The person who answered the pay phone had simply let go and let it fall the length of the cord. When it did, it banged against the wall several times.

"Hello? This is Rachel. Who—who is this?"

"It's me." He hesitated. "Johnny Morocco. You have to contact Thomas. I want to meet him at Flat Rock tomorrow afternoon. It's a matter of life and death for him. You've got to impress that on him. If I see him, I can help him, but I've only got a day to do it." There was no response from the other end of the phone. "Rachel? Did you hear me?"

"I did. But I want to know why you're doing all of this. Who you doing it for. Thomas or you?"

That was a question he had asked himself several times in the past few weeks. He had spent most of his time on this and had not made any money other than a few bucks serving some papers on a soon-to-be divorced doctor. He knew he wouldn't make any money until he finished with Thomas, and he didn't know how that was going to end, but he did know that it was going to end soon.

"We can talk about my motivation later. Right now, you've got to promise me you can reach Thomas and get him to Flat Rock tomorrow afternoon. Can you do that?"

"I think I can, but I don't know for sure."

In the background Johnny heard someone calling her name and telling her to come back to work.

"Look, I have to go. Can I reach you someplace tonight?" She held her breath waiting for an answer.

"I—I'll pick you up at your house. Seven. Same as before." He hung up before he had a chance to reconsider.

The movie was over by five. Johnny walked back to the parking lot across from Big Town and got into his car. With over an hour to kill, he decided to grab something to eat. He drove across Edgewood, turned on Courtland and began to look for a parking place. He found one not far from the cafeteria where he planned to have supper. Johnny pulled his car into the space and got out. He was searching in his pocket for a nickel for the meter when a black four door car pulled beside him and the front passenger's side door opened.

Before he could say anything, he saw the glint of the streetlight overhead as it flashed on the knife heading in his direction. His only choice was to duck and slam the other car door against the person with the knife. Johnny heard the knife when it hit the pavement but he did not have time to search for it. He was immediately thrown against his own car as a dark skinned man began to pummel him. He tried to block the punches but the man was too big and too fast. Johnny got in one, maybe two good shots but the rest of his actions were purely defensive. He heard someone yell from down the street.

"Hey, what the hell you doing down there?"

Johnny wanted to take a minute and tell the person who asked that he was getting his ass handed to him in no short fashion and, he could use a little help, but he thought better of taking the time to respond.

He took several shots to the stomach and was being propped up for even more punishment, when the back door of the car opened. Johnny knew without looking who would be sitting in the seat.

"Don't kill him. I want to come back and do it myself. Let him hurt for a while and wonder when he's gonna die." Victor spoke through a broken nose that was packed full of cotton. He was missing at least two teeth and both his upper and lower lips were split.

"Can't work alone, can you Victor?" Johnny managed to gasp as he took a right hook on the chin. The last thing he remembered was Victor's promise to return as he slid to the pavement.

"Hey, mister, you okay?" Johnny felt someone trying to stand him up.

"Yeah, I think I'll live, but I'm not sure if I want to." Johnny almost fell as he struggled to his feet. From inside the cafeteria someone brought him a wet cloth and a glass of water.

"You want me to call an ambulance or the cops?" The man who was helping him stand asked.

"No, I'll be okay. Just open the door and let me sit inside the car." By then, a small crowd had gathered on the sidewalk and was offering Johnny advice on how to deal with the thugs.

"Dirty bastards. You should have shot them. I see that gun you got underneath your jacket," one man offered. "Anybody that'll kick a man in the head when he's down like you were has lost his right to live among civilized folks."

Johnny drank the water and was handed another wet

towel. He wiped blood from his face and looked in the car's outside mirror. He had a cut over his right eye that was bleeding with no end in sight.

"Looks like he got you with a blackjack or brass knuckles over your eye. That's about the only way to get a deep cut like that," another of the bystanders offered.

A man in the crowd pushed his way to the front. "A cop is coming. I can see their car down the street at the red light. You want me to stop them?"

"No. This was just a misunderstanding. I'll be all right." Johnny pressed the cold wet cloth against his cut and climbed back in his car. He cranked it and pulled out into the street behind the Atlanta Police cruiser as it rolled slowly down the street.

Thirty minutes later Johnny pulled up in front of the house where Rachel lived. He stopped the car and checked once again to see if he had been followed. Since leaving the street where he was beaten he had driven around in circles, taking side streets and doubling back to make sure he lost anyone who might be behind him. If his suspicions were correct, this was one time he did not need to be followed.

Satisfied that he was alone on the street, he opened the car door and eased himself from the seat. Across the street from Rachel's house, he saw two men in their twenties watching his every move. He didn't blame them. A white man in their neighborhood at that time of night was unusual and probably up to no good.

He took his time and walked up to the front door. Before he could knock, Rachel opened it.

"Oh, my God. What happened to you?" She took his arm and quickly but gently pulled him inside. "Did somebody beat you up?" She led him to a chair and he took it without protest. "You weren't in a car wreck were you?" Rachel knelt in front of him.

Rachel had dressed for a night with Johnny. She wore a light blue dress with thin straps over each shoulder. She had brushed out her hair and it hung loose down below her neck and barely kissed her uncovered shoulders. When she leaned forward, Johnny could not help but look down and into the front of her dress. It fell away revealing the top swell of her breasts encased in a white bra.

"Let me get you something for that cut." Without waiting for a response, she left the room. She soon returned with a bottle of alcohol and several bandages. She also held a small bottle of iodine.

The cut was almost in line with a similar cut he had received in a match in Italy. The Military Police set up a match between some of the military and their German and Italian Prisoners of War. Johnny drew a scrappy German who wanted to fight bare knuckled, but the organizers of the matches refused. Johnny had him by about two inches in height and ten pounds, but the German fought like his freedom depended on the outcome. He cut Johnny in the third round and for the next two rounds Johnny was looking sideways. He caught the German with a combination left hook and a right uppercut that almost lifted the man off the canvas. When the two blows connected in rapid fire, the only thing left was an eight count and a cut man telling Johnny how bad it was going to burn as he cleaned the cut.

"This is gonna sting." She opened the alcohol and soaked a piece of white cloth and then touched it to the cut.

Johnny felt it but did not respond as she dabbed at the open wound. "You probably need some stitches, but I know you're not going to the Grady to get any. Are you?" She lay the alcohol pad aside and pulled the rubber stopper from the iodine bottle. "I'm gonna soak a pad in this and it's really gonna sting this time." True to her word, she tipped the small bottle on the pad and then placed the red coated pad against the cut. This time Johnny could not help but wince when the iodine touched the open wound. "I told you it was gonna sting. Mama used to blow on the cut when she put this on me or Thomas." She smiled. "You want me to blow?"

Johnny closed his eyes and leaned back in the chair. "Did you get in touch with Thomas?" He put pressure on the bandage to stop the small flow of blood that was still coming from the cut.

"Same as before. I could only leave a message but I think he got it. I imagine he'll be there tomorrow when we get there."

"We? Who said anything about you going with me?"

"You're in this mess because of Thomas. I want to do what I can to help. And besides, you're in no condition to go anyplace by yourself. You start bleeding again, you might bleed to death." She kneeled down in front of him again and began to untie his shoes.

She had both shoes off before he realized what she was doing.

"No, don't take my shoes off. I need them to drive—"

"I—I don't think you should drive anymore tonight." She stood. "You can stay here. You'll be safe and I can take care of you."

Johnny looked up at her. She stood with her head slightly bowed and her hands behind her back almost as if she was apologizing for the suggestion.

"What about your mama? What'll she say if—"

"Mama and Aunt Emma are staying with their sister in Chattanooga for the next few days. They left on the bus this afternoon." She reached out and touched the bandage. "You're not afraid to stay here, are you? Nobody in the neighborhood will say anything or cause you any trouble."

Johnny took her hand in his. "You don't have to do this. If you'll help me to my car—"

Rachel didn't let him finish before she pulled his hand to her face and held it against her cheek. She closed her eyes and moved ever so slowly as she turned her face and kissed the back of his hand. When he didn't pull away, Rachel reached out and took his other hand in hers and led him into the bedroom.

Johnny sat on the edge of the bed as she helped him undress. Once he was naked, he lay back on the soft bed. He watched as the pale moonlight danced through the open window and fell gently on Rachel. She dropped her dress and, then in seconds, she too was naked and lying beside him.

"You don't have to say or do anything you don't want to." Rachel lay on his outstretched right arm. She snuggled closer and turned to face him. Her breasts were both soft and firm as they touched his bare skin. "You ever been with a colored girl before?"

Johnny turned to face her. He did not respond.

"I know it's strange the first time, but I'm more white than colored, so that'll make it easier for you. You don't even have to kiss me if you don't want to."

Johnny pulled her closer and cupped her face in his hands.

Rachel closed her eyes and smiled as the bulldog broke his chain.

The next morning, Johnny awoke to the smell of coffee. He tried to sit up, but he was in pain from his eyebrows to his kneecaps. There were few places on his body that did not hurt, although there were some areas that felt better than others. He tried for the second time and managed to pull himself to a sitting position with the pillows behind his back. He was still positioning himself

when he looked up and saw Rachel standing in the doorway.

She wore a thin housecoat that she had loosely tied at
the waist. It hung open enough to see that she wore nothing beneath it.

"How do you feel?"

"I think I may live. Is that coffee I smell?"

"Coffee, biscuits, ham and eggs. All waiting for you to
tell me you're ready to eat."

"Help me stand up, and I'm ready." Johnny swung his
legs to the side of the bed. When he did, the covers slid
back and revealed that he had slept naked the night before.
"Whoa, I'm sorry. I didn't realize—"

Rachel walked toward him. "Nothing to be ashamed
of. It's not like I didn't sleep the same way beside you
last night." She stood beside the bed, the housecoat open
even more now that she was moving. "We're going to see
Thomas this afternoon. We have all the time we need to
eat breakfast if you have anything else you want to do
first." She untied the cloth belt around her waist allowing
the housecoat to open completely. Without waiting for a
response, she dropped the housecoat and slipped back
into bed beside Johnny.

∞

The drive from Rachel's house to the golf course
where they were to meet Thomas normally took about an
hour if he took the highway heading south from the city's
center. This time, Johnny took the long route. He left the
house, by way of the back door, cutting across the yard
next door. Once in the yard, he found himself alone with
a large dog on a long chain. The dog was a mixture of
unknown breeds. His mother had obviously been a large
animal. His father might have been even bigger.

The dog lunged at Johnny as soon as he saw him. The yard was small with a wooden fence at the back. Just in front of the fence was a clear patch of ground about ten feet wide and thirty feet long. It was neatly turned earth and was where the homeowner had recently planted their garden. At one end several tomato plants, each several feet tall reached for the morning sun. All along the rest of the patch, the earth was tilled and laid out in rows. Johnny swerved to avoid destroying the homeowner's work as he ran for the fence. On any other day, the run would have been no challenge, but after the beating of the previous night and the care Rachel had provided throughout the night, he was in no condition to outrun an angry dog. With inches to spare before the dog's chain reached its end and yanked him backward, Johnny cleared the small fence and was in a vacant lot.

The dog, angry at missing his prey, continued to bark as Johnny slowed his pace and made his way to his car. As he approached the street where he had parked the night before, he stopped and lit a cigarette. He took the time and the action to slowly survey the area. Secure in the knowledge that there were no more cars on the street, and none at either corner, he walked the half block to Rachel's house.

Back inside, Rachel had dressed and was ready to go.

"What about work? Don't you need to call somebody or something? I don't want you to lose your job."

"Don't worry. I told them yesterday that I had to take Mama to her sister's house in Chattanooga. They're not expecting me at work today." She smiled as they left the house together.

Johnny drove through some of the short, narrow streets in her neighborhood. If anyone was following them, he would have not been able to follow and keep up. Most of the streets were so narrow that if a car was parked on the side, the passing car took up the remainder of the street. The houses were a combination of shotgun and dogtrot houses built at the turn of the century for the mill workers at the Fulton Bag Cotton Mill. Long since released from the iron hand of the mill, the houses and their owners had maintained the mill village look.

Many of the houses were still heated with wood or coal stoves and the residents used them for cooking as well. The smell of wood fires hung like a toasted fog over the streets early in the morning and late at night. In the winter, the aroma would be augmented with that of the coal burning in the fires to heat the homes.

Once out of the city, he took Highway 41 through Hapeville and south to the golf course.

As they passed the turn off for Plunkett Town, Rachel spoke for almost the first time. "Last night was...I mean...if you need to, you can forget it happened. It doesn't have to mean anything."

"Why would I need to forget it happened? It did. Nothing more, nothing less. It happened." He pulled out his cigarettes and offered her one.

They made the drive to the golf course and Johnny pulled into the driveway. On Saturday or Sunday his car would have immediately been surrounded by boys, both white and colored who wanted to caddy for him. Very few of the younger boys were there during the week, so only three ran to meet the car.

"Hey mister, I can carry the bags for you and the lady. I'll give you my special price for the two of you." The boy ran beside the car as he spoke.

"Don't listen to him. Ain't no way he can carry two bags. He's only eleven years old. I'm almost thirteen. You want a strong boy, like me." His competition ran beside him and gave his sales pitch.

Johnny ignored both of them as he drove to the main

parking lot. He pulled in, stopped the car then turned to face Rachel. "You told him to meet me in the same place as last time, right?"

"You know I didn't talk to him directly. I can only leave a message, but that's what I said and I told them it was really, really important. That's all I could do." While Rachel spoke, Johnny looked toward the shack where he had met Thomas the last time he was here. Standing just to the rear of the shack, was a large man wearing a brown hat, a large cigar in his hand. Johnny recognized him as Broadway.

"I see Broadway back there. Thomas must be with him." Johnny turned to face Rachel. "I think you may want to wait in the car." He hesitated.

"That's okay. I understand. I'll be all right. Don't worry." She busied herself by digging for some unknown object in her purse.

Johnny left the car and walked around the clubhouse and to the equipment shed behind the caddy shack. Several golfers were standing inside the clubhouse. They were leaning against the long wooden counter where the club manager traded jokes and golf stories with them. He could hear the laughter coming from inside as he walked past them.

Just outside the door and ahead of him a party of two was on the first tee. Johnny took a second as he passed to watch the first one tee off. The golfer was a man in his mid-forties. His hair was already turning gray and his middle was beginning to turn soft. He took two practice swings and then laid the club head against the ball before drawing back for his swing. Johnny was impressed. The swing was clean and there was a solid thwack as the club hit the ball. The tee flew up and to the right as the ball took flight. Johnny shaded his eyes with his hand as he watched the ball fly true down the center of the fairway, hit and bounce once before rolling to a stop. He estimated the ball lay over two hundred yards from the tee.

"Nice shot, Dick. Do that again and you'll be on the green in two." His golfing partner approached the tee with driver in hand.

"Thanks. If I can keep from three putting, I may have a decent game today." The other man walked over and stood by his caddy as he waited for his friend to send his ball down the fairway.

Johnny shook his head as he continued toward the building.

"Over here."

Johnny heard Broadway call to him as he got closer. "Is Thomas with you?"

"He's close by, but he ain't here right now." Broadway stepped out from the back of the building. "Thomas's just a little gun shy if you know what I mean. The last time you come to see him, the boy almost got hisself kilt."

Johnny could not argue with that reasoning. "It's not going to happen this time. I need to see him for about five minutes. That's all." He looked around. "Do you think there's a big screwdriver in that shed?"

"They's all kinds of screwdrivers in there. You want a Phillips or a slot head?"

"It doesn't matter. Just get me one that has a good shaft."

Broadway disappeared inside the dark tool shed and reemerged in a minute with two screwdrivers. One had a shaft at least ten inches long and the other was only six inches. "Which one of these you want?"

Johnny took the longer of the two and stuck it in his back pocket. "I'm going inside the clubhouse for a minute. When I come back, I want to see Thomas out here.

This is no time to mess around. If he's not here, you tell me now."

"Thomas said you was a good man, and I got no reason to believe otherwise, but you need to be a bit nicer when you telling folks what to do." Broadway took a drag from his cigar and starred at Johnny. "I'll go find him, but I'm doing this for Thomas, not 'cause you said so." He turned and walked toward the wood line where Thomas had been waiting the last time.

Johnny walked back to the clubhouse. When he went inside, there was only one person at the counter. The manager was showing him a new putter and both of them were engrossed in tapping balls across a piece of carpet on the floor by the counter. Johnny eased by them and went to the locker room.

Once inside, he walked to the restroom. As he walked he took a quick look around. There was one person sitting on one of the long green benches in the center of the room. Around the walls were the lockers where golfers put their shoes and other items when they were on the course. Many of the doors were open, a few were closed and an even smaller number had padlocks on them. He watched as the man finished tying his dress shoes and then put his golf shoes in the top of his bag and left.

Johnny quickly pulled the scorecard from his wallet and checked the number on it. He moved to locker number twenty seven and pulled the screwdriver from his pocket when he saw a lock securing the door. He inserted the screwdriver between the arms of the lock, gave a downward twist and the lock popped into two pieces and fell from the hardware holding it to the door. He quickly picked up the two pieces and put them in his pocket.

Johnny was not certain what he would find in the locker but he had a good idea. When he opened the door, he found several articles of clothing, some hanging on hooks and others just stuffed in the locker. Most of those stuffed and laying on the bottom shelf of the locker looked to be recently worn. A light jacket was draped over a package lying on top of the dirty clothes. When Johnny saw the wrapped package he knew he had been right to return to the golf course and the locker. He took a quick look around to make sure he was still alone in the room and then slipped the package beneath his own jacket. The bulge was large enough that he had to cross his arms over his chest as he walked out past the men who were still rolling golf balls on a piece of carpet on the floor.

"Can I help you with something?"

"No, I was just looking for a friend. I think he may have already teed off."

"What's his name? I'll check the sign out book." The manager did not have a friendly face.

"We call him Dick at work, but it may be Richard," he said remembering the name of the golfer on the first tee when he came in.

"Oh, yeah. He and Fred are probably on the third fairway by now. You just missed them. They'll come by the back of the clubhouse when they go from the forth green to the fifth tee. You can probably catch them there."

"No, that's okay. I'll talk to him later." Johnny walked back into the sunshine.

When he got to the tool shed, Thomas was standing with Broadway and Heavy. "Mister Johnny, I can't be—"

Johnny stopped Thomas in mid-sentence. "Listen to me Thomas. I've got Rachel in my car. I'm going to take both of you to back into town and to the train station. Do you have any cousins in New York or Chicago or Detroit? Anyplace out of Atlanta?"

Thomas looked at Broadway. "What about Aunt Roberta? She's in Chicago, ain't she?"

"Yeah, my mama went up there to visit her a couple of years ago. She said she was living in a housing project that was a big as a regular city."

Thomas turned to Johnny. "We call her Aunt Roberta, but she's really a cousin. Her daddy was—"

"Thomas, listen to me. I don't care if she's the ghost of your great grandmother. That's where you're going." Johnny looked around. "Broadway, is there any place I can pull up to with my car so Thomas won't be seen getting in?"

"You think somebody done followed you down here?"

"No, I just don't want to take any chances. He's been through a lot and it's not over yet."

Johnny saw Dick and his partner placing the flag back in the cup on the forth green. He knew if they stopped by the clubhouse for a beer on the way to the next tee, the manager would tell them someone was asking about them.

"We have to hurry. I'll pull up as close as I can get to the clubhouse and I want Thomas to walk between the two of you when you bring him to the car." He looked at Broadway. "It's the best way for us to make sure he's not seen."

Johnny kept the bulge in his jacket covered as he walked back to his car. When he got there, he saw one of the caddies who had followed the car into the parking lot standing beside it talking to Rachel.

"Okay, Jason, we have to leave now. You take care of yourself." Rachel smiled at the boy as he backed away. It was obvious from his smile that he was enamored with her.

"Friend of yours?" Johnny asked as he opened the door. He opened his jacket and placed the package on the seat between them, He turned the key and pressed down on the starter with his foot and waited for the engine to catch.

"No, just talking to pass the time. Did you find Thomas?"

"Yes. We're going to pick him up now." Johnny put the car in gear and drove to the rear of the clubhouse. He could see inside and noticed Dick and his friend talking to the manager.

When he got as close as he could, he gave a short half-toot on the horn. In seconds, Broadway and Heavy were walking toward him with Thomas squeezed between them.

"Open your door and lean forward. Let Thomas pull up the seat and get in back."

Rachel did as she was told when Thomas got even with the car. He slid easily into the back seat, Rachel leaned back and closed the door. "Why don't you lie down in the back seat till we get on the highway, Thomas? I think it might be safer that way."

Thomas slid down and lay across the floor in back. "Mister Johnny, you keep talking 'bout how it might not be safe. You know I didn't shoot that man at Big Town. Why won't nobody believe me? They burned down Aunt Emma's house, scared her nearly to death and now you got me laying in the back seat while you takes me God knows where."

"Okay, Thomas, here's how it is. I know who killed the man at Big Town and so do the police now."

Rachel turned to face Johnny. "Then why are we doing this to Thomas?"

"Because sometimes it doesn't matter what the truth is, it's what people believe. The man that was killed had a lot of money that belonged to the man who killed him. That's what they wanted, only they didn't get it. They think you have it."

"Me! I don't have nobody's money. Mine included."

"I know you don't, but they believe it and they're not going to stop looking for you until they find the money. Even Detective Brewer thinks you have it and he's looking for you." Johnny pulled onto the main road and slid in between two large truck filled with produce heading to the Farmer's Market. "What you're going to do," he hesitated and looked at Rachel, "both of you are going to catch a train tonight and go live with Aunt Roberta in Chicago."

"But how we—" Thomas rose up from the floorboard.

"How did you find out about Aunt Roberta?" Rachel asked.

"Thomas told me. You're going to catch a train because you have to leave Atlanta. If you don't, some very bad people are going to hunt you down and kill you."

"You know we don't have the money to move to—" Rachel was cut off in mid-sentence.

"If I'm right, you have more money than you ever thought possible. Here, open this." Johnny handed the package he had placed between them on the seat to her.

Rachel took the package and opened it. Inside was another brown paper wrapper tied with string. When she untied the string and pulled off the paper, her lap was filled with money. "Oh, my God! Did you rob the golf course when you were in there?" She began to flip through the bundles of well used bills. There were stacks of hundreds, fifties and twenties. "I can't believe this. It's not…I've never seen so much money."

"Let me see! Let me see!" Thomas had raised himself and was looking forward over the back of the seat.

"Wrap the money back up. Take out five hundred dollars in fifties and twenties. Give Thomas a hundred in twenties and put the rest of it in your purse."

"What am I going to do with that much money? I've

never had four hundred dollars at one time in my life."
She was still mesmerized by the money and had not
picked out the bills.

"You don't have four hundred dollars. You have everything in your lap. If you and Thomas are going to be
hunted for the rest of your lives, you may as well have
the money."

"But what if we give it back?" Rachel began to count
the bills.

"Do that and they'll be convinced you killed Charlie,
and they'll kill you for that. Either way, if they find
Thomas, he's a dead man. With the money, you can buy a
new life someplace for both of you." Johnny looked over
his shoulder as he spoke. "You understand me, Thomas.
You can never come back to Atlanta. Don't ever call anyone or write them. After today, you have disappeared."
Johnny looked at Rachel. "You too, Rachel. After today,
you have to forget everything about Atlanta. It's like it
never existed."

She looked at him as he drove. "Do I have to forget
everyone, too?"

CHAPTER 28

The parking lot for Terminal Station was on the same level as the entrance to the gigantic building. It was a masterpiece of architectural elegance from the early part of the twentieth century. Built on the site of the railroad junctions, the embryo that grew into the city of Atlanta, it was a favorite for tourists and travelers. When he pulled into the parking lot, Johnny selected a spot not far from the front of the building.

He opened the car door, stepped out and pulled out a cigarette. As he lit it, he looked around to make certain he did not see any of the players from Big Town or anyone else he did not need to see at the time. When he determined the area was safe, he nodded for Rachel and Thomas to get ready to leave the car. Rachel had slid down in the seat and Thomas had resumed his position on the floorboard when they hit the city limits.

"When you get inside, go to different windows to buy tickets. If they have a shop in there, I'll buy a bag to put the money in. You don't want to travel all the way to Chicago with all that money wrapped in brown paper." He was talking around his cigarette as they opened the car door. "Rachel, you hang on to it and don't count it, don't tell anyone about it and don't let it out of your sight." He looked at Thomas. "If I hear that you did any of those things, I'll find you and kill you myself." He crushed his cigarette on the ground. "Let's go."

The inside of the cavernous building was intimidating the first time anyone saw it. Every footfall on the stone floors echoed throughout the structure. Wooden benches sat in perfect alignment in the middle of the terminal's open space. Each bench was about eight feet long. Some had single travelers sitting, reading books or newspapers. Others had families with children running and playing in front of their parents. Several benches had people stretched out, as they waited for the next train or the next day of their life.

Johnny knew they would have to split into two groups as soon as they entered. To the right of the entrance were the ticket windows. Men stood behind steel frames and issued tickets to travelers. The loudspeakers were calling a train to New Orleans when they entered. Just beyond the ticket counter, Johnny saw a large sign that said *COLORED WAITING ROOM.*

"Mister Johnny, I know I can't shake your hand out here, but I want you to know I will always be grateful for what you have done for me and Rachel. Ain't no man, white or colored 'cept you, would have done that. You took a real chance and I 'spect as long as they looking for me, they gonna keep a watch on you, too." He smiled and headed for the ticket counter.

"You wait here. I'm going over there and get a bag or something for you." Johnny left Rachel standing by the front entrance.

She watched Thomas buy his ticket and then turn quickly and look her way before he walked to the waiting room reserved for him.

Johnny returned with a small suitcase. "Here, take this and go to the bathroom and put everything in it." He handed her the case.

Rachel stood for a moment looking at the signs above the ladies room. One was marked for *WHITE ONLY* and the other was *COLORED*. The two entrances were separated by thirty feet and a hundred years. In her hand she held enough money to start a new life in a new city. She could leave all her past behind her once she made the first step. She turned to look at Johnny. He gave no indication of what she should do even though she knew he realized why she was hesitating. Rachel made her selection and went into the room.

She emerged ten minutes later after having secured the money and reapplied a limited amount of make-up. She walked past Johnny and went to the ticket counter where she purchased her one way escape to Chicago. Once she had the ticket envelope in her purse, she turned back toward Johnny, smiled and walked to the larger of the two waiting areas.

As Johnny was leaving the terminal, he saw a young man in an army uniform come and sit on the same bench with Rachel.

છગ૭છગ૭

Johnny was listening to a game between the Yankees and the Red Sox. The Yankees were a two run favorite, so he took the Sox and the runs. It was the middle of the eighth inning and he was winning.

It had been almost two months since he had the conversation with Brewer. He heard that Joe Skinner's body washed up about twenty miles downriver in less than a week. Otis Hightower's was never found. Johnny knew that Victor was still a threat, but so was crossing the street at Five Points. He decided to worry about it when and if it happened.

He had just finished a bottle of beer when he heard

someone yell his name. "We got anybody here named Mister Johnny?"

Amid a few good natured comments he got up and walked to the pay phone. He took it from the man's hand and spoke into it.

"This is Johnny."

He heard the operator tell someone to deposit eighty-five cents for three minutes and heard the coins as they dropped through the phone box at the other end of the call.

"Johnny—is that you?"

"Uh, yes. Are you okay?"

"I'm fine. We both are. How are you doing?" There were no hospital laundry sounds behind Rachel's voice this time. "I just wanted to tell you that I'm taking a course to become a hairdresser," she said. "I've always wanted to do that. I think I'm good at it, too. And—and the other person with me is working at a restaurant. They let him wait on people now. He really likes it."

"I'm glad things are working out for you."

From the area where he had been sitting, someone yelled, "Hey, Johnny, Boston just scored again."

"Will you do something for me?" Rachel asked.

"Maybe. What is it?"

"Give me your address. I want to mail you something."

Johnny could hear a catch in her voice, and he was sure she was crying. He gave her his address and listened as she repeated it, though she was now clearly crying aloud.

The last thing he heard her say was, "Thank you."

e/ɔe/ɔ

Five days later, he found a notice from the post office

between the door and the frame on his room. The post-man had left it and his landlady stuck it in the door while he was out. The next morning, he stopped by the post office to check on the notice.

He placed it on the clerk's counter. "I got this yesterday. You have something for me?"

"Hang on, let me check." The clerk took the slip and returned from the back room with a small package and a form for Johnny to sign.

As he signed he looked at the return address. It simply said Aunt Roberta, Chicago. He took the package out to his car and sat in the driver's seat as he opened it.

Inside was a note that read: We have enough. *This is for you.* Beneath the note, he found ten thousand dollars in cash.

Johnny had no idea how much was "enough," but ten thousand was plenty for him.

THE END

About the Author

Paul Sinor is a published novelist and a produced screenwriter. The first book in his latest novel series was published in March of 2015. His other published works include one novel and a book on marketing screenplays. Eight of his screen plays have been produced as feature films, and he currently teaches screen writing at the University of West Florida in Pensacola. He has a MFA in Creative Writing and is a member of the Mystery Writers of America.

Sinor is a retired US Army officer and spent five years as the army liaison to the television and film industry in Los Angeles where he worked on such films as *Transformers 1-3, GI Joe, I Am Legend, The Messenger, Taking Chance* and numerous television episodes.